REVONTULI

BY ANDREW EDDY

Booktrope Editions
Seattle, WA 2013

May 2014

Dear Nick,

what a crazy business we have chosen! Best of luck with Hong Tng and I hope you like Revontuli.

Best,

Andrew

Cover Designer: Lorna Nakell

Proofreader: Dawn Pearson

This is a work of fiction. Names, characters, brands, media, and incidents are either the product of the author's imagination or are used fictitiously. Any resemblance to similarly named persons living or deceased is unintentional.

PRINT ISBN 978-1-62015-189-1

EPUB ISBN 978-1-62015-285-0

Library of Congress Number: 2013919529

For Christiane

In the northernmost part of Europe lies a land of forests, lakes, and rivers called the Finnmark. For centuries it's been a meeting place of East and West. Its people are the Sami, the 'People of the Reindeer'. In western culture, we have long known them as Lapps. The Sami traditionally roamed with their herds across a wide area covering parts of Norway, Sweden, Finland, and Russia. The village of Karasjok lies in a rich valley that leads to the Tana River, on the border between Norway and Finland, best known for its salmon and brown bears. It is as far east as St. Petersburg or Istanbul.

Revontuli is Finnish for 'Fox's Fire', or northern lights.

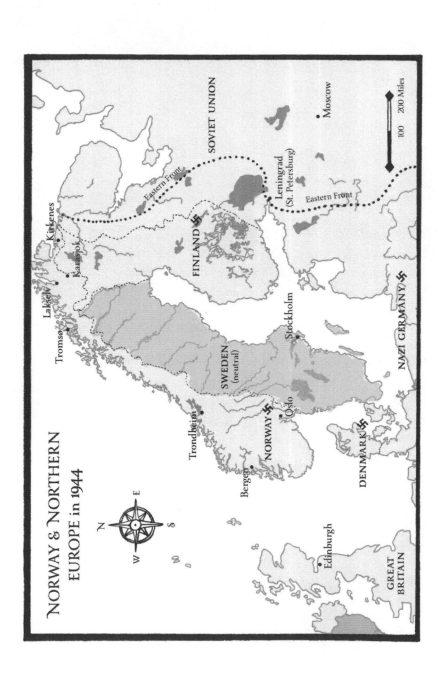

NORWAY & NORTHERN
EUROPE in 1944

SOVIET UNION

Moscow

100 200 Miles

Eastern Front

Leningrad
(St. Petersburg)

Eastern Front

Kirkenes

FINLAND

Karasjok

Lakselv

Tromso

Stockholm

SWEDEN
(neutral)

NAZI GERMANY

Trondheim

Oslo

NORWAY

Bergen

DENMARK

N
E
S
W

Edinburgh

GREAT
BRITAIN

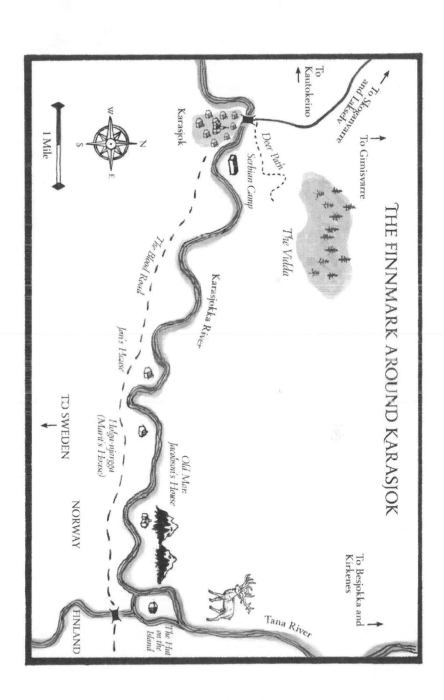

CHAPTER 1

Traundorf, Southern Bavaria, 1 July, 2013

THE CEMETERY WAS NOT BEHIND THE CHURCH, as is so often the case in Europe. It was a short walk up a path on the hillside that looked out over the valley. Long ago, there had been a chapel, but the roof and walls had given way to vines and bushes, until only piled stones and an arch could be seen emerging from the forest's edge. It was hard to see where the forest stopped and the churchyard began. The villagers continued to use the graveyard on the hill long after the chapel was only a ruin, even after the new church was built in the valley below, fifty years ago. The tallest of the markers are visible from the village, crowning the winding path that leads up from below.

Marit started up the path. It was sunny and hot, and she could hear her own rhythmic huffing and puffing as she took each step. Her legs strained against the slope, but she kept a steady pace, leaning more heavily against her walking stick and sweating beneath the scarf that covered her head. The swallows from the park had followed her, and she smiled as they flitted back and forth through the bushes on either side of the path. She was happy for their company.

The sounds of the valley became more distinct as she climbed, each one marking a different note in a pastoral symphony: the cars from the road that ran around the village on the far side of the Ache River, accelerating as they left the houses behind them; the cabinet maker sawing lumber in his workshop; a tractor spreading fertilizer over a field, or maybe cutting hay. She heard each one alone, a separate layer on backdrop that was the forest and fields where she walked.

Gradually, each faded, before becoming lost in the growing sounds of the alpine meadows: first, the chirping of the birds, then the crickets in the afternoon sun. A brook off to the right, probably the same one that ran into the village, cascaded noisily down a rocky face into a shallow pool of water. A cow's bell clanged high above her as she finally reached the top of the path and the gate to the cemetery.

She paused and turned back toward the valley, both to catch her breath and admire the view. It was three hundred feet down to the houses below.

She looked at the beading sweat on her wrinkled hands. Her veins were swollen rivers, bulging and pulling at her skin instead of carving valleys through the ridges. Her heart beat strongly in her head. She was still breathing very heavily, but the sounds of the meadow were louder than her breathing now. *Perhaps it is not just the steep walk*, she thought.

She had arrived, and the determined serenity of the last weeks gave way to a gripping anxiety that the birds and the sun and the view could not truly quell. In her heart she was seventeen again, but her body could not forget nearly seventy years of waiting. Sixty-nine years since she had held him and been held, since she had touched his lips and seen the smile in his eyes that revealed the softness and gentle life of these mountains she was seeing for the first time.

It is a beautiful country, she thought, looking out again over the valley, *very different from Norway—not as rugged, not as untamed, but also beautiful*. A different beauty, a shaped, tailored beauty. *God's country*, Hans used to say. *Yes, this was God's country*. A lot more like her native Norway than California. After the long years in America, it was good to be back in Europe.

Behind her, the small graveyard was a world unto itself. Every plot was meticulously manicured, with fresh flowers laid out at many of the markers. Beyond the small iron fence that ran around the yard and lost itself in the woods, there were meadows and pastures that fell off toward the valley below. The meadows were awash with the flowers of the mountain. At her feet lay the entire narrow valley: Traundorf directly below, held close to the hillock by the winding arm of the Ache River, sliced in two by the stream that flowed down from above. The river flowed from right to left, and behind it were a few houses, as though they had slipped through its strong grasp and spilled over to the other side. The road ran through the valley, and beyond were more fields and the majestic Oberstein Mountains. Even at this distance, the mountains loomed over her, dark in shadow. She faced them bathed in sunlight.

Marit turned and pushed the gate open. It answered with a loud creak. Hans' plot was not hard to find, toward the back, a single marker, at the end of a row.

Grass had not yet grown to cover the freshly turned earth. His wife was not there.

Just Hans, beneath a simple marker.

Hans wanted to be alone, and he was.

Marit laid her walking stick on the ground and sat down next to Hans. She breathed more slowly now, but still her heart raced. She ran her fingers through the blades of grass next to the grave, as though she were stroking his hair.

He was with her for the first time since coming to the village from her American home, for the first time since parting almost seventy years ago, in faraway Norway. She bent her head forward slightly and wiped the tears that began to trickle down her cheeks.

Tears.

She tried to remember when she had last cried, but it was a long time ago. She couldn't remember when, and she couldn't remember the feeling. They flowed steadily now: tears of joy, not the grief she had expected. She had grieved quietly for Hans for most of her life. Around her she again sensed the heat of the afternoon sun, but the warmth also came from inside now, from the knowledge that he was here.

CHAPTER 2

Karasjok, Late September 1940

MARIT HEARD THEM FIRST from the hill above the town as she came back from Mrs. Upsahl's house. The Upsahl farm lay a few hundred feet away, on the hillside above the village, with open fields and a few cattle. The cows wandered in and out amongst the empty reindeer pens that waited for the herds to come back from the sea fjords in the late fall. Walking down the path on her way into town, Marit heard the rumble of the motorcars as they came into the valley on the opposite side of the river. There were a few motorcars in Karasjok. Harald Edvardson the local butcher had one. So did Mr. Larssen, the mayor. The bus came came every Tuesday along the same road, but today was Saturday, and the roar of a half dozen motorcars driving at high speed over the dirt road from Lakselv sounded strange and unfamiliar. It seemed to Marit that the birds stopped singing, and that even the flowers bent away from the foreign noise.

Marit set down the milk jug she'd collected for her mother, took her dress into her hands, and hiked it up above her knees. She ran down the dirt path—slowly at first, but with growing speed as the noise grew louder. She arrived in front of the school dripping in sweat despite the cool fall air. The convoy of military vehicles reached the bridge. It accelerated across the straight, narrow passage. Milly stood at the roadside, next to the school.

"The Germans," she said. "They are here."

The rumors had raged for months. Ever since April when the Nazis violated Norwegian neutrality, the people of Karasjok had expected them to arrive. When the government fell in May, and the city of Tromsø was stormed the same month, people knew it was only a matter of time. Yet the summer came and went with no sign of Germans in little Karasjok. Perhaps they were afraid of the blackflies. Far from even the regional capital of Tromsø, in a remote river valløy better known for its salmon than its inhabitants, life in Karasjok went on much as it ever had. The village had almost forgotten the Nazis. Anticipation focused instead on the return of the nomadic Sami, who would bring their reindeer herds into the valley when the first snows fell.

The motorcade stormed across the narrow bridge and came to an abrupt halt in front of the schoolhouse. The road here broadened to form a circle and then spread out in several directions. It became many small paths for ox-carts and horses rather than for motorcars.

Mr. Dahlstrøm must have heard the roar too. Marit watched him standing in front of his school under the blue cross of the Norwegian flag. His small, round glasses gave him a scholarly look that left an impression of weakness in front of the smartly dressed Germans. Still, he held his head high. He came from the south, and spoke good German. He would know what to tell them.

Men jumped out even before the cars had fully stopped and made a rough square around the cars, their guns pointed at the small crowd that clustered around them. From the lead car, a tall man in a long, black jacket stepped out and came up to Mr. Dahlstrøm. He put on his large cap and seemed to tower over the young schoolmaster, though Marit noticed he was in fact only slightly taller.

"We will be commandeering the school," he said in German. "As barracks for the men. Do you speak German? " he added, almost as an afterthought.

"Yes, of course. I am the schoolmaster."

"Where is Herr Larssen?" The German glanced in the direction of the small administrative building beside the school.

"He is out hunting. He will be back later today. We were not expecting you."

"Send for Herr Larssen immediately. We don't like to be expected, but you should be ready nevertheless." While they were talking, one of the young Germans removed the flag from the pole in front of the school and unfurled a new one, with a large, black swastika in the center of the Norwegian cross. Mr. Dahlstrøm looked straight ahead and pretended to ignore what was going on behind him.

Marit turned to Milly, Milly's eyebrows were arched in large semi-circles that made her usually large eyes even bigger, staring out from under her Sami bonnet.

"I'm scared, Marit," she whispered, barely audibly.

Marit looked around at the stunned faces of the villagers. "You are not the only one. Come on. Let's go find my grandma. She'll want to hear all about this."

The young girls milled along the edge of the square to get behind the motorcade and headed toward the far side of town. As they turned to leave, Marit stopped to look back at the men who stood at attention while their colleagues filed into the schoolhouse. She stared hard at the closest boy, only a few years older than herself. His strong, blond hair stood on end, making him look taller. He had no helmet. He was sweating, even though it was not very hot. His eyes darted back and forth, trying to avoid direct eye contact with the villagers. He looked almost as nervous as they were. She smiled at him, but he frowned back. Still, in his blue eyes, she wondered if she hadn't caught at least a hint of kindness.

Or maybe only fear.

"Come on!" Milly pulled Marit's arm and they broke into a run toward the Enoksen farm.

They ran down the path that led east along the Karasjokka River. The midday sun was warmer, and before long they tired. It took almost an hour to cover the five miles that lay between the farm and the village of Karasjok. Milly, despite her obvious excitement, could not keep up with Marit, who travelled the path every day when her mother did not let her use the boat. They rounded the last corner and came quickly down into the meadow that surrounded the group of buildings several hundred feet up the gentle hill overlooking the river. Star, Marit's husky, greeted the girls eagerly as they ran into the meadow. Her large tail swung back and forth in a broad sweeping motion.

Bera, Marit's grandmother, stood behind the main house, hanging clothes on a line.

"Babi! Babi!" Marit called out to her.

Marit's mother Lidy also came out of the hut at the sound of her voice. If she was surprised to see Marit back so early, she said nothing.

The girls came running up to Bera and collapsed at her feet. Marit reached over to stroke Star's belly. Lidy walked over slowly, but her eyes betrayed her keen interest. They were green, like Marit's, but the similarity stopped there. Instead of the sparkling curiosity that showed in Marit's eyes, Lidy's were cold, hardened by pain and struggle.

"The Germans have arrived. Six cars. At least thirty men. They've taken over the schoolhouse." Milly's voice was strong. She had recovered her courage now that they were far from the village.

Lidy looked to Marit.

"Yes," said Marit. "It's true, Lidy."

"What did the mayor say?"

"Nothing. He's still hunting. The schoolmaster greeted them."

The older women looked at each other in silence. The arrival of the Germans was not good, but not necessarily bad. Lidy and Bera were both Sami. Only Marit's father, Mr. Enoksen, was Norwegian. He had passed away several years before. The Sami were used to living under someone else's rules. Marit tried to judge the effect of the news on them, but they hid their feelings well.

"Let us see what Mr. Larssen says when he gets back," Lidy said. She ran her fingers through her hair from front to back. It was chestnut brown, like Marit's, but streaked with gray. It looked as though Lidy put the grey there with her fingers, adding a few strands every time she repeated the gesture. Marit looked away. Bera returned to her washing. As far as the older women were concerned, the discussion was over. Star put her paw softly on Marit's leg.

"Come on, Milly. Let's go down to the river," Marit said. The two young girls set off at a run to the river, with Star close at their heels.

"Where's my milk jug?" Lidy called after them, but Marit pretended not to hear.

The meadow came down to the water's edge in a soft slope, and the dry yellow grasses gradually thinned until they became a bank of sand and stones. The Enoksen boat lay to the right where there were fewer rocks. Marit and Milly sat to the left on a large boulder that served as a bench looking out over the meandering river.

"Why do you call your mother Lidy?" Milly asked, as they sat down.

"I don't know. I always have, I guess. When my father died, it was just Bera and her in the house with me. Bera calls her Lidy ..."

Marit's voice trailed off. She wanted to say that it seemed strange to call Lidy "mother", but somehow the words seemed harsher than she wanted them to be, so she stayed quiet instead. It wasn't that Lidy was a bad mother. She just wasn't a very warm or expressive mother.

"I wish my father was still alive," Marit finally said, as if that answered the question. "He would know what to do about the Germans."

* * *

The news ran through the valley like a fall wind, faster in places, then swirling in tight eddies, stirring people up like dried leaves caught in a thermal spiral. Rumors of a much larger German force spread too, and it brought a slew of questions that nobody could answer. The Sami, for the most part, took the arrival in stride. In the Norwegian community, however, faces ran long. Hopes that they might be spared some of the humiliations of the south and the coast were crushed, and the distant news of warring armies suddenly seemed very real.

By nightfall, they began to gather in the church. Almost every family in the valley had sent someone. Most of the Norwegian notables were there: the schoolmaster, the lawyer, the merchants and the butcher. Only Olaf the innkeeper was visibly absent. Most of the church was filled with the Sami farmers and artisans from the village and the valley. They sat quietly, women to the left, men to the right, looking for an indication of what was to come. At least a hundred people packed the benches and more were streaming in.

Reverend Framhus paced back and forth at the rear of the church, flashing a forced grin as people filed in. Marit noticed the sweat beading on his brow, and how he kept watching the door to see if his brother-in-law, Mr. Larssen, had arrived. He unfolded a few more chairs at the back, but stopped immediately when Erik Larssen stepped inside the church. His shoulders slumped and he left the floor to the mayor, who tried not to hear the litany of questions and comments that came from those near and far from him.

"They've shut the school!"

"Why did they send so many?"

"What do they want?"

Erik Larssen's eyebrows arched, and his lips twisted into a frown. He had been mayor of the village for almost twenty years, but nothing compared to this. People looked to him for reassurance, but Marit doubted he could offer any this evening.

Marit watched as he stood next to the altar, leaning slightly on the low rail, finding his words. Not everybody liked Erik Larssen, but no one questioned his authority or ability to lead the village through the crisis. Marit could see the trust they placed in him, and how they looked to him for a clear vision of what to do. The wooden arch that stretched across the nave of the church framed Erik Larssen. Two carved lions sat atop the frame, leaping towards each other, but they seemed frozen, impotent. Behind them, the painting of Christ in his torn robes was more somber. Christ's sad eyes and the humiliating crown of thorns set the mood of the gathering.

Before Erik needed to call for quiet, a slow hush fell over the room. He spoke in Sami, instead of Norwegian. Most of those there could understand a fair bit of both. Marit wondered about his motives in choosing the native tongue, an unstated message of solidarity between the Norwegians and the Sami.

"I've spoken with the German Commandant. He is an SS Officer." He paused to let this sink in, but neither Marit nor the others understood what this meant. "He is not part of the regular army. They are not invading. They are occupying. The Germans have been sent here to organize the road network. They will use Karasjok as a base for a while. There will be more people coming. Many more people. Prisoners too. The Germans are going to open up a new road to the border, and another running along the river towards Kautokeino. They will be here for a while, and there will be many of them." Some of the faces now began to register a reaction.

"Where will they stay?" someone asked from the back. "They've already taken the school. The hotel is too small for more than a few of them."

"They've taken the hotel as well, which is why Olaf isn't here. The hotel will be Sturmbannführer Lechmann's headquarters. The school is closed until further notice and will be an army barracks."

There was an uneasy shuffling around the room.

"They will be staying with us, Leif. With all of us. They arrived with a detailed map of the valley. They are placing their men in strategic locations in and around the town, as far down the Tana River as Besjokka in Finland—and there are others from elsewhere further down, I'm sure. Eventually they'll build barracks for most of them. But for now, they stay with us."

"We don't want them, Erik. I won't have them in my house, with my wife and children."

"Their quarrel is not with us."

Several of the men near the front of the church began shaking their heads in violent disagreement. Erik straightened up and took stock of the room. Marit thought most would listen to him. He sighed heavily, as if the weight of the occupying Germans was already on his shoulders.

"I don't want them here. No more than any of you do. But we don't have a choice. The government in Oslo has ordered full cooperation. We are allies of the Nazis now, and to refuse them access to the village is treason."

"May God forgive you for saying such foolishness." It was Harald Edvardson, the butcher. He spoke in Norwegian and looked directly at Erik. He stood up, though he didn't need to in the small church. Harald was almost twenty years younger than Erik, but it was not the first time these two men had clashed. One was imbued with the impetuosity of youth, the other hardened by the trials of life.

"Erik, these men come to enslave us and our friends, and destroy the lives we have built here. They have no respect for human life or rules. They mean to bring an end to everything our fathers have fought for. We did not gain our freedom from Sweden only to serve a German master. And ..." he paused a moment, "they are Godless."

"They've left us the church, Harald. If you want to fight them, against our own government, without allies or money or guns, you can fight them alone."

"We are not alone. The British have not fallen, and the Sami still pass freely through the woods and along the paths of the high plateau." He turned purposefully toward the Sami who filled most of the Church. Except for the schoolmaster, the merchants, the administrators and the priest, the whole village was Sami. "We can take to the woods for the winter, and ensure they spend a rotten time in our village."

Several of the Norsemen from the village looked at each other skeptically. A winter in the woods was folly, even for the hardy villagers. Only the nomadic Sami really felt at home in the frigid snows, huddled in their small huts surrounded by reindeer. Even the Sami from the village preferred their warm houses to the rustic comforts of a *lávvu*, the round tents their nomadic cousins slept in all winter.

"The British! They mined our waters and violated our neutrality. It's the British that brought the Germans to Karasjok in the first place," Erik growled back at him. "London is in flames, and the British can hardly defend themselves. As for our Sami brothers, I don't know that they have any intent to fight the Germans." This last bit he said in Sami again, instead of Norwegian.

Harald turned to look towards the Sami that sat silently throughout the church. Most were looking down at their feet. A few shuffled uneasily in their seats under his gaze. It was clear they would not be taking any stand, for one side or the other.

"Pikka? Jan-Peter?" Harald called on two of the more senior Sami in the front row. Neither looked back at him.

Harald did not bother to sit down again. He pushed his way to the end of the row and stormed through the narrow passage that cleared before him, walking past the glares of the men and women and the urging look of the pastor, out into the night. Several others streamed out behind him, but no one spoke. The meeting ended almost before it had begun. The wind blew through the dried birch leaves, creating a rustling that sounded like thousands of tiny feet running away. And behind the wind, under the moonless sky, came the distant muffled howls of the wolves that roamed the hills above the town.

CHAPTER 3

Karasjok, June 1941

THERE IS A BEND IN THE RIVER, just past the Enoksen farm. The river begins to run a little faster past the town, but in the bend it slows as the near bank pulls back and opens into a broad pool. In the summer, the fishing is good, and the children come to swim in the cool waters to get away from the heat and the bugs. The water is just deep enough to swim. The shore is shallow and the rocks are flat. Out near the deeper water, there is an old boulder that the children jump off when the elders are not around. It towers a good eight feet above the water on the steep side. For the older Sami, the boulder is sacred. For the children, it marks the beginning of the deeper water. It's the center of a revolving circle of jumping and clambering as they leap off the high end and swim round to scale the backside and start all over again. Sometimes, in the winter, the ice seems to move it a few feet downstream, but when the children check again they always find it hasn't moved at all, unless it crawls back in the night with the help of the Moon.

Marit and Milly went down to watch the boys push each other off the rock and jostle in the cold waters. After a few minutes, the boys came back to shore and collapsed exhausted in the weak evening sun.

"The water's still freezing from the snows. And running fast. I've had enough," Jan smiled at Marit, as he wrung his wet trousers and put on the shirt he'd left on the bank. "I'm like an ice pan."

"No one sent you out," Marit said.

Milly gave her a sharp jab in the ribs.

"No, but the sun was warm just after noon, and we wanted to be the first into the water this year." Jan hesitated a moment. "I'm surprised how cold it is."

"You weren't even swimming," Marit teased him. "Just splashing like reindeer calves. It's better that way. The current is strong out there."

"Not too strong for us," said the other boy, Sakku, standing taller. Even straight up, he wasn't quite as tall as Milly. Yet it was Marit, four inches shorter, to whom he looked for a reaction.

"I wonder why we come to watch them," Milly said tauntingly. "They won't ever do it."

"Do what?" Jan asked.

"Swim the river, of course."

Jan looked at Sakku, then at the current and turned back to the girls. "You're nuts."

"The current here is much slower than further down. The water isn't that deep. I can almost ford it here."

"It's still freezing. And fast. And you'd have to swim back, or walk four miles half clothed to the village to cross at the bridge. Unless you want to steal Old Man Jacobsen's boat."

Old Man Jacobsen had the only farm on the other side of the river this far downstream. It sat under the steep hills of the far side, and the children all thought it was haunted. Old Man Jacobsen himself was probably close to one hundred, and no one was quite sure whether he was dead or alive. He could sit for hours staring out into space.

Jan sat down on a large rock.

"He's scared," Marit told Milly.

Milly shifted back and forth, putting her weight first on one foot, then on the other. No one said anything for a moment. In the distance, from the hill above the flood plain, the children could hear the prisoners from the German war camp that were opening the road to the Finnish border, a slow but constant hammering against the rocks, punctuated by the occasional dumping of a wheelbarrow. The far off sounds only underscored the quiet on the riverbank.

Sakku tossed a rock lazily into the water. "The trouble with you girls is you're all talk. Maybe if you could swim, we'd rise more easily to your challenges."

"I *can* swim," Marit protested.

Sakku looked down on her with a condescending smile. "Girls can't swim. You always think you're better, Enoksen, but you're just like the rest of them."

"Come on, Marit," Milly said, reaching for Marit's arm. "Let's let these two freeze out here."

The sun was already low in the sky, although it would not go any lower this time of the year. It cast long shadows, in a cold, piercing light. Marit stepped towards the shore and began to take off her shoes.

"Marit? What are you doing?" Milly seemed panicked.

"Relax, Milly. She's bluffing. Even Jan can't swim the river in the spring, and she knows it." Sakku sat down and tossed another stone into the current. Marit stripped off her stockings from under her dress and rolled up her sleeves as high as they would go. Her brown hair shone in the sun as she set her bonnet down next to the leggings. Neither boy moved until she started into the river.

Milly just stared, blankfaced, her hand slightly over her mouth.

Marit was out as far as the pile of rocks when Jan and Sakku realized she wasn't stopping. She didn't even slow down. She wasn't walking anymore. She reached out over the cold water in long broad strokes, aiming upstream so that the current would help her cross. Her dress weighed her down, but she made good progress. She was closing the distance to the far shore with strong methodical strokes. The current was stronger closer to the far shore though, and it was harder to keep ahead of it. It pulled her toward the sand spit that marked the turn in the river. If it brought her past it, she could be swept downstream into the faster flowing Tana River a few miles east. Just when it seemed she would not reach the shore, she rose suddenly, finding her footing, and walked up the sandy bank to sit in the sun. Her small body cast a long shadow along the beach, reaching up to the edge of the pine forest behind her.

Three hundred feet away, the boys jeered. "You're crazy, Enoksen. You could have drowned." Jan's voice was resentful. Marit could hear the anger, even from the across the river.

Milly was jumping up and down excitedly. "Marit swims better than a boy!" Marit saw her clap her hands together again and again. She stood up and began walking back upstream along the narrow sand bar. She stopped after a few hundred feet, where the strong current was narrowest.

"Go further up," Jan shouted as she started back into the frigid waters. "Go further up!" His shouting seemed far off, drowned by the water's many voices.

Marit leaped into the river. It felt even colder now. Her wet dress seemed made of stone, and her heart raced wildly as she floundered against the current. Her arms moved like lead in the water, losing speed as the river grew stronger and reached out to wrap a thousand watery arms around her. In the distance, the boys were shouting something, but she could not make out the individual words. The rushing of the water was growing louder, either from her panicked flailing or from the current. She was at its strongest point now. She tried to see her friends on the shore, but her head kept dropping below the water. The current pounded her against a rock and she felt a sharp pain in her left side. Her body shuddered and suddenly the current took control, slamming her against another rock. She felt a third strike, this time in her back. Her dress pulled up against her neck and seemed to strangle her. She was being dragged backwards, swallowing water. Reaching down, she found a boulder and twisted herself around. With a kick, she scambled forward across the current.

Then, in an instant, it stopped. The waves rushed by in the distance, but the water around her was calm. Her dress slackened, and Jan placed his arms around her waist. She flinched when he touched her left side.

"Are you okay?"

She turned to face him. His arrogance was gone. Instead he had a worried look on his very wet face.

"Yes, I'm okay." She stood on her own and slowly dragged herself to the shore. She tried to keep her bottom lip still. "I told you I could swim."

Marit threw herself onto the rocky shore and lay for a moment, staring upward. Her arms were trembling and her teeth started to chatter. She tried to stop shaking, but only shook harder.

"She's going into shock," Jan said. "We have to get her undressed." Milly stood staring, rigid as a pole.

"Sakku, take off your shirt and pants. Milly, you get her dress off fast, and lie close to her. If she stops shaking, we'll put Sakku's things onto her. I'm getting help." He turned and broke into a dead run, straight towards his father's farm, less than a mile away.

Milly was crying now, in short bursts, trying to wipe her nose in between. Marit kept shaking.

"Rub her skin, Milly," Sakku said, looking over his shoulder. Milly wasn't taking her dress off. She just stared, rubbing Marit's arm a little and wiping her nose again with her sleeve. "Milleeee!" Sakku kneeled beside Marit. He pulled the dress over her head and put his hands onto Marit's naked chest. He rubbed her vigorously. In his panic, he seemed not to notice her taut breasts. Her skin was like ice, cold and pallid. Milly shifted behind Sakku and started rubbing each of Marit's legs. Marit shook a little less.

"Are you feeling any better, Marit?" Sakku asked. Her eyes rolled a little. "Don't worry. Jan's gone to get help. He won't be long."

Despite the light, the evening cold began to set in. Even the dry teenagers were shivering. Sakku took his shirt and put it onto Marit, and slid his pants onto her as well.

Marit heard Jan's horse, the hooves pounding against the rough trail at a breakneck pace. The beating rang in her head, growing louder until she thought the ground shook. Jan stormed into the clearing by the shore and swung off his horse in a single motion. He was carrying a blanket, which he wrapped around Marit without hesitation. Jan's father came riding up behind him a few seconds later. Neither said anything. The two put Marit onto Mr. Erikssen's horse, and Jan's father jumped up behind her. He placed his hand against Marit's neck, and then on her wrist, before he started off at a gallop back towards the farm.

Jan turned to his two friends.

"We're taking her back. My mother has started a fire. My father says she has to get warm quickly or her body won't recover from the shock. I have to get back."

"What about us?"

"You can walk back. Your parents will be wondering about you for sure by now. If Marit gets better, I'll bring them word."

"Jan, I gave Marit my clothes." He was standing in his underwear, shivering in the evening air.

Jan smiled. "Well, I guess she won't mind if you borrow hers then." With that, he rode off, already some distance behind his father.

Sakku stared at the wet dress piled into a mound on the rocks by the shore. He kicked a stone into the river and swore loudly. Milly bit her lip before bursting into a loud laugh. "I'm sorry, Sakku. I'm worried about Marit. But I would do anything to see the look of your parents when you come home late in a wet dress."

*   *   *

The fire was roaring in the woodstove of the small living room as Mr. Erikssen rode up to the farm and took Marit off the horse. She was too weak to walk, so he carried her into the house, still wrapped in blankets, and laid her on the floor on a reindeer skin next to the fire. Mrs. Erikssen felt her brow and her hands, and shook her head. "Alright, now leave, both of you." She stripped off her own clothes and then the blankets and Sakku's shirt and trousers. She took off Marit's wet undergarments, and lay her naked on a reindeer skin rug in front of the fire. She lay down at her side, pulling her close, wrapping the rug around them.

Marit was wide eyed. "What are you doing?"

"I'm warming you up, and don't think I'm happy about it. You were a foolish girl, but I think you'll be alright."

"How's Jan?"

"He's fine. A little wet, and very concerned. Shame on you, Marit Enoksen," she added. She meant to scold her, but it came out softly, almost as an endearment.

In a few minutes, Marit's body temperature had risen several degrees. She was shaken, but not in shock. The women dressed and Marit sat in her boy clothes, huddled in the deerskin, close by the fire. Mrs. Erikssen brought her a mug of warm herbal tea. Mr. Erikssen was back in the room, sipping fish soup quietly at the table. Jan was nowhere to be seen, and Marit didn't ask where he had gone. She watched the fire crackle, and was happy the Erikssens asked no questions. *There would be a time for that later*, she thought. Sure enough, it was only minutes later that Lidy came in, followed by Jan. Her mother's glass eyes left Marit cold again, but she noticed Lidy's hands were shaking too. Perhaps there was worry as well as anger behind Lidy's impenetrable expression.

Mr. Erikssen rose and raised his hand before Lidy had spoken her first word of reproach. "Mrs. Enoksen, thank the Lord, she's fine. I'm sure she's happy to see you, but she'll stay here tonight, until she gets some of her strength back." He looked Marit squarely in the eye and winked.

Lidy seemed to melt as she rushed past the old farmer and threw her arms around Marit. "Yes, Mr. Erikssen, thank the Lord."

"And Jan," Marit added.

She looked around, but did not find Jan in the room.

"He's tending the horses," Mr. Erikssen said in response to her unasked question. "We need to lay you a bed near the fire, and you need to rest. Get some sleep, child."

Mrs. Erikssen brought some pillows and Marit let her head fall back into them. Without another word, she closed her eyes and let her thoughts wander. Sleep called to her. She could just make out the individual words that the adults were speaking, but not their meaning.

"It happened yesterday," Mr. Erikssen was saying. "Like a lightning strike. No one expected it …"

It?

"… twenty divisions. Planes, tanks. Like the Western Front, all over again. They will push all the way to Moscow," Mr. Erikssen went on.

"Maybe some of the Germans will leave," Lidy said.

"More likely that even more will come. They have been preparing for this. This is why they are building the road to Finland, and the new railway line they want to put through. This will be their highway. They will follow it right to Leningrad, to Moscow even … We already have German political prisoners in the camp outside of town. Now we will have Russians too."

Mr. Erikssen sounded resigned. Everybody had noted the new camp they were building on the left bank of the river, just before the town. For now, it was empty, but it was big enough to house hundreds of prisoners. It was the third such camp in or around Karasjok. "And if they do not get to Moscow, and the Russians push back, war will come here."

"Here?" Lidy looked at the Erikssens in alarm. "To Karasjok?"

Marit came a little more awake at her mother's surprise. It was not the first time people were afraid the war would come. But even the arrival of the Germans had brought less change than people thought. Most of them were engineers, not fighters. After a few months, people became used to the Germans. Marit tried to imagine what it meant that the war might come. Hadn't the war come already?

Jan's father peered long and hard at the wall of the little house, speaking as much to himself as to Lidy.

"Yes, even here, to little Karasjok."

CHAPTER 4

Karasjok, July 1942

THE NEW PRISONERS ARRIVED in the dead of the night, marching along the road that crossed the desolate *vidda*, the barren plateau that separated Karasjok from the woods and mountains around Skoganvarre just inland from the fjord and Lakselv. Marit could only imagine the impression the *vidda* made on the men in the eerie summer night light, with stunted birch and alder casting shadows two to three times longer than the trees were high. Without the reindeer, without the elk, the summer *vidda* was even more desolate, but birds did flitter here and there, and field mice scurried along ditches that ran either side of the narrow road. The Germans who marched the prisoners across the plateau eyed it with a mixture of fear and respect. They knew from their colleagues in Karasjok that more than one German had had a little too much to drink and gone off wandering in the *vidda*, only to be lost in its endless mazes and deceptive terrain. Just a few hundred feet off the road, the seemingly flat land was so traversed by ditches and small ravines that the road itself was no longer visible, and moving forward required that you follow the lay of the land, not the direction you wanted to take. Only the Sami herders knew the paths of the *vidda*, and they kept those secrets to themselves.

Marit was sleeping over at Milly's house in the village. Milly's parents ran a small saddlery where they made harnesses and other tack for the horses and reindeer of the valley. Milly's room was just under the rafters above the little house, and from her small window they could see across the river to the high ground where the German soldiers had been unrolling barbed wire and building two watch towers for the past week. It was clear to everyone in town what they were building, but nobody asked about it, and none of the Germans said anything about it. It was an unspoken covenant—a pact of silence many times repeated over the course of the war.

Tonight, though, nothing could cover the noise of the three hundred prisoners as they marched down the north road into the far side of the village. They walked in silence, but the soldiers carried packs with pans that clanged, and occasionally a shout would go up from one of the German soldiers: "*Schneller! Schneller!*" Even the muted scuffled of the three hundred pairs of feet made enough of a din that Marit couldn't help but hear them.

In the dim light, the girls peered across the river and saw the column winding its way down into the valley. They walked two astride spread over several hundred feet, with soldiers every forty feet to either side of the main column. For a quarter of an hour the girls watched as the column wound its way down into the village, turned left just before crossing the bridge, and went up again out the east road towards the new camp just outside of town.

The girls could see the camp too from the window, or at least the towers. They watched in surprise as bright lights lit up the field at the approach of the prisoners. Even though the sun already shone from the west, the lights from the towers drowned the long shadows and made the camp much brighter than the surrounding fields. There was more yelling now, and Marit and Milly both heard muffled noises from the neighboring houses. A light came on at the Alriksons, where the schoolmaster was living now. A door closed two houses further down at Old Widow Nansen's place.

The next morning, the village got its first close up look at the prisoners. They were thin and unshaven. Their clothes were very dirty. They walked without chains over the bridge and onto the new road the Germans had started building to the Finnish border. Another road had been started in Finland, built by Russians taken from the Eastern Front. The two roads would meet over the Tana, twelve miles downstream.

Marit and Milly stood just outside the bakery and watched the long line file by in silence. Several of them looked up at the girls with pleading eyes, but they said nothing. At the end of the line, two of the German soldiers pulled the last two prisoners aside and pushed them over to the bakery. Marit and Milly looked at each other partly shocked, partly scared. The four men came over to the bakery and passed inside.

"Come on," Marit said before Milly could protest. She pulled the door open and followed them inside.

One soldier was standing close to the two prisoners. The other one was trying to talk to the baker. The baker spoke no German, and the German spoke no Norwegian or Sami.

"They will work with you here," the soldier said raising his voice. "They will bake bread." The baker shrugged and looked past the soldier to the two men.

"Marit," he said smiling. "You speak some German. Can you tell me what he wants?" Jon Johanssen wasn't intimidated by the two soldiers, and wanted to get back to his work.

"He wants the prisoners to work with you," Marit said in Sami.

"What?" the baker looked at the two men in their ragged clothes. They almost certainly had lice.

By now the soldier too became interested in Marit.

"*Sprichst Du Deutsch?*" he asked.

"Yes, I speak a little," she answered in German.

"Very good. Tell him the prisoners will work in the bakery every day. They are to cook bread for the new camp. There are three hundred men that need bread once a day." The soldier seemed relieved to have someone to talk to.

Marit translated for Mr. Johanssen, who lifted an eyebrow and started to frown.

"Three hundred men?"

"The prisoners. They arrived last night. They aren't German. They aren't Russian," Marit explained.

"We're Serbian," one of the prisoners said in German with a strong accent.

The soldier standing next to him rammed the butt of his rifle into the prisoner's ribs and watched him crumple forward.

Marit felt her own stomach rise in her mouth but swallowed hard and fast. The prisoner held his arms across his stomach.

"I won't have enough flour for all these men," the baker said, losing some of his confidence as he watched the prisoner struggle back to his feet. "I have flour for a few days, maybe a week. I'll need more."

"Don't worry," the first German guard said to Marit. "They don't eat very much."

The two guards laughed at the joke and went back outside, leaving the two prisoners with the baker and Marit.

"Alright," the baker said. "We'd better get to work. Marit, I need your help to translate today, at least until we can figure out what is going on." The baker seemed uncertain what to do next, and Marit could see that he was more shaken than she had first thought.

"I can stay."

"Good. Tell them to get washed. And tell Milly to come in."

Mr. Johanssen pointed to the window where Milly had cupped her hands around her head trying to peer through and see what was going on inside. Even the prisoners laughed, which broke the tension like river ice in the spring.

"I'm Milos," the one that spoke a little German said. "And this is Danik." The other man just smiled. They were probably in their late twenties, but their skin was wrinkled and their hair was graying. "We're from Belgrade. I told the Germans I used to work in a bakery."

Marit grinned. "But you don't know how to make bread."

"Exactly. I'm glad the guards left." Milos' lips parted and revealed two missing teeth; he was clearly proud of his white lie.

The prisoners were partisans from Yugoslavia. The Germans shipped three hundred of them by boat. They walked all through the night from the fjord at Lakselv and were already working today. They were the new work crew for the border road.

Marit explained to Mr. Johanssen, and he explained back what they would do. It wasn't very hard work, and both of them snacked liberally on the dough as they rolled it out and kneaded it down. Marit was beginning to understand why Milos had lied to the soldiers.

Marit stayed all day with Milos, Danik, and Mr. Johanssen. By late afternoon, there were several large sacks of bread waiting out back by the oven. It was Milly who ran in first, warning the guards were coming back.

"They're coming down the road—the whole lot of them. The prisoners and all the guards too."

The column stopped at the bakery and the two guards from the morning came in together. They motioned for Milos and Danik to pick up the bags of bread. They each took two, and the baker took the last bag himself. The German who'd spoken that morning stepped forward and put his gun against Mr. Johanssen's chest. He motioned to set the bag down.

"*Nur vier*," he said. "*Vier sind genug.*"

"He's says four bags are enough," Marit whispered.

The baker set the fifth bag down.

The two young girls and the baker watched as the column started up again, winding its way through the town and over the bridge.

"I can come tomorrow too," Marit said to the baker.

"If you like," he smiled back.

The girls stepped out to follow the column a short ways towards the bridge.

A few houses down, by the schoolhouse, Mr. Dahlstrøm spoke with one of the German officers. Marit wondered what Mr. Dahlstrøm had to say to these men.

Marit came back to the bakery every day that week, and every day the following week as well. There hadn't been any school since the Germans first took over the school house, and Bera and Lidy said she could work in the bakery for a few weeks if she didn't fall too far behind in her chores. She had to go to town anyway for her German lessons with Mr. Dahlstrøm. Lidy didn't like it, but Bera felt someone needed to speak the language of these men, and Marit was the only option. Marit was even learning a little Serbian from Danik and Milos, and could now bake several different types of bread. She had almost forgotten that Danik and Milos were prisoners until the Friday morning of the second week.

"Tell Danik I need him to get me more flour," Mr. Johanssen said.

"I'll go with him," Milos said.

They walked out the back door and headed across the courtyard to the barn where the flour was kept. Minutes passed. Neither Danik nor Milos reappeared.

"Tell them to hurry up. I want to make the next batch before lunch."

Marit stared out the window at the barn where the sacks of flour were.

"Go tell them," Mr. Johanssen said again.

She went out the back door, her chest tightening. Somewhere inside of her, she knew already she would not find them. Inside the barn, she could see the flour stacked in piles ten and twelve bags high.

No Danik, no Milos.

She walked back to the bakery, her feet heavy.

"They're not in the barn," she said almost under her breath.

Mr. Johanssen looked at her with a mixture of fear and anger.

"Go get the Germans."

"What?"

"You heard me."

"We can't tell the Germans!"

Mr. Johanssen grabbed the collar of her dress and pulled her close to him, "We damn well can tell the Germans. If the Germans come back and they aren't here and we haven't told them, you and I and everyone else nearby will be dead. Don't you understand? Now go, run!"

Marit stumbled out of the bakery and into the street. She sprinted a short way toward the schoolhouse and saw one of the officers coming out of the building. She came over, out of breath.

"Yes?" He wasn't unfriendly. Maybe even curious.

"I was working at the bakery ... with the prisoners. We can't find them. They've gone."

In minutes the calm of the village was transformed into a chaotic whirlwind as soldiers ran left and right yelling out things in German which the villagers did not understand. Soldiers were going in and out of people's houses, and occasionally the soldiers took someone out of the house when they left. Mr. Johanssen was kneeling in the street in front of his shop. His shirt was off and one of the soldiers was beating him. There was blood trickling down his back.

Marit was standing slightly behind Mr. Johanssen, choking back tears. Several of the villagers stared from the windows of their houses, but except for the people being corralled into the street in front of the schoolhouse, no one was venturing out.

Eventually, the soldiers decided that Marit and Mr. Johanssen really didn't know where the two Serbians had gone. Marit was allowed to go home, and Mr. Johanssen went back to his bakery where his wife welcomed him with tears.

Marit had seldom covered the ground between the village and her house so quickly. The path ran parallel to the river, but a little higher up now ran the road, the Blood Road, as the villagers had baptized it these last days, as the nature of the work and its toll on the workers became more obvious.

It had felt like every soldier in the valley was rifling through the town, but as she ran along the path she could see the Serbians still hard at work, and several soldiers chatting by the roadside. The prisoners shoveled the crushed stone into the trucks that carried it to where it filled the marshes and gullies the road ran through.

Marit approached the farm. She could see Milly outside with Lidy. They were getting ready to go down to the water's edge where they kept the boats. Both women dropped what they were carrying and ran to her as soon as she came into the farmyard.

"My God, child. Dear God." Lidy held Marit close to her, closer than she had in many years. Marit could feel Lidy's body heave up and down as she cried softly into Marit's hair and stroked her back. "I thought they were going to kill you."

"No, Mother. They just want the prisoners back. They aren't going to kill either me or Mr. Johanssen. Although, I was very afraid for a bit."

Milly tried to smile and make light of things. "Marit Enoksen, adventuress extraordinaire. Nobody gets into trouble like you, Marit."

Marit found it rather brave of Milly to talk like that in front of Lidy, but Lidy just smiled and held Marit more tightly. Milly and Lidy seemed to understand each other, and know what to expect from one another. Somehow, somewhere inside, Marit felt a hint of jealousy that Milly could communicate so well with Lidy. Whatever Lidy and Milly had been expecting from Marit, it wasn't that she would run back alone unharmed to the farm.

Marit did not return to the bakery the next day. The day after that was Sunday, and the baker did not work. In church, nobody said anything about the prisoners to Mr. Johanssen, and he didn't stay after the service to talk with the other men as he always did.

By Monday, Marit had reassured Lidy enough that she was allowed to go back into the village to see how Mr. Johanssen was faring and to tell him she would not be helping in the bakery every day anymore. She could help from time to time to be sure that the baker could understand and be understood, but she could not come every day.

Nobody in the village was talking about the escaped prisoners, even though everybody must be thinking of them. They could not survive in the *vidda* without help, even in the summer. Everybody knew this. Perhaps they had already fled southwest, to the Swedish border. It was a long walk, and without knowledge of the woods, they would certainly get lost. Even the more obvious paths were poorly marked, and those were patrolled by the Germans.

In the bakery, Mr. Johanssen had two new prisoners. Neither talked very much, and the atmosphere was very different from that of the previous week. Mr. Johanssen was tense and treated the prisoners as prisoners, not as friends or allies against the Germans. When Mr. Johanssen went to get the flour in the barn, one of the men took Marit's hand. At first she wanted to scream, but he looked calmly into her eyes, and placed a small wooden carving in her palm.

It was a horse.

It was still rough and not quite finished, but its features were clear. It was a stocky horse, with big shoulders and thin legs, and a short neck and large head. He held her hand a moment longer, and said simply: "Milos. *Danke.*"

Did he think she had helped him escape?

She clutched the horse. She could feel her heart beat in each of her taut fingers.

She had done nothing. Why does he thank her?

She put the horse into her pocket and left the bakery. A few streets away, she found Milly outside with her little brother playing in the yard with a red ball. Milly's brother Sven was only eight, but he liked to kick the ball back and forth with his fifteen- year-old sister, and was pretty good at it. Milly sat down in the tall yellow grass when Marit came over.

"You're not working at the bakery anymore?"

"No," Marit said. "Lidy forbids it, and I don't think I want to. I go in to help Mr. Johanssen from time to time, but that's all. I can't stop thinking of Milos and Danik, and what has become of them."

The horse burned in her pocket. Her hand was holding it again.

"What *has* become of them?"

"How should I know?" Marit asked defensively.

"I just thought ..."

"What did you think?"

"Nothing. It's just you said you were thinking of them."

"Look!" Milly's brother called out.

Several of the other children from the village were running towards the bridge. A few of the older villagers were stopped by the roadside, watching a small procession coming from the southwest along the path that followed the river there. They were headed for the bridge.

Marit knew who they were before she could make out their features.

Her heart felt like a stone in her breast. The two prisoners were bound just above the knees so that it was hard to walk except with little steps. From their hands behind their backs came a long lead, each of which was held by a German soldier who yanked erratically on the rope so that the prisoners sometimes lost their balance and fell. A third soldier took up the rear and kicked the prisoners when they stumbled.

"*Schneller! Schwein!*"

"What are they saying?" Milly's brother asked.

"Faster. Pig."

No one in the village said a word. Neither of the prisoners looked up at Marit as they passed by the three children on their way to the bridge. They seemed only half alive, covered in mud to protect them from the flies and gnats, and now caked in dust from the walk back from wherever they were found.

Marit clutched her wooden horse in silence, and let her legs find the way back to the house.

That evening Marit convinced Lidy and Bera to let her sleep at Milly's again. She came back to the village by boat and left the boat tied up by the bank not far from Milly's parents' shop.

The two girls went to bed early and sat at the window trying to see or hear what went on in the camp. It was too far, though, and as the village went to sleep, the girls had to admit they could hear nothing.

"I can't stand it," Marit said. "I have to go see."

"What?"

"I have to *see*." Marit was already out of her bed, pulling her clothes on.

"You knew you would do this when you asked to sleep at my house, didn't you?" Milly's face flushed red, but her voice trembled a little too. She was as much scared as angry.

"Yes. I did."

"You've been waiting 'til everyone is asleep to cross the bridge and see the camp?"

"Yes."

"Damn it, Marit. I'm not going with you. You're going to get killed."

Marit clutched her horse tightly and realized why she had been unable to show it to Milly, even though she wanted to.

"Maybe I will, Milly. It's best you stay here then."

Milly rolled her eyes in frustration. "Marit! I don't want you to go. Please. It's too dangerous."

"I'm going. I'll be back before anyone wakes up."

It wasn't really dark outside, even though it was the middle of the night. The sun was on the horizon just behind the cemetery that overlooked the town. The streets were empty. The houses and occasional trees left long shadows, and there was an eerie silence that made the cold light feel darker. She could her distant laughter inside the bar at the inn, and then music—probably the German soldiers. She darted from building to building, hoping she would not meet a German patrol or one of the villagers wandering home after a late night drink. She met no one.

On the far side of the bridge, she shunned the broad path that led right to the camp, less than a mile outside of town. She knew another one that led up the ridge above the camp, which offered a nice view over the entire field where the prisoners were kept. The trail was a deer trail, and wound its way nicely between the trees and through the brush. She was sure now she would not be seen. The Germans had never made a rule about going near the camp. They must have thought they didn't need to. It was clear that the camp was off limits, and no one was eager to be found nearby.

Before long, she came to the place she was looking for. There was a tall pine tree with easy branches to climb, and it was a denser pine than many of the others. Several of the branches grew close to each other and made large clumps in the tree. She climbed to the largest clump halfway up the tree and settled herself down between the boughs.

From her vantage point, she could see the entire quadrangle of the camp. It was about six hundred feet long and one hundred and fifty feet wide on the inside. A second perimeter of barbed wire ran another thirty feet outside the first perimeter. There was a tall guard tower at one end, and a shorter one near the only gate in or out. Next to the gate was a small hut. Inside the perimeter, there was a single building, built fairly low to the ground. It was hard to believe it could house 300 men. In the yard, a single pine tree had been spared. They had topped it and shaved off the branches. It made a thick pole that stood about eight feet high. Milos and Danik were tied to this tree, one on each side. A strong spotlight shone down directly on them from the roof of the barracks. She couldn't tell from this distance which one was closer to her, but she guessed it was Danik. His beard was shorter and his shoulders not quite as broad.

After a few hours, the village began to come awake. A few boats moved along the river, merchants taking their wares downstream to the Tanafjord, or upriver towards Kautokeino. Marit remembered her promise to go back to Milly's house, but she was as tied to her tree as Milos and Danik were to theirs. Marit stayed in the tree all through the morning, watching the prisoners gather for inspection, then march out of camp to the Blood Road for their day's work. She stayed in the tree all through the day, watching Danik slump a little more every hour, until it seemed it was Milos from the other side of the tree who was trying to use his hands to pull Danik up a little more.

The hours did not seem long to Marit. If anything, she wanted them to be longer. She wanted the sun to stop in the sky. She hoped her two friends might somehow feel that time could stop, and the inevitable end might never come. Her legs ached, and the bugs bothered her. They were small blackflies, and they crawled under her hair and along her neck. They didn't sting; they bit. The wind had died down, and there was an uneasy stillness that hung around the camp like a rock hung on a bird's neck.

At the end of the day, the other prisoners marched back into the camp and lined up in rows of eight around the tree. One of the Germans stepped forward and was saying something, but she couldn't hear him from her tree. He held a long riding crop and used it liberally across Danik and Milos' chests and groins. Marit wondered if this was the man Milos had said they called Donkey, because of his big shoulders, large ears and repetitive yelling.

Marit wanted to look away, but her tired eyes were wide open and something inside of her kept them fixed on the scene that played out in the field below her. By now Danik was slouched completely over his bonds, and did not react to the beating. After a few minutes, one of the other soldiers ran forward with a knife and cut both of the men free. They collapsed to the ground, exhausted. The officer drew a pistol from his holster and stepped towards Milos.

Marit closed her eyes, but it was already too late. She knew what he was doing.

Nothing could drown the noise of the single shot fired from that gun. It rang in her ears, and the vision of her dead friend came through her closed eyes and burned itself into her mind. The ringing did not stop until it was replaced by the second shot. Marit's eyes were still closed, but she could clearly see the officer lifting his pistol from Danik's temple, checking to see if it had any blood on it, and mechanically putting it back in the holster at his side.

When she did open her eyes, her fingers were locked around the little wooden horse, and the men were filing into their barracks--except the two that lay prostrate, arms splayed, at the foot of the topped pine tree.

CHAPTER 5

Karasjok, August 1942

MARIT OFTEN WONDERED whether it was Karasjok that changed after the first escape attempt, or whether it was Marit in her tree above the camp who could never again find the Karasjok she left the night before.

She stayed in the tree for several hours more, until her hands had welts from clinging to the branches, and her neck bled from the bites of the blackflies under her sweat- drenched hair. Her hands smelled of vomit, though she couldn't remember being sick. She didn't go back to Milly's that day. She wandered back to the village, and crossed the bridge as if she was walking into another place. The Germans in their uniforms stood out now, as though they were paper cutouts moving across the painted backdrop of a town. The triste brown uniforms did not fit with the strong yellow of the grasses along the riverbank or the deep blue of the Sami tunics that most of the men in the village wore. Marit found her boat, tied up where she had left it, and pushed it out into the current.

She didn't start the little motor at the back. Instead she let it drift, dipping her paddle into the water only to keep the boat from turning or drifting onto the shore. After a time the boat came to their farmstead. jcover it from the rain.

She walked across the fields towards the farmhouse, letting her feet find the path, her mind somewhere else, anywhere else.

A tree, a copse.

A magpie.

The new road, the Blood Road, up on the hill above the farm, where the Serbians broke rocks and moved wheelbarrows.

The Erikssen's horses in the next field over.

Horses. The horse.

When she did come through the door, only Star seemed relieved and happy to see her. Lidy swore profusely. Bera said nothing, but took a cloth from the line and dipped it into the water bucket, and rubbed her neck and arms to take away the caked blood from the fly bites. Bera looked down Marit's back and saw dozens of the little red welts, oozing blood that drew lines in the sweat. Marit thought she heard her softly humming a familiar Sami song, a *joik*.

Marit could hear Lidy, but she wasn't sure what she was saying. Only Star had a voice, softly licking her hands and staring wide-eyed into her soul. Star's dark pupils seemed larger against her very pale eyes, and in the blackness of the pupils Marit found an understanding that surprised her.

It was as though Star too had been there. Star did not need to be told of the tree or the field. Star could see everything and know everything and never question what to make of it.

It was. That's all. It just was.

* * *

They were in the bedroom, gathered around Marit's bed: Bera, Lidy and Milly. Dr. Olson too.

"One week. Eight days," Lidy corrected herself. "She drinks water. That's all."

Star was curled in a small ball at the foot of the bed, oblivious to the discussion that went on around her.

"She needs to eat," Bera said.

"Milly, has she told you anything about what happened that night?" Dr. Olson asked.

Milly shook her head.

"What is this horse she's clutching?" Lidy asked. Milly shook her head again. She was trapped between the two adults. Her eyes were misting over, but she just shrugged and looked back to Marit, who sat upright in her bed, staring out the window.

"She won't let go of it," Bera said. "She's been holding it since she came home."

"She should get out of bed. There isn't anything wrong with her. Maybe if you asked her to work at the bakery again, or somewhere else in the village."

"That's out of the question," Lidy said. Her eyebrows came together and her voice dropped to a whisper. "That's what got her into this mess in the first place."

"Maybe it can help her get out of it. She can't just sit in bed and waste away."

"Harald Edvardson needs help. His sister has been sick. I can speak with him if you like. It would give her something to do. With the school closed ..."

"There's plenty for her to do here. That's not the problem."

"I'll work with Harald Edvardson." Marit's voice brought a stunned silence, followed by a shout of joy from Milly and a litany of reproach from Lidy, which seemed her own way of expressing her relief, if not joy. The doctor turned to Marit and smiled; even Bera began saying something. They were all talking at once, and Marit could not make out what any of them were saying.

"I'll work with Harald Edvardson," Marit said again. "Would you speak with him, Dr. Olson?"

"Of course, child." He was packing up his bag. It was hot in the room. Marit wondered why they all stood around her bed like this. She put her feet onto the ground and patted Star, who rose to greet her. Their chatter petered out. Bera went back to her chores. Lidy walked the doctor to the door and then outside to the gate in the lower meadow that opened onto the path to the river and the doctor's boat. Milly gave Marit a quick kiss, realizing her ride back to town was already out the door, and before long, Marit was alone again in the room with Star, still holding her wooden horse.

Harald Edvardson.

The butcher. His sister wasn't sick. Everyone in the village knew she was not sick. Arnfrid Edvardson spent her days hanging around the German barracks, flirting with soldiers instead of helping her brother in the shop. That was why Harald Edvardson needed help.

* * *

Harald Edvardson's shop was several doors down from the school, which was now the barracks for the German engineers that filled the town. They worked on the road to Finland, on the road to Kautokeino, on the widening of the Lakselv road, even on the railway that was to link Lappland to the south and to Finland, with Karasjok as a major stop. The small town bustled. From around 1200 inhabitants before the war, it had swelled to over 2000 now. Of course most of the new arrivals lived in camps outside the town, but they were seen in the village as well. There were Serbian prisoners at the bakery and the Todt barracks. There were Russian prisoners working on the Blood Road and at the smithy. There were even prisoners helping to build boats down under the bridge at the old boat house.

In late August, there was a second attempt by another Serbian to escape. He left the road crew and ran off through the pines. The men moved between crews, and he wasn't missed for hours. Two days later they found him hiding in the hills near the cemetery. He had stolen a chicken from the Upsahl farm. Mrs. Upsahl became scared and called the Germans to come see if there was anything dangerous in the forest behind the house.

As with Danik and Milos, they tied him to the pine and shot him. This time Marit did not see the events firsthand. She heard them from Arnfrid, and tried not to listen, hoping that the visions of Milos and Danik would not come back.

But they did.

They had never left, in fact. They lived in the shadows of her mind, lurking there until her mind wandered out of the light, always ready to reappear, never really gone. Donkey in his gray officer's dress. The crop. The gun. The single shot. Another single shot.

"Marit?"

It was Arnfrid. Marit looked up at the back door of the small shop. Mr. Edvardson was out front dealing with clients. Arnfrid stood in the doorway, staring at Marit. *How long had she been there?*

Before the war, Marit had always liked Arnfrid. She was a few years older than Marit, and Marit admired her long blond hair and deep blue eyes. She would help the schoolmaster, and Marit wanted to be like her. She was taller than Marit, but had similar features: a straight, attractive nose, strong cheeks and slightly rounded eyes that accented their color—blue for Arnfrid, green for Marit. Like Marit, Arnfrid was half Sami, half Norwegian, only in Arnfrid's case, it was her father who was Sami. Arnfrid had her mother's tall, strong build, but her father's penetrating eyes.

"Marit," she asked again. "Are you alright?"

"I'm fine. Just thinking."

"Sometimes it is better not to."

"Not to?"

"Not to think. Really."

Marit wanted to like Arnfrid again. *Why did she spend her afternoons with the off-duty Germans?*

"I promised the garrison some sausages," Arnfrid said after a moment. "Have you made any new ones?"

Marit was stuffing dried blood into intestines as they spoke, but she said nothing. She only stared at her hands.

"I'll wait 'til you finish," Arnfrid said in a remorseful tone that Marit didn't quite understand. *How could she sound sorry for Marit if she was taking the sausages to the Germans?*

CHAPTER 6

Karasjok, October 1942

"THEY'RE HERE! THEY'RE HERE!" Marit ran as fast as she could over the freshly fallen snow, which was already over a foot deep in the courtyard outside the old farmhouse. "They're here."

Bera stepped out into the snow and let her eyes adjust to the darkness. She peered out over the field below the house and across the river. The wind carried the first confirmation of Marit's news: the crisp clang of a cow bell.

"Over there, Babi. They're just about to cross." Marit pointed to the place where the path came out of the woods on the far shore, and sure enough, a few more reindeer cows emerged. They were not hard to pick out now, even by starlight, small patches of darkness breaking away from the large mass of the woods and forming little droplets on the white river.

In a few minutes, there were close to a hundred reindeer working their way across the ice. Jakob, Marit's uncle, was on skis next to the lead reindeer. Two or three of the deer had bells, and the clanging mixed with their huffing and occasional grunting to make a virtual symphony that warmed Marit's heart.

Pulling up the rear of the herd, Marit thought she could make out the little caravan driven by her cousin Andarás. The caravan was led by a strong reindeer that pulled Andarás on a sled. A tether ran from his sled to another reindeer, which pulled another sled, which led another reindeer, and so on until all of the baggage train was linked together. Marit counted five reindeer with five sleds. That would mean they brought their *lávvu*, the traditional Sami tent. Jakob and Lidy fought every year about where he and his son Andarás would stay. Lidy insisted they stay in the farmhouse, which was modern and convenient. Jakob was happier in the *lávvu* and, after trying the farmhouse one season to please his sister, was more convinced than ever that the *lávvu* was a better option.

Lidy opened the gates to the large pen and waited for Jakob. He crossed the river with the first of the herd and worked his way across the field below the farmhouse. To either side of the herd, Marit could hear barking. Those were Jakob's dogs. Star heard them too, and ran out to help herd the reindeer over to the pens. Jakob was out in front of the herd, coming up the hill and whistling instructions to the dogs, all at the same time.

In minutes the courtyard was transformed into a raucous, moving sea of grunting reindeer. There were well over a hundred animals.

"I brought Pikka's herd too this year," Jakob explained to Bera and Lidy. They were eyeing the reindeer suspiciously. A third of the animals had distinctly different patterns carved into their ears. "He will be by next week to take them to his place."

Jakob walked up to Bera and gave her a broad smile, revealing his small teeth and a few holes where others were missing.

"Hello, Babi," Jakob said. Marit watched Jakob greet his stepmother. Babi's hands rested a long while on Jakob's cheek. No one was really sure why they called her Babi, but everybody called Bera Babi. It had become a mark of respect.

Jakob turned a little to face his half sister.

"Hello, Lidy."

Marit, who had held back until Jakob could greet her elders, threw herself headlong into her uncle's arms.

"You're going to knock me over soon!"

"Hello, Jakob! We missed you," Marit said for everyone.

"Still just as pretty. Bet you've been into trouble again."

Marit blushed but did not answer.

"Hey, what about me?" Andarás said from the caravan at the back of the pen, where he was still unhooking the caravan ropes and putting the deer in with the others. Marit ran over and hugged him as well, while the three others continued to chat quietly.

"How was the trip?"

"Uneventful. There's more snow than last year, which is good. We didn't lose any deer, even on the lake crossings. Dad said we did well, given it's just the two of us and the dogs for so many deer."

"You brought the *lávvu*," Marit said in a teasing voice.

Andarás smiled. "Dad's not sleeping in Lidy's house again."

They both started laughing, hard enough that even the other three noticed.

"When you've finished rolling in laughter," Jakob said in a strong voice, "you can bring the *lávvu* round to the sheltered spot above the house and we can set it up for the night."

Lidy looked at him sternly, and Bera smiled.

* * *

Setting up the *lávvu* was very quick work. The cut wood poles were driven into the snow and lashed together with ropes at the top and the bottom. The coverings, instead of the traditional reindeer skins, were woolen weave in large, long rolls that were simply unrolled around the frame of poles. An opening was left at the top, and a flap served as a doorway, facing away from the wind. Andarás and Jakob made a little ridge of snow along the bottom of the woolen blankets to make sure the wind did not blow in, while Marit and Lidy gathered wood to start the fire. They wouldn't need it to cook over since they would eat in the house, but the *lávvu* was a lot more comfortable warm than cold. In an hour the tent was up, and the wood was stacked for the fire. The four of them retreated to the warm comfort of the farmhouse where Bera was cooking dinner.

Marit followed behind the others, taking wood for their own fire on the way. By the time she had stacked enough wood behind the kitchen, the others were already gathered round the woodstove and eating from large bowls.

"Babi, nothing changes here. You still make the best deer gulash in the Finnmark." Jakob was serving himself another large bowl by the fire, conscious of the quiet that had settled over the house.

"Some things change, Jakob," Lidy said.

"Lidy means the Germans," Marit explained as she stepped into the room out of the shadows. Lidy seemed surprised by her sudden entry.

"You don't have the same Germans?"

"They opened a new camp this summer for Serbian prisoners."

"You don't have to talk about it, Marit," Lidy said again. Her voice was almost a whisper.

"*I* don't have to talk about it?" Marit asked accusingly. "*You* brought it up."

"So the Germans opened another camp. There are dozens of camps across Lappland now. Big, small, Russians, Serbians, even Germans—political prisoners," Jakob stated matter-of-factly.

"They shot several prisoners here—for trying to escape."

"Better that they stay then ..."

"They're starving, Jakob," Marit pressed on, her eyes welling up. "They're hardly dressed. They won't survive the winter."

"Marit was there when they were shot," Bera said, not lifting her head from the gulash. "She knew them."

Jakob started to answer and stayed quiet instead. The only noise to be heard were spoons dipping into bowls of gulash. When he did speak, he sounded more philosophical than before.

"It's a war, Marit. People die. Even Sami people ..." His voice trailed off. Perhaps he wanted to sound stern, but his concern for his niece shone through. He locked eyes with Bera and seemed to read her concern too.

* * *

Marit had decided against going back to the tree over the camp, but she could not get the fate of the prisoners out of her mind. She stayed late at the butcher's shop to watch them come back in the evening from the Blood Road and stumble over the bridge. They had only summer shoes, and several limped heavily now. A few had coats or sweaters, but most wore only another shirt over their clothes. It was cold already, but only just below freezing. They would not survive the deep cold of the true Finnmark winter that came with the January winds. Marit wondered if they were meant to. There were only a few kilometers of road left to link to the Russian built road in Finland. The bridge over the Tana River was finished. The Germans seemed to be playing a strange game of attrition: as the last miles of road neared completion, fewer and fewer workers worked more and more slowly, bringing the progress to a near standstill. *Would the road be finished just as the last prisoners froze to death in Karasjok?*

Marit sat in the window of the butcher's shop and watched the prisoners file by in their thin, ragged clothes. It was early evening, but it had been dark for many hours already, and the wind was blowing strongly from the east. It was going to be a cold walk home to the farm.

Marit decided to take the Blood Road back. It was more sheltered from the winds than the path along the river. It ran along the south ridge in the valley. It was only a short walk down the hill from the road to the farm.

A few miles outside of the village, Marit realized she was not alone on the road. For the first part of her walk she noticed nothing. It was a gradual realization, not that she could hear someone else, but that nothing else was making noise. The trees swayed in the wind, of course, but there were no birds or small animals as there often were.

When the snow began to fall in large flakes and cover the road, Marit's suspicions were confirmed by a set of tracks leading the way through the newly fallen snow. Someone else was walking the road ahead of her. In a half hour or so, maybe less, both sets would be covered by the snow and wind, but Marit could clearly make out the delicate outline of a woman's boot.

Marit picked up her pace, almost running along the road, trying to catch up to the ghost walker. The wind shook the branches of the trees, even in the shelter of the forest. Outside, along the river, it must be blistering. It was the first storm of the season, and a bitter one for mid-October. The weather made it hard to follow, even with the tracks through the snow.

After a few minutes, Marit could make out a black shadow moving quickly across the snowy road. She slowed her pace a little and followed from a distance. They were almost at the level of the Enoksen farm when the shadow suddenly turned and darted into the trees.

Had she seen her?

Marit didn't think so, although she couldn't be sure. She came to the place where the tracks turned: the quarry, where the prisoners dug and crushed the stone for the road. A deer trail ran along the edge of the quarry and into the woods. Marit followed the tracks along the narrow trail. After a few moments she came out into a clearing.

The ghost walker was up ahead, tying something to the lower branches of one of the pines that grew interspersed with the aspen. It was hard to see with the moon behind the clouds, but the light reflected on the freshly fallen snow. Marit thought she saw several packages hanging from the pine tree. It was an odd sight, like an austere Christmas tree, oversized and under-decorated. Long lengths of string held long narrow packages.

Marit edged closer to the woman, trying to stay behind the trees, but wanting to see what she was doing. Suddenly, the woman turned and looked toward Marit. In the half-light, it was not easy to see each other, but they recognized each other immediately. Both women were startled. Marit's deep, green eyes stared, transfixed by Arnfrid's pale but beautiful face. For a moment, they were locked in a gaze that could not be broken. Then, without warning and without a single word, Arnfrid turned and ran across the clearing back toward the road.

Marit came up slowly, making sure that Arnfrid did not look back. The tree was close now, a few feet away. The packages swung back and forth slowly in the wind ...

They looked like sausages.

Marit looked more closely. She pulled one close to her.

Sausages.

The tree was decorated with sausages.

She looked quickly down the path, and caught Arnfrid's shadow disappearing into the forest.

Marit left the tree and wandered back to the road, again following Arnfrid's footsteps. At the road, the tracks turned left, back towards the village. Marit turned right instead and followed the road a short way to the trail that led to her farm.

Arnfrid, who spent her days at the garrison, being friendly with the Germans, was smuggling sausages to the Serbians? She wanted not to care about the Serbians, about Arnfrid, about sausages. *Why was she helping them?* If they found her out, she would be put in a camp herself. Or simply shot. They had shot three men and a woman from Lakselv earlier that winter, for trying to help a British spy who'd come ashore off a fishing boat. Arnfrid was feeding prisoners. There wasn't much of a difference. And Marit could only guess at what else she was doing.

Marit felt a strong sinking in her stomach. She'd seen Arnfrid, and Arnfrid had seen her as well. If she said nothing, she too was helping the Serbians.

Her mind flashed back to the topped pine tree, and she swallowed hard again, choking on her own breath, or on fear maybe.

It ran up her stomach, became caught in her throat, and shook her entire body.

She turned quickly and ran as far as she could from the sausages, searching for the trail that led back to the farm, and the comfort of her home.

※   ※   ※

Marit sat on the church bench and tried not to think that every pair of eyes in the small building was staring at her. In the week since seeing Arnfrid, she had gotten out of helping at the butcher's shop with one excuse after another. She had even cancelled her German lesson, for fear she might run into Arnfrid near the barracks. She avoided going into town, but the sausages were in fact not far from her own home.

The sausages she herself had stuffed hung just up the hill, minutes from her house, waiting for the Serbians she was known to have befriended to come find them.

To pick them off and eat them.

What if one of the prisoners was caught eating a sausage?

What if a guard wandered into the woods to follow a prisoner, to be sure he wasn't trying to escape again?

There had been one more escape in September, and now, one month later, there was still no news of him. Maybe this time he had really escaped. Had he been caught, they would have shot him, like the others. In the village, no one mentioned him, but Marit imagined he was not far from anyone's mind.

Bera sat next to Marit and held her elbow. Bera's fingers were strong, and her grip was reassuring. Still, Marit longed to be outside with Star, not in the cramped church. Star, like all the other dogs, waited in the churchyard. The inappropriately named "dog passer", usually the blacksmith or the mayor's uncle, would stand guard at the church door, herding the people in and keeping the dogs out. Still, in Karasjok, the dogs were never far off.

Reverend Framhus was reading in Norwegian from the gospel. It was the story of the crowd that could not stone the adulteress, and gradually turned away. Marit found some comfort in the parable, even if making sausages seemed a far cry from adultery.

In the front row, listening attentively, Marit noticed one of the new German officers. He lived at Jan's house, just one farm over. She had seen him once before when she brought something over to Mrs. Erikssen, and again in the town, from the butcher's window. He was tall and blond, and his hair washed over his head in a great wave. He smiled more than the other Germans. He was looking intently at the minister, as though a harder stare could bring forth the mystery behind the words and switch the Norwegian into German. She liked the look of him, even though he was German.

She felt Bera's grip on her arm strengthening and turned to look at her, catching her cautioning eye.

Was she staring? She let her thoughts drift again as the gospel ended and Dr. Framhus began his long sermon, made longer still by the translator who stood beneath the pulpit under the double lion arch and repeated everything in Sami. Most people there could probably have understood the Norwegian, yet the sermon was always translated into Sami. None of the ministers Marit had known spoke Sami. Dr. Framhus, like his predecessor, was from the South, and spoke in clear, rhythmic Norwegian: *bokmol*, the 'book language'.

When mass was over, Marit was intent on leaving quickly to avoid any discussion with Arnfrid. Arnfrid wasn't in church, however, which was somewhat surprising. Probably over at the barracks again. Her brother was there in church, with their mother. Marit stood apart from the after-church crowd and stroked Star's long coat. Suddenly

Star set off on her own, running forward toward the church door. The dog stopped at the bottom of the steps and greeted the German, who seemed surprised. Marit was quick to look away. When she turned back, the German was in conversation with Mr. Dahlstrøm, and Lidy was walking over slowly with Bera and Star, ready to go back down to the cold river for the boat ride home.

"What was that all about?" Marit asked Star. Star opened her mouth and panted approvingly, looking back twice towards the blond man before walking around behind the church towards the road and the river. "Alright, keep it to yourself." Marit stole a quick glance back, but the German was lost in the crowd of Sami men gathered in front of the church, discussing the week's business, the preparations for the winter market and the long winter that had set upon them so suddenly.

A street away from the beach, where the boats were usually pulled up, Marit saw Arnfrid; not with the Germans as she had thought. She was alone, waiting near the boats, waiting for Marit. Lidy and Bera didn't slow their pace.

"Hello, Arnfrid."

"Hello, Mrs. Enoksen. Babi."

"You've been without our Marit all week," Lidy said, looking at her daughter. "Seems there's been one thing after another."

"I hope we'll have you back this week, Marit. My brother is falling behind."

Marit stole a glance in Arnfird's direction and was caught by her eyes. They weren't aggressive or threatening. They seemed reassuring, if perhaps also a little worried.

"Marit will be back tomorrow," Lidy said.

"Yes, tomorrow morning," Marit managed in a soft voice, as Lidy nudged her.

The three women walked on and climbed into their boat.

"What is the matter with you, child?" Lidy demanded, as they pulled into the slow current, the motor sputtering.

"What do you mean?"

"Why are you avoiding Arnfrid? Or do you take your mother for a fool?"

Bera stared out over the water, looking over Lidy's shoulder, and Marit reached over to take her arm into her hands. She wanted to open her mouth, but as she did, something inside clamped it shut again. She squeezed her grandmother's arm a little harder and lay her head on her shoulder, trying to ignore her mother's plea.

"Don't answer me," Lidy said. She turned away from Marit and looked out over the far bank.

To the left as they motored slowly down the river, Marit could see the tower of the camp looming into view, and above and behind it, the grove of pines that grew on the hill.

* * *

"So you've come back to work after all. I wasn't sure you would after hiding all week." Arnfrid stood just inside the doorway of the shop, far enough in to let Marit off the street, but close enough that Marit could not avoid confronting her.

"Am I supposed to feel guilty for avoiding you?"

"I'm sorry, Marit. But you shouldn't have followed me."

"Well I did. I didn't know it was you."

"You're too nosy for your own good, and now you are in over your head."

"I won't turn you in."

"Very good of you. But you know what that means for you, don't you?"

"Yes." Marit's voice was almost inaudible.

"They're going to die anyway, you know that, don't you? The food I bring them isn't enough, and their clothes aren't warm enough ..."

"Then why do you do it? Why do you take the risk?"

"They'll kill us both if they find out," Arnfrid said, to be sure Marit understood.

Marit stared, trying to speak but losing her voice again. She pulled her hand from her pocket and produced the wooden horse.

"It's from one of them?" Arnfrid asked in a whisper.

Marit nodded.

"The Serbian baker," Arnfrid said as the pieces fell into place. "You were his friend."

"He couldn't bake bread," Marit said, wiping a tear from her cheek and smiling. "I taught him as the baker taught me. After Milos escaped, one of the other prisoners brought it for me."

Marit's heart lifted as she put the horse back into her pocket. She could see that Arnfrid was no longer afraid she was going to tell the Germans. Their exchanged secrets formed a sort of blood pact that neither wanted to break.

"I'm sorry I misjudged you," Marit said, looking into Arnfrid's deep blue eyes. "I thought you were sleeping with the Germans."

"I am," said Arnfrid. Her voice cracked as she spoke, and she swallowed hard.

The girls sat in silence for a minute, neither knowing what to say. Arnfrid was first to speak again.

"They are not all bad, the Germans. There are those who turn a blind eye to what I am doing for the prisoners, but not without a price. If they are happy, they keep their colleagues away. They don't want me to get caught." It was Arnfrid's turn to wipe a tear from her face.

"I hate this war," Marit said. "I hate what it has done to us. And I hate the Germans. I don't understand why God has not protected us."

"He has, Marit. He has. Things can still get a lot worse, and before it's over, maybe they will."

Arnfrid seemed relieved to be at last opening up to someone. She wasn't through with her confidences. "Come on," she said suddenly, grabbing Marit's hand.

They left the shop and ran together out the door into the winter snow. The sun was up, but not very high, even if it was already well past nine. It sat perched on the horizon, threatening to leave at any moment. Arnfrid ran down the street to the bridge and kept running to the other side until Marit called from behind and begged her to slow down. There were a few people milling about: some Sami farmers and a few off duty soldiers. Arnfrid kept walking up the road that ran above the prisoners' camp, and darted into the woods along the same deer trail that Marit had taken to the pine grove.

About half way to the pine trees, she turned right down a steep path that ran straight down the hillside. She walked as swiftly as a deer and Marit had trouble keeping up. She stumbled as they scrambled down the path and almost lost her footing. Eventually, they both stood at the bottom of the hill, only a few hundred feet from the camp, but well hidden in the birch trees that grew densely along the base of the hill. Arnfrid put her fingers to her lips so that Marit could clearly see them, and then turned to walk along the edge of the forest. After a few minutes she stopped. They stood in a small clearing. There was no one anywhere nearby. She edged her way forward to the side of a large pit. There was earth on top of the snow, and the pit steamed a little in the cold air. Marit caught up to her and without realizing it reached out to take Arnfrid's hand.

Marit leaned forward to look down into the pit. The earth around it was piled three feet high on all sides. It was almost full. The bottom was uneven. As she looked closer, Marit could see things coming out of the ground.

A foot.

An elbow.

A shoe.

Marit opened her mouth to scream, but Arnfrid already had her hand over it. She grabbed Marit and pulled her back into the forest as quickly as she could. In the woods, Marit bent forward and was sick, but Arnfrid did not stop dragging her until they reached the bottom of the trail back up the hill. They sat down together and Marit took a handful of snow to wipe her face clean. She took some more and rubbed it on her plaid dress.

"Why did you show me that?" Marit said after a long pause. She stared at Arnfrid, trying to hold back the tears.

"Because you have to know. In case something happens to me. We both have to know."

They walked back up the hill in silence, keeping close to the trees and not speaking again. Even back on the road, they walked side by side without saying a word.

CHAPTER 7

Karasjok, December 1942

THE MOOD IN THE VILLAGE in December 1942 was strangely optimistic. While most of the village felt pity and concern for the Serbian prisoners, the very desperation of the situation shook many out of their helplessness. No one said it, but the news from the Russian front seemed to be close to everyone's thoughts. The Russians had broken the Axis lines at Stalingrad, and caught 300,000 Germans in a noose. In the dead of winter, it was only a question of time before they gave up.

Weeks.

Maybe months.

But there was no escape.

Suddenly the hunter had become the prey, and even in far northern Lappland, the change in balance was obvious. Several villagers, whom Arnfrid had suspected might know of her secret sausage hangings, approached her. They did not want to warn her off, but to offer help. While the atmosphere was still far from revolt, the village took pride in saving a few lives, or at least putting off death for a few more weeks.

It was a bitter blow when the road to the border was finished. In the darkness of the long winter night, just as suddenly as they had appeared, the Serbians were moved out to another camp, somewhere down the new road towards Kautokeino. Karasjok was left to itself, the Sami villagers, the Norwegians and the garrison of German engineers who charted out the Arctic railway and the Kautokeino road … a long and lonely wait for spring.

* * *

"I'm sorry," Marit said in a shaky voice. "I was looking for Mr. Dahlstrøm."

"It's alright, Marit," the young German said, looking up from the table. They were alone in the room that Mr. Dahlstrøm rented as both his quarters and makeshift tutoring room. "Mr. Dahlstrøm stepped out for a few minutes. He'll be back soon," he said in a lilting accent.

"How do you know my name?"

"You're Marit Enoksen. Everybody in the village knows you. You live on the next farm over. I'm staying with the Erikssens a little closer to town."

"I've seen you there," Marit blushed. He was the German from the church. The one that Star liked.

"My name is Hans. Hans Bauer." He smiled.

"I'm surprised you know so much about the village. Most of you only care only about the camp and getting back home."

"This is not so unlike my own home, in Bavaria. The hills here are smaller, and the houses too. But our village is also very small."

"Please tell Mr. Dahlstrøm I can come back another time for my German lesson."

"I think you're having one now." His eyes smiled at his joke—deep blue eyes, the color of the late September sky at dawn, just before the first rays turned everything rosy pink.

"What are you holding?" Marit asked.

"Bizet. It's Carmen."

"Bizet?"

"It's a record. Haven't you seen one?"

"No."

"That's why I'm here. Mr. Dahlstrøm lets me use his gramophone. This is a recording of the Habanera. It's an aria from Bizet's Carmen."

Marit tried to look as though she understood. He talked to her as though she were a child, himself hardly much older. But there was a softness in his voice too.

"Would you like to hear it?" he asked.

"Yes."

He stood up from the table and took the black disk with him to the far side of the room. The gramophone was a small box on the sideboard. He lifted the top of the box and set the record on the platter. Turning the crank on the side of the box, he wound up the machine. As the record began to spin, he lifted the arm and placed the needle on the turning disk. It crackled at first, and then started, a few notes from the strings, and a deep, enchanting voice, in a foreign language. The flutes joined in behind the voice.

Marit closed her eyes. It was a slow, winding music, like a river flowing softly downwards, around many bends. She was lying on the bottom of a small boat, her arms stretched above her head, and the clouds danced around her in strange and changing shapes as she floated further downstream. The river ran quickly and she picked up speed at every turn, as she came closer to the shore. Her boat drifted fast and spun round.

The clouds moved as quickly as the river. There was a bear that became a dog, and then a fox. The fox dissipated until he was flames running along a broad swath of meadow.

Big, generous white clouds.

She could not hear the water; she floated almost above it as the clouds pulled her ever nearer ...

The static from the needle woke her from her reverie as the aria came to an abrupt halt.

"Did you like it?" he asked.

She kept her eyes closed a moment, but sensed him nearer. She heard his slow breathing, and felt his eyes watching her. He couldn't be more than a foot or two from her. She didn't dare open her eyes, for fear he might step away. In her mind, he wore a deep blue tunic, like her father used to wear, with the red band along the collar and the wrists.

"It's beautiful," she began to answer when she heard him walk away to stop the gramophone.

"It's a song about love."

Marit blushed, suddenly embarrassed that she liked it so much. "What is she saying?"

"She says that love is like a rebel bird that no one can tame. You can't control it. It's French."

"Am I interrupting anything?" Mr. Dahlstrøm asked, stepping through the doorway into the room.

Marit took a large step away from Hans and looked down at the floorboards. Broad knotted pine boards.

"I was introducing Marit to Bizet."

"And working on her German too. *Ausgezeichnet!*"

"I can come back later, Mr. Dahlstrøm. Thank you for allowing me to use your gramophone." He bowed toward Marit and again towards the schoolmaster, and was gone.

"Why do you let him come here?" Marit asked.

"What do you mean?"

"You let him come. You could say no. Why are you nice with them?"

Mr. Dahlstrøm stared for a moment at Marit, choosing his words. "Hans is a good man, Marit. He treats the villagers nicely. We would do well to have a few friends on the other side, especially if things get worse for them."

"But he's German ..."

"Yes. So was Goethe, and Schiller and Beethoven." Marit didn't know Goethe or Schiller, but she understood Mr. Dahlstrøm's point. "Being German doesn't make him bad. You are here today to learn German. How can you speak a language if you hate everything it represents?"

Marit wanted to say something. Anything. She couldn't picture Hans in a tunic anymore. He wore the formal dress of German officers. All German officers. She could only close her eyes, trying to block out the vision of Donkey wiping blood from his pistol.

Schwein.

Of course Mr. Dahlstrøm was right, but the world looked so much clearer in black and white.

"Marit, there is no doubt that what the Germans are doing here is wrong. The Nazis are evil, and the way they treat the prisoners is wrong, but we must also recognize good when we see it, and acknowledge it and help it grow. It is the only way things will change."

"And you think this German is good?"

"He has shown some good. He is not alone. Not every German is a Nazi. Many of the Germans and Austrians in the village have shown some good. Of course there are fanatics. Some of our own Norwegians have become quite fanatical about helping them too. Hans does seem good to me."

"Then why doesn't he stop them? How can he let it happen?"

Mr. Dahlstrøm shrugged.

"A great writer—Burke I think—once said, 'All that is necessary for Evil to triumph is that good men do nothing'. He had to say that because good men so often do nothing. It is not always easy to row against the current."

Mr. Dahlstrøm looked to Marit for a reaction, but she did not understand. If there was one concept Marit couldn't fathom, it was the difficulty some people have rowing against the current.

CHAPTER 8

Traundorf, Southern Bavaria, Germany, 1 July, 2013

"GUTEN TAG," **MARIT SAID** to the young girl behind the desk at *Hotel zur Post*.

"*Grüss Gott,*" she smiled back. *May God greet you!*

Yes, thought Marit. *I'm in Bavaria.* She was still breathing heavily from the walk up to the cemetery.

"Will you be staying long, Mrs. Enoksen?"

I don't know, thought Marit. She took a step backwards and sat down on the large pine chair next to the reception desk.

"Mrs. Enoksen?" The girl came around the counter. "Are you alright?"

"Fine. Yes, of course. Forgive me. I am fine." She could hear her breathing in her head.

Deep breath in, slow breath out.

The poor girl probably thought she was going to have a heart attack.

Barely seventeen. Very cute with her blond locks and deep green eyes. Marit's eyes too were green. But her hair had been chocolate brown, before turning gray. Marit looked at her bags stacked next to the counter.

"We'll have your bags brought up to the room. It's ready now. It looks out over the valley. On the church side. Will you be staying long?"

"A few days, I think."

"The room is available until the fifth. I can call around to find you another if you would like to stay longer. It is high season, and can be hard to find a room. Many of the innkeepers only speak German."

"That won't be necessary. A few days should be fine."

I used to speak German, she thought. She wondered if some of the words would come back now that she was here. It was so long ago. Marit struggled to stand and find her balance. "I would like to make a call to America. What time is it in California?"

"It's almost eight in the morning, Mrs. Enoksen. You can call from the room. Dial 00-1. If you need anything, dial 9 for the reception."

"Thank you."

The room did indeed look out over the valley, which was narrow near the village, but broadened and sloped downward as it ran west. The sun was still high in the sky, even though it was almost evening. It bathed the whole valley in a comforting light, much softer than the Californian sun.

The little inn was just a few houses off the main square where the church stood. She could see the steeple from her window. The bed and desk were newly carved pine, with a little heart in the hollow that the back of the chair formed as the two sides came together in the middle. The curtains were checkered red and white, and tied up with slim green strands of woven cloth.

Mary was probably already at work. Or was it Saturday? Marit picked up the phone and dialed Mary's work number.

"Hello?"

"Hello, Mary."

"Mom! Are you alright?"

"I'm fine, Mary." Her voice had a finality to it that left little room for questions.

"I wish you hadn't gone, Mom. I'm worried."

"You worry too much."

"You're so far away. If anything happens ..."

"There are plenty of people here happy to take care of an old lady."

"Have you met anyone?"

"No."

"Did you find what you're looking for, Mom?"

"Not yet. I only just arrived ... It's beautiful, Mary. A lot like Karasjok. Well, Karasjok before the war anyway. The river is much smaller, and the village a little bigger. The mountains are taller too. And there are no reindeer, of course. But it is a good country."

"Mom, what are you doing?"

"I told you. I'm looking for an old friend."

"You said he was dead."

"Yes."

"Some reunion, Mom."

"I saw his grave today. If he is still alive anywhere, if part of what he left behind still lives, it is here. At least I hope it is."

"Mom, who is he?"

Marit stared out the window. *Part of what he left behind was in California too.* She tried to speak—she wanted to—but her mouth was sealed by the passage of time.

"I'm sorry, Mom," Mary said after a moment. "You don't have to say."

"I'll let you know if I find him," Marit managed to answer.

"Come home soon, Mom."

Marit set the phone back down on its cradle.

Home.

Sixty years hadn't made Southern California feel like home. It was as far from home as she could imagine.

Dry, sunny, hot, with strong winds blowing in from the sea. Even the pine trees looked different there.

Home was buggy and humid in the summer, and cold the rest of the year.

Mostly home was dark through the winter, and light all day long for those short summer weeks.

Mary couldn't know that Europe was more her home than even she herself realized.

Even after all the years.

Even in Bavaria.

A knock at the door brought her back from her thoughts.

"Mrs. Enoksen?" The girl from the front desk stuck her head into the room. "I found the address you were looking for. I'm sorry. I'm from the next village over. I don't know everyone in Traundorf so I asked the cook. Bauer is a pretty common name here, but he knew who you meant. He was at the funeral for Mr. Bauer Sr. just two weeks ago. The son's name is Hermann. He has been living in the house for several years now. Mr. Bauer was quite ill these last years, since Mrs. Bauer died. The farm is just outside the village. Dorfstrasse 29. You can walk. It's not far."

"Thank you."

The girl was very sweet. She reminded her a little of herself, so many years ago. A little sweeter.

Maybe Mary was right. What was she doing here? What could she ask Hermann Bauer that she did not already know?

It was a ten-minute walk down the main street of the village a few blocks south of the river. As she came to the edge of the village, she could see the farm on the left. The old house fronted on the street with three levels of balconies above the door. It went back at least one hundred feet, becoming the barn as was the fashion in Bavaria. Behind the house and barn were a few outbuildings, and then the rolling hills that led in steps up the walls of the valley.

To either side of the door was a plaster fresco of a man and a woman. Under the roof, the builders had carved and painted into the massive beams the year of their work: 1789. The shutters were painted a deep green, which contrasted nicely with the cream colored whitewash over the plastered ground floor, and with the rusty brown barn boards of the upper stories.

It was exactly as Hans had described it.

She pushed the wooden gate and started up the path towards the front door. As she reached up to ring the large bell, the door swung open. A tall man stood before her. He was well over sixty, though his hair still had darker patches. His skin and face were wrinkled and his eyes cold.

"What do you want?" he asked in passable English.

"*Grüss Gott!*" she said.

He didn't answer.

"I'm looking for Hermann Bauer," she tried again.

"You've found him."

"My name is Marit Enoksen. I was—"

"I know who you were. What do you want?"

It was hard to believe that this man could have anything to do with Hans. He didn't look like him. He didn't behave like him. He didn't even sound like him.

"I wanted to ask you some questions."

"I can't think of anything I have to tell you."

"I've come a long way. From America. I spoke with your father, just before he died."

"I know. You shouldn't have come. There isn't anything for you here."

He closed the door just as abruptly as it had opened. It was a beautiful door. Large boards held together by old nails and hung on huge hinges. Marit ran her hand slowly along one of the old hinges. It was long and traced a slow curl as it reached out to hold the door. The door stayed shut.

It might be a long four days, she thought to herself, as she walked slowly back to the village. *A very long, lonely four days.*

Back at the hotel, the girl with the blond curls was smiling at her. "You had a visitor."

A visitor?

"Mrs. Enoksen, you had a visitor while you were out."

"But I don't know anyone here."

"He left this." She reached under the desk and handed Marit a small piece of paper folded in half. Marit unfolded it with a shaking hand. The message was written in English, in large, bold print: MEET ME AT REINHARDT'S FOR DINNER.

The girl was still staring at her, smiling.

"Do you know who Reinhardt is?" Marit asked.

"You mean where, Mrs. Enoksen. Reinhardt's is a restaurant in the next village. It is a popular place with the locals. They make excellent deer gulash."

"Ah."

Meet me at Reinhardt's for dinner ...

The girl stared on, as though she had nothing else to do.

"Is it far?" Marit asked.

"Mrs. Enoksen?"

"Is it far to Reinhardt's?"

"A little far to walk. If you'd like to go for dinner, I can arrange for a ride to pick you up." She blushed, probably realizing that Marit hadn't mentioned dinner.

"Very well," Marit answered. At least she wouldn't have to eat alone. And she would meet somebody. Anybody would be welcome after the reception from Hermann that afternoon.

The dining room at Reinhardt's was wood paneled and a little dark. Marit would have had trouble finding her host, if she had known who to look for. A large fire burned in a fireplace in the middle of the room, set up so that it could be seen from every side. Tables were arranged around the chimney in concentric circles. Along the walls and down a few halls that led away from the room, smaller tables were tucked into booths with long hanging lamps that provided muted light. The restaurant was busy but not full.

"*Haben Sie reserviert?*"

"I'm meeting someone," Marit answered in English.

"Ahhh. You must be Mrs. Enoksen. Please follow me."

She cut a path through the tables and led Marit to a small booth tucked away at the back of the room. A man in his eighties sat erect at the table and stood up as she approached.

"Good evening."

"Good evening." If he expected her to be startled or surprised, she made sure that he was disappointed.

"I'm Johannes, an old friend of Hans'. I'm sorry for the mystery. I came to find you at your hotel, but you were out, and I wasn't sure what message to leave."

She gazed for a moment deep into his eyes. They were soft and gentle, with a slight spark. A little like Hans' eyes. *Truly God's country,* Marit thought.

"Thank you for the invitation. I was a little surprised by the message, but I'm happy for the company. I didn't know anyone knew I was coming. Should I remember you? Were you also in Karasjok?"

"No. I was in the war, but in the submarines, in western Norway, and later in France. I was captured by the Americans, and did not come home for many years."

They sat down as he was talking. He seemed old all of sudden, sitting in the darkened restaurant, talking of the war, so long ago. His eyes were framed by a tired, scarred face. He was almost bald, except for the thin strands of very gray hair that he combed elaborately across the top of his head. He was wearing the traditional green vest of the Bavarians, with carved horn buttons holding down his lapels on each side.

"I miss him already," Johannes said.

"I've missed him for sixty-nine years."

Johannes sighed audibly. "He was looking forward to your visit. He asked me to meet you. He said you were very beautiful."

"Maybe I was," she smiled. Her eyes were still a piercing green, and they flashed when she was excited. But tonight, she was discouraged. It was a long way to come to find an old war buddy and deer gulash.

"Hans asked me to help you, Marit."

"Help me do what?"

"Help you do whatever it is you are doing here ..."

Marit stared for a moment into the space between them, which seemed greater all of a sudden.

What am I doing here?

The waitress was already bringing food. The deer gulash. Beer for Johannes. The girl asked her something, and she nodded. Soon she was back with more beer.

"I contacted Hans this spring. It has been so long. I wondered if he was still alive."

"And he was ..." Johannes chuckled. "I'm ninety-two this fall. We aren't getting any younger." He sat upright, and Marit had trouble believing he was really ninety-one years old.

"I was surprised at how easy it was to talk again. I even found some of my German words, although we spoke mostly in English. I don't know when he learned English."

"After the war. Hans was head of the local milk producers. He travelled a lot, actually. Even to Norway."

"Hans and I agreed it would be nice to see each other again. He said he wasn't well, but I'm not that young anymore. It took a while to organize the trip. He wrote a telegram before he died, which someone sent to me ..." Marit wiped her eyes.

Receiving the telegram hadn't made her cry, but everything seemed so much more difficult here, so foreign. For a moment, the tombstone in the cemetery up the hill flashed through her mind. She fingered the worn piece of paper in her pocket and brought it out. She did not need to read it. She remembered every word.

"If you get this, I am no longer among the living. STOP. I'm sorry. STOP. Would have loved to see your eyes in person one more time. FULL STOP."

"I'm not sure who sent it. Maybe the lady at the old age home ..."

"It was the *in person* that grabbed me. I decided maybe I should see what Hans had been living these last sixty-nine years *in person*. We probably should have talked more about it on the phone, but the phone seemed so cold. I wanted to see him. To know it was really him, not just a ghost with a voice. To share like before. Silly, isn't it?"

Her voice trailed off.

"I was happy Hans sent the telegram." She tried to finish her thought. "So I came anyway."

"I saw Hans two weeks ago—the day he died. I was there when they sent for the priest. He was in good spirits. He was surprised the end had come so soon. He thought he would see you again first, but he was at peace."

Marit listened in silence, unwilling to interrupt Johannes' train of thought.

"I can take you to his room, if you like. His room in the home; he moved out of the farm two years ago. He must have told you. They haven't moved anything yet. Hermann has not been in, and the old age home does not want to just move everything out."

Marit gazed into the space between them. *His room.* Of course, he had a room. In a home. He slept in a bed and read books and ate meals. He did not live in her head. He lived here, or at least had lived here. For over sixty years.

"I'd like that very much."

"We can go tomorrow after church. It's right here in the village."

"Tomorrow's Saturday."

"We go to church every day here. At least those of us who are old enough not to have anything else to do. But you're right. Sunday is better. That's visiting day at the home."

Johannes went on talking, but she could not quite hear him over the growing noise from the other tables. Her thoughts were drifting.

After church ... "I don't remember Hans talking about a church. He said he used to walk to the next village to go to church. I wondered about that when I got here. I can see the steeple from my bedroom."

"That was before the war. It's a new church, built in the 1950s. Very modern inside, although it's not obvious from outside. Most of us old timers don't like it much. Maybe you will though. Hans was quite involved in the design. He was instrumental in getting it built.

He was on the committee that chose the artist that did the windows and the statues."

Her thoughts drifted to the Old Church, in Karasjok. It had lived on with her in America, just as Hans had.

In her mind.

"Marit?"

"I think I should be getting back. I'm tired," said Marit.

"I can drive you," Johannes said smiling, swallowing the last of his beer. "Don't worry. Beer makes us better drivers in Bavaria. I still have my permit, and it isn't far." He stood and offered a hand to help her out of the booth. His large fingers felt strong as she held them, and his hands were steady.

"What time is church?"

"Ten o'clock."

"Alright, Johannes. Sunday, we can go to church, and then to the home."

CHAPTER 9

Karasjok, April 1943

STAR WOKE FIRST. She stood at the foot of Marit's bed barking at the top of her lungs. Marit almost fell out of the bed. It took only seconds for Marit, Bera and Lidy to dress and run to the window.

Marit wasn't sure how late it was, but it was still very dark outside. Dark enough that the eerie red and orange glow just upriver from the farm sent rays high into the sky and sent shivers down Marit's spine: Jan's house.

Marit grabbed her coat and pulled on her boots before running out the door. Star passed ahead of her and ran down the snow covered meadow towards the Erikssen farm. It was more than half a mile, but they ran quickly. The snow had been melting and the path was well worn. Still, by the time they arrived, the flames shot eighty feet into the sky. The house and barn were both infernos, every window pouring forth flames. The roof of the barn had caved in. The second story of the house would follow soon.

Star ran over to Jan and his mother, who stood a fair distance back from the buildings. Mrs. Erikssen knelt in the melting snow, crying uncontrollably. Her usually broad shoulders folded forward, her head in her hands. Jan stood above her, his hands on her back, staring at the flames. Jan's younger brother Per-Erik also stood a few meters off, watching the flames.

Marit came up slowly and touched Jan's shoulder. He turned with a start. She could see long streaks running down his soot-covered face; the blaze burned brightly, and was reflected in his hollow gaze. Marit's mouth froze and Jan turned back to his mother. Marit looked left and right, but there was no sign of his sister Ana, of Mr. Erikssen or the German officer.

"They're inside," said Jan, almost inaudibly. "Father, and Ana. He went back in to get her." The roof of the house came crashing down as he spoke, and they all moved back to get away from the suddenly much hotter fire. The roof brought down the top story in a shower of embers and heat. If anyone had harbored any hope that they might still be alive in that inferno, it was extinguished.

"Let's get a little further back,"said Marit. Mrs. Erikssen was walking now, sobbing more softly. The fire devoured the house and barn with a ravenous, insatiable hunger. There was no living creature that could survive that heat. "What about your German?" Marit asked. She didn't want to sound so pejorative, but she was afraid also of showing too much concern for the foreigner.

"Hans is on duty tonight."

There was a coldness to Jan's voice, even though Marit thought he liked Hans, as though he resented that Hans was not there to burn in the fire, like his father and sister. Or maybe if Hans had been there, his sister would have gotten out. Lidy and Bera were arriving, along with several men from further upstream. The Erikssen horses were standing a short distance away from the people, oblivious to the blaze and curious as to why they were not in their barn.

It was unlikely Jan would have had time to save the horses. Marit shuddered at the thought. Both the barn and the house had burned together, and the horses were safe. Someone had lit the fire and let the horses out. Jan left his mother to Lidy and turned to Marit, as if to answer her thought.

"Somebody lit the fire." He didn't say that they were after Hans. He didn't have to. "I was still awake. I saw the barn go up first, and when I came out, the horses were already outside. Then I saw they had lit the summer kitchen too. I tried to put it out. So did Father. When we saw we couldn't, I ran out with Mother and Per-Erik, and he went upstairs to bring Ana out. We should have just gotten Ana out first."

* * *

The knell could be heard from up and down the valley. Funerals always seem to be held on still, windless days, as though the contrast to the raging elements which so often lead to death was in itself important: a howling inferno, a torrential flood or a winter's storm. Marit was glad to be in the church and not at the farm. The Enoksen farm was only a half mile downwind of the Erikssen's, and the acrid smell of the burned buildings lingered in the air even three days later. It was only burned wood, but Marit imagined Mr. Erikssen and Ana in the house, trapped and choking, and this made the smoky odor even more nauseating.

In her mind, Donkey was in the house too, with his tall riding boots and pistol. He ran from one end of the living room to the other with a long torch, lighting curtains, upturning tables and laughing.

Marit looked out across the pews and saw the faces of her neighbors, and most of the leaders of the community. Per Erikssen was popular, both with the farming Sami and the nomadic Sami who followed the herds. He would visit their tents when they came into town, and drink their spirits. He had been champion at the reindeer sled races twenty years back in Kautokeino and no one had forgotten. Hans, the German officer, sat near the front beside Per's window. He stared forward, expressionless. He was visibly moved by the event, if not the ceremony, of which he could understand nothing.

In front of the altar, two coffins lay side by side, one so much larger than the other. Both lids were already nailed down. The tiny pine coffin was a magnet for the villagers' gazes. Everyone tried to look away, but even Marit felt the compulsion to look again and again at the little yellow box, and imagine the charred bones and disfigured body of little Ana.

Reverend Framhus spoke slowly, choosing his words. The fire was suspect. It was the third fire this year in a house sheltering a German officer. Not only had Per died, but Hans, the officer on duty that night, far from home, had only discovered the blaze when its smoldering ashes floated in the morning breeze to greet him as he walked along the river path. More than one onlooker felt it should have been Hans' funeral, not Per's.

"Per was an honest man, who lived an honest life. God lays a bountiful table for such men. He has promised it. Per was not a rich man. Per was a working man. Every hardship Per endured is a stone laid on the path towards his redemption."

Marit's mind stopped at redemption.

Redemption?

What had Per Erikssen done that required redemption? He had lived his whole life honestly, and earnestly. Why did God take him so early, and why had Per to redeem an original sin he knew nothing of?

Marit turned to Lidy and saw that she was nodding in agreement. Redemption.

We were all struggling to overcome the terrible weight of something we had never done. Hans too was nodding. Perhaps he was beginning to understand some of the Norwegian. More likely, he felt the general tone of remorse and wanted somehow to share the feelings of the mourners.

Reverend Framhus had finished extolling Per's virtues, and was now condemning in no uncertain terms the use of violence, any violence, to achieve one's goals—even if the goals might be justified. Violence served no useful purpose. Violence had cost a four-year-old child her innocent life.

What would redeem her, Marit wondered, *if she too was fraught with original sin?* Marit imagined a whole village of sacrificial lambs, lining up for the slaughter as Reverend Framhus told them all to turn the other cheek. It was more complicated of course. Somebody's violence and hatred for the Germans had led to Per and Ana's death. But the alternative to the growing violence was to do nothing. Despite the Reverend's words, the tension in the church was palpable and the tiny casket was like a lightning rod.

No one wanted to sit and wait for things to change, or for the Germans to grow even less tolerant of the Sami and the Norwegians, and to dictate more draconian terms to what was after all an occupation.

* * *

The mayor, Erik Larssen, stood in the square behind the church, deep in conversation with Lidy, who shook her head again and again.

Marit, Milly and Bera were a few meters away, watching intently.

"What are they saying?" Marit asked her grandmother.

"They want the German boy to live with us."

"What? Are you sure?"

"That is why your mother shakes her head so. It isn't proper." Bera smiled broadly.

"Then why do they ask it?" Milly said.

"Our farm is the only other one left along that stretch of the river, and better placed too. Erik Larssen had to speak with the Commandant already last year to ensure the German was placed with the Erikssens, not with us. Jakob and Andarás will be gone within a week with the herd. Anyhow, they slept in the *lávvu* again. There is room with us for one more."

"Well, he is attractive," Milly said with a mischievous look.

Marit pretended not to notice. She looked for a moment at her mother, and then back at Bera. The old woman smiled, revealing a few gaps between her teeth.

"Your mother thinks we can't take care of ourselves with a German in the house, and your uncle by the sea with the reindeer."

"What about Mrs. Erikssen, and Jan?"

"The mayor met with her yesterday. She doesn't want to rebuild the farm. She can't work it alone, and Jan is only sixteen. She will live with Old Widow Nansen for a while, and Jan is going to board at the Alrikssen place. They have a huge herd, and lots of cattle. They need more help. He may even go with the herd to the coast this year. He's never made the trip. He can bring his horses and learn a little more from Alrikssen until he builds the farm again himself in a few years. When he finds a wife …"

Marit's head was spinning. Jan moving to the other side of the valley, maybe leaving Karasjok for the year. Hans moving in with them …

"What will people say, with a German in our house?" Marit asked herself aloud.

"What does it matter?" Milly said.

Bera only smiled more broadly. The comment was not one typical of Marit. That was Lidy talking through her daughter. Lidy's discomfort clearly amused Bera.

"So, is he coming? To live on the farm?" Marit asked.

Bera didn't have to answer. She looked piercingly at Marit. "You don't dislike him, do you?"

"I don't know him."

"But you'd like to. He comes to church every Sunday." She drew in close to Marit and lowered her voice. "My eyes are not so old, child, that they cannot see where yours wander. And they can still recognize a handsome boy," she chuckled.

"He's German!"

"Yes. Blond and broad shouldered. A very handsome German, and with kind eyes ... I bet he is hard working. We need a man on the farm."

"Where will he sleep?" Milly asked. Marit thrust her elbow into Milly's ribs, but she only giggled harder.

"We will make a room for him behind the stable," Bera said. "When your father was alive, there was a boy who lived there. There is even a small stove. More comfortable than our *lávvus*, even if you are sleeping alone ..." Bera laughed.

Milly took her leave, presumably to find someone to share the news with. Lidy walked back towards them, her shoulders lower and her head down.

"The German man will stay with us at the farm." She was dejected. Bera and Marit were not as morose. Neither said anything, but there was a distinct smile on Marit's face as the three turned to walk back to the reindeer sleigh for the ride back to the farm.

*   *   *

"How was the funeral?" Andarás was in the pen with the herd, calling out to Marit and Star as they came over. Marit wondered why Andarás and Jakob never came to church, but never asked them about it. It was another point of contention with Lidy, who called them heathen and said that their pagan worship would only bring bad luck to the family. She never mentioned Bera's traditional practices, or the strange fusion Bera had found, like her father before her, marrying Sami and Norwegian religion.

"Sad."

"Sure."

Andarás was marking the last of the new calves. He had the calf pinned to the ground and was carving each of the ears, notching them in the distinct pattern that would identify the calf as one of Jakob's herd. He stood up and wiped the blood from his hands.

"When are you leaving?" The snows were melting fast. It was above freezing, and the winter had not been particularly cold. Most of the other herds had left the week before.

"We'll be gone by tomorrow. Jakob wanted to be sure Lidy was going to be okay. But if we wait longer, we'll have trouble on the lake crossings. The river is already looking soft in places." Andarás climbed out of the pen and looked at Marit. "Are you going to be okay?"

"Sure. Marit Enoksen—tough as nails!"

"I know you like the Erikssens."

"The German officer that lived with them is going to come live on the farm with us."

"What?"

"It's the only place left this far downstream from the village, unless you count the border hut. And there's already one German there."

"Jakob's not going to like that."

"Finally. Something Jakob and Lidy can agree on."

"Funny."

"We don't have a choice. Anyhow, he's nice. I've met him."

"He's still German. Jakob says the war is changing. Things are going to get worse here. There might not be any 'nice' Germans left when things get worse."

"So Jakob is a war strategist now? Or just a soothsayer like grandma?"

"I mean it, Marit. Be careful."

"I will."

CHAPTER 10

Karasjok, June 1943

SHE WATCHED HIM FROM THE FARMHOUSE WINDOW. The cold weather of May was already forgotten. Hans had worked up a strong sweat planting the new posts in the wooden pen. Even though the temperature was not as hot as summer, he was working hard. He paused a moment to undo the buttons on his shirt, but did not take it off.

Bera was outside too, sitting in the sun in a chair, carding wool from a large basket at her feet. Lidy had insisted she would be better inside, but there she sat, hardly a few feet from Hans. She sang a ballad as he drove the piles into the ground. He didn't speak, but Marit noticed that he struck the posts in time to her grandmother's rhythmic *joik*. Bera was expert at *joiking*, sharing old ballads and rhythmically calling out truths as the Sami had always known them. The music must have been strange to Hans, but he seemed to like it.

"What are you watching?" Lidy asked suddenly from the other end of the room. Startled, Marit dropped the bowl she'd been holding. The spindles she'd collected for Bera spread across the floor. Marit kneeled to pick them up, leaving her mother's question unanswered.

Lidy was relentless. "He's only here for the war, Marit. And he's on the other side." Lidy too had noticed Marit's interest in Hans. Only Hans seemed oblivious.

"You told me the Sami were neutral, didn't you? You said this was Norway's war. The Germans work with the Finns, and that's our home also." Marit stared hard at her mother, unashamed of her feelings.

"He's occupying our house," Lidy said just as firmly.

"Yes," Marit answered, "and he's fixing the reindeer pen for the arrival of next season's herds."

Marit picked up the last of the spindles and took the bowl outside to her grandmother. Lidy did not step aside and Marit passed within a breath of her mother's stern face. Neither Hans nor Bera stopped as she came out, but Marit thought that perhaps Hans' hammer was swinging a little harder than before.

Marit set the bowl down next to Bera, and sat down to listen to her *joik*. It was a beautiful tale that Marit knew well.

Babi's voice rose and fell, rose and fell, like a raven in a fall wind, staying in the same spot but moving up and down very quickly. The raven came back, again and again, before moving on or veering off to one side and alighting, quite suddenly, on a bush or a tree. At that point Bera cleared her throat, or took a deep breath, and the raven would take flight just as suddenly.

Marit was surprised by how well Hans beat the posts to the rhythm, mimicking the drum that Babi only brought out for very special divinations or celebrations. Today, in the sun, the *joik* sounded happy, almost a joyful expression of the return of spring. This too surprised Marit, for much of the *joik* was a sad song. The hero struggles, and almost fails. Yet Babi seemed able to weave sadness and joy together in a way that one led to the next, and was always the shadow of the other, like a windmill with blades of yellow and blue, spinning wildly until one only saw green. Yellow is the color of the spring sun, that brings the thaw, and chases away the winter blue that seems captive in every snow drift, in every ice pan on the river, in the light of every dawn and dusk. Until spring, one cannot find the yellow.

"That's beautiful, Babi," Hans said, pausing as she stopped, and resting his sledge hammer on the ground at his feet.

Bera smiled, but said nothing. Even though Hans had learned some Sami from the Erikssens, she spoke mostly with eyes to him, and he listened very well.

"What does it mean?" Hans asked Marit as Bera continued carding.

"It's an old Sami *joik*. One of the oldest. It is a story about the sun. Babi likes to sing it in the spring when the sun comes back."

Hans set down his hammer and sat down next to Marit.

"The Sami believe everything around us is alive. This *joik* tells of the son of the Sun, who travels to the land of Giants in search of a wife. The Giants are unfriendly, and ask the hero to accomplish many difficult tasks. In the end, he outsmarts the Giants, and takes the prettiest of the Giants' daughters back to the Sami country. She becomes the mother of all the Sami people. It is the victory of the Sun over the Moon and the stars, the victory of light over dark."

"So Babi sings to the Sun?" Hans asked in German.

"No. *About* the Sun. Never *to* the Sun, or the Moon or the Northern Lights."

"Why not?"

Marit blushed. "If they are mocked, they can strike you down." Marit stood up abruptly to signal the end of the discussion. She brushed the dirt from her tunic, unsure of what she'd said, afraid of sounding silly.

"I don't think Babi would mock any of them," Hans said seriously, picking up his tools as he got up. He looked from Babi to the warm sun overhead, and back down at Babi. "Still, I guess I'd better stick to opera. It's less dangerous."

"Really?" Marit asked as he started off towards the barn. "Don't most of these singers cry over stabbed lovers or their own despair and pain?" She bit her lip, but didn't really regret saying it.

Hans smiled broadly and walked off toward the barn without saying anything, never turning to see if they watched him walk away.

*   *   *

Marit did not often go down to the river alone. Certainly not for swimming. She was busy with the work from the house, and her studies. Lidy said she was fortunate that Mr. Dahlstrøm had agreed to tutor her. With the school occupied by the German garrison, none of the Sami were getting instruction. The money Lidy paid him for the tutoring was meager enough. Mr. Dahlstrøm must believe in Marit if he agreed to continue.

Marit had finished early. It was hot. Very hot. She decided she could go down to the river to the broad pool in the bend, and swim out to the boulder that they jumped off in simpler times, when the world seemed a smaller, kinder place.

There was no one near the river. Late June was often hot, but in the early afternoon, without any breeze to speak of, it was almost stifling. She looked around again to be sure she was alone, and took off her dress, which she laid neatly on a large stone near the water's edge. She slid off her undergarments too, and left them on top of her dress. It was risky to swim naked in the summer, because it was never dark, but the fall water was far too cold to enjoy the feeling of nakedness. She ran into the water and let the cool current wrap itself around her like a flowing tunic.

Marit loved the sensation of lying naked in the water. It made her feel one with the current, one being with the Lady of the River. The water came inside of her, and she was the river. With her eyes closed, she could project herself upstream all the way to the bridge at Karasjok, or downstream into the Tana River and the rapids that led to the fjord.

A branch snapping under someone's foot woke Marit abruptly from her reverie.

"Hello?" Marit called out, suddenly uncomfortably aware of her nakedness, trying to sink deeper into the water. "Is someone there?"

There was someone in the bushes at the far edge of the beach. She was sure of it. Nothing stirred. Nothing moved. But she was sure. She wished Star had followed her down to the water's edge. She paused on the water, turning on her stomach, wondering what to do. "Is someone there?"

Marit searched the bushes again, but there was nothing to be seen but the rushes and the tall grasses along the riverbank. Finally, disgusted, she stood up in the water and faced the bushes. There was a sudden rustle, and she heard someone running quickly up the path away from the river.

She walked slowly over to her clothes and pulled them on. Whoever it was, they were gone. Marit made a mental promise to herself not to swim naked in the river without being more careful.

*　*　*

"Babi's reindeer gulash," Marit said in German, ladling a large portion into Hans' bowl. He bowed his head quietly, answering as a Sami would. He made a small sign of the cross before eating, and kept his head low. "I went swimming this afternoon," Marit said to him in German again.

"I know."

"You do?" she said, surprised. It couldn't be him. She knew inside it couldn't be him. She passed a bowl to Bera, who took it silently.

"I saw you walk down to the river after we finished the pens, and I saw you come back wet while I was writing my reports."

Marit stared deep into his eyes, but found only the gentle, placid blue that had left her mute the first time they met.

"I'm going to have to learn German to speak at my own table," Lidy muttered in Sami, softly enough that Hans might not understand.

Marit glared back and served Lidy a bowl of the gulash, before taking her own and sitting down at the table.

"The pens are finished," Hans said to Lidy in Sami. His accent was terrible, but he wasn't hard to understand. "Tomorrow, I have to go back to the road."

"Thanks for helping," Marit said softly, embarrassed by her mother's silence.

Lidy spoke out. "How's Jan?"

"What do you mean?"

"Well, what did he say to you?"

"I don't understand."

"He came by this afternoon after you went to the river. I told him you'd gone swimming. He didn't find you?"

"No."

They finished the gulash in silence, each of them alone with their thoughts.

CHAPTER 11

Karasjok, July 1943

HANS WAS STANDING IN THE LIVING ROOM, at the door of her bedroom. It was late morning. The house was quiet. Tidy and Bera were out. From her bed, Marit could hear him standing there, a foot or so from the door. She knew every creak in every board of the house. He was waiting. *But for what?*

A double knock.

"Yes?" Marit answered, trying to sound disinterested.

"It's Hans."

Marit set her book down on her pillow and went to the door, which she opened wide. Hans was in the doorframe. His head had to stoop a little to see her clearly. Most of the doors in the house were too low for Hans. Star was beside him, panting softly.

"It's Saturday."

"Yes."

"We're going to go for a hike, Star and I. We wondered if you would like to come along."

"It'll be lunch soon."

"Yes. I thought we could bring something with us."

Star was standing at his side as though she were his dog, not hers. Marit eyed her suspiciously.

"I see you've already convinced Star. What did you promise her?"

"Sausages, of course."

"Alright. I'll help you put some things together and we can walk along the river path towards the Tana River."

"I don't know that one."

"It's on the other side. It's prettier, because it's in the sun and the path is quite hilly."

She stepped past him, trying not to notice how close she needed to come to him to get by. He stepped back as she passed, but a moment too slow to assuage her discomfort.

In the kitchen, she opened a knapsack and filled it with some bread, a few sausages, and a deerskin of water. She knew Hans would like some beer, but there was none in the house. Lidy didn't even like wine around, and Babi drank only strong spirits. She said that beer and wine were for weaker souls. There was some reindeer cheese from the last batch she had made with Babi, and she cut off a large slice and wrapped it in a cloth.

"All set?" Hans asked.

"All set."

"Did you tell Lidy?"

"Lidy and Babi left this morning for the town and said they might be gone most of the day. Peter, the blacksmith's son, died of fever this week. They were bringing some food over to his wife and sitting with her."

They walked down the path over the lower meadow, the sun was already high in the sky and very warm. A soft breeze kept the bugs at bay, and the dry grasses of the meadow hid a thousand crickets that chirped softly in the summer sun. Neither Hans nor Marit spoke, and they didn't need to. The warm air and sparkling river in the distance said enough.

At the beach, Hans helped Marit remove the canvas from the old boat. The newer canoe had been taken by Lidy, even though it was the one she had rented to Hans. It was Saturday, and she knew Hans would not need it for work. The old boat was shallower, and not as long. It was a little wider and had fittings for oars. There was no motor, but they weren't going far.

Marit finished wrapping the tarp and stowed it under the front bench. She gestured for Hans to get in and he did so, still not completely at ease in a river craft. Marit pushed the boat out into the deeper water and settled onto the middle bench. She fitted each oar and then turned the boat effortlessly in the slow current. There was a small beach a few hundred feet downstream and she made for it, feathering her oars across the water and pulling them towards her in a slow, rhythmic motion.

Marit could see Hans watching the sun dance on the water. He stared dumbfounded at dozens and dozens of funny spider-like bugs running along the surface.

"What are they?" he said.

"Water crawlers," she answered. "They run across the top of the water swallowing up smaller bugs." Their feet did indeed run on top of the water, and with each footfall, a small ripplet was sent across the still water. There were so many feet making so many ripplets that the entire river was a patchwork of concentric circles breaking against each other, a million intertwined rings, like an ephemeral net cast to catch a dream upon the water's surface before it sank away.

"They're beautiful, in a funny sort of way." Hans seemed fascinated by them. "I wonder why I never noticed them before." Star was on the bench next to him, peering over the edge of the boat, as if she was about to eat the nearest of the crawlers.

"They only come out on the hottest days of summer," Marit explained.

The boat beached itself nicely on the riverbank and Marit removed the oars and scrambled out. Hans helped her pull it up and tied a lead to one of the bushes near the shore.

"This way."

Marit led them up a narrow path that passed under some low branches before widening. She struck a course up the steep hill on the north bank of the river. They climbed in silence for thirty minutes, weaving their way up the hill, always within sight of the riverbed, which gradually sank at their feet until they were several hundred feet above the water, and many hundred more downstream. The forest was sometimes dense pine, sometimes a mix of alder and birch and pine. Occasionally, the forest cleared as the land leveled off a bit and there were meadows with raspberry bushes.

"In the fall, this is the best place for blueberries," Marit said as they crossed one of the meadows. A short distance ahead, Star froze. Marit stopped instantly, and Hans came up behind her.

"What is it?"

"I'm not sure," Marit answered. There was a rustling noise in the raspberry bushes to the right of the path, a little further down the hill. Star sniffed the air.

"Look!" Marit pointed in the direction of the noise. There was a large black bear in amongst the bushes, eating berries.

Hans quickly opened his knapsack and pulled out a small hand gun.

"You don't need that," Marit whispered. "There is nothing here that will hurt you."

"I'm more comfortable with a gun in hand when I meet bears."

"He is upwind of us, and he is eating happily. You need not be afraid."

"You're very brave."

"Not really. Sami believe bears are the dogs of the Gods. It is forbidden to hunt them except under very special circumstances."

"That is a very big dog," Hans said, putting his gun into his coat pocket instead of his knapsack.

They watched the bear eat for a while, and decided they should press on. Now the river turned a little south and the land at their feet widened. There was a farm down below, and a few cattle grazing along the riverbank.

"Old Man Jacobsen's place," Marit said.

"I know. 'No one knows if he's dead or alive', or so they say, right?"

"You listen well."

"Have you ever seen him?"

"Who?"

"Old Man Jacobsen."

"Of course."

"So you know he is alive."

"No."

"I don't understand," Hans said, looking perplexed.

"That's because you haven't seen him." She laughed and started walking again. "Some people say he is a *Stallo*. They're a sort of troll: half Sami, half giant. They live for thousands of years. But he's not a *Stallo*. He's not big enough," she said, smiling. "It's very steep for the next part. It goes almost straight up."

Hans just followed, effortlessly walking behind his guide, happy to take in the sights and sounds of the forest. Star ran on ahead, disappearing for minutes at a time, and then reappearing in a rush, almost knocking them both to the ground as she darted past them to see what was happening further down the path. The trees were mostly birch now, although there were patches of pine and a lot of alder too. When the trees were thick, the bugs became much worse, and they walked even faster to chase them away. It was not long before they emerged into the warm breeze at the summit of the hill, a large granite outcropping, barren and beautiful in the hot summer sun. Three small birch grew from a large crack in the middle of the hilltop. The rest was bare rock.

Marit walked over to the edge that was steepest and peered down several hundred feet to the river below. There was a second peak almost the same height, and a little less rocky, a few hundred feet further east. She imagined she could connect them with a wire and walk along it over the deep ravine that split the hills in two.

"Wow," Hans finally said in Sami. "It was worth the hike."

"I thought Germans liked hikes anyway."

"Bavarians do. I'm used to slightly taller mountains, but also cooler weather and less bugs."

Marit noticed that Hans too had a knapsack, and he opened it and took out a large wool blanket which he spread across the rock. Marit opened her own knapsack and took out their lunch. She smiled when she saw that Hans did indeed have a drinking skin of his own, from which he served himself generously.

"Do you want some?" he said offering up some of his beer.

"I brought water, thanks."

"That's Finland, over there." She pointed out over the arm of the river that joined another river. In the distance, there were endless forests, but on the far side of the river there was more pine and less birch, and the trees seemed denser than in the valley.

"I know. This is where we built the road to. Look," he pointed. "Just past the second bend to the south. That's where the bridge went in. The Tana River is narrower there, and the water runs over a shallow rapid that was easy to put pillars down into. It's a great bridge for fishing."

"That's where my family is from," Marit said, looking at the vast expanse of rolling, wooded hills in Finland.

"I thought you were half Norwegian." Hans had taken out a large hunting knife, and was gingerly peeling away the skin from the sausage and feeding large clumps of it to Star.

"I am. But the Sami half is Finnish Sami, like most of the village. We came to build the church in the early 1800s. There was work for people and another way of life than always following the reindeer."

"You don't like following the reindeer?"

"It's a hard life, to always be on the move. I like the *lávvu*, and the songs and the wilderness, but I also like a home. I love the farm."

"*Holga-njargga* … it's a funny name for the farm. What does it mean?" Hans asked.

"I don't know. It's just a name." She sat cross-legged on the blanket, staring out over the valley, vaguely looking back towards the farm.

The wind had dried the sweat from his brow, but his blond hair was still damp. It was cut short, and stood out proudly. He was very at home here, and Marit found she liked that.

You ask too many questions, she wanted to say, but something held her back.

"There's always something in a name," he said. "Take Lidy, for instance. What does that mean? It doesn't sound very Sami to me."

"It *is* very Sami. Lidy is short for Lidnu. It means eagle owl."

"See? There's always something in a name. Eagle owl. I like that. Eyes that never sleep, and claws that can rip you apart. That's Lidy." Hans laughed at his own joke, and Marit flushed.

"Marit is just Marit," she said.

"Not true. Marit is Mary. Like the Virgin Mary. Mary symbolizes purity and honesty, and courage in the face of adversity."

"Sounds like a lot to carry."

She rose suddenly and started gathering the food. He was only a few feet away, and the discussion about her name made him seem threatening somehow. She wondered what the name Hans meant, but didn't want to say anything, for fear that he might answer, and maybe come closer.

"Hans means 'Grace of God' in German. But in Sanskrit it means 'swan'. I like that better," he said, as though he could read her thoughts. Marit didn't know what Sanskrit was.

"I think you are more bear than swan," she said, turning her
back and putting the rest of the food into the knapsack.

If he was uncomfortable at her bringing an abrupt end to the
lunch he didn't show it. He finished drinking and stood up, dusting
off the blanket. He folded it and stood again looking out towards
Finland and beyond.

"What do you see there?" Marit finally asked, when the silence
became too loud for her to hold back any longer.

"My friends. In Russia. I'm glad I am not with them, but part of
me wants to be. It is not easy for them."

"It is easier here."

"It is—for now ..."

Marit didn't like his strange tone. He was friendly, but complicated.
It was clearly easier here. The sun was warm. There were no cannons,
no planes, no tanks. Just trees and rocks and the spirits of the ancients,
weaving themselves into every living thing and keeping them safe.

It was a lot easier here.

There was a rustle in the woods at the edge of the clearing. Star
stood frozen, eyes fixed on the place where the path came out of the
woods and onto the rock face. Hans too was alert, and Marit was
surprised to see he had pulled the hand gun out of his jacket again,
pointing it downwards but ready all the same.

"Is it the bear?" Hans asked.

A man stepped out onto the rock and stared at them both without
moving any closer. He was twenty or thirty feet away, but they could
clearly see his features in the sun. He was tall for a Sami, but not as
tall as Hans. His face was wrinkled to the point that it was hard to
guess his age, though he must be very old. It was hard to find a clear
form from beneath all the creases.

His eyes were piercing. They looked past Marit, and into her all
at once, until her spine tingled and the hair on the back of her neck
stood up. They pinned her to the rock and held her there, so that it
was hard to turn to see Hans. It was hard even to breathe. He stared
at Hans until it seemed his eyes would burn the rock on which he
stood. He didn't seem to notice the gun that Hans pointed at him, or
Star, or Marit. He stared unmoving at Hans, and Hans stared back.

They stayed like that for a minute or more, immobile, the wind blowing around them, whispering to them.

As suddenly as he came, the man turned without saying a word and walked back into the woods.

Hans holstered the gun and Star went a few feet towards the man before coming back towards Marit and sitting at her feet.

"Old Man Jacobsen," Marit said, letting out a deep breath, and realizing for the first time that the combination of the apparition and Hans' gun had made her heart stop. She was breathing heavily.

"Alive," Hans said half to himself. "Definitely alive. But I see why they say what they say."

CHAPTER 12

Karasjok, October 1943

IT WAS LATE OCTOBER, and the snows were already thick on the ground. Across the lakes of the *vidda*, the ice had come early, and Bera expected that Jakob and Andarás would be back any day with the winter herd. Marit kept a near constant watch, sitting by the window looking down towards the river. The ice was thick enough to cross, and had been for almost a week. Star too knew that the herds were near, for she was more nervous than usual. Her thick coat was ready for the cold winter nights, and she longed to sit by the fire in the *lávvu* and listen to the masters tell their tales.

This year, the waiting took on a different feeling, with Hans in the house, sharing the meals and watching the waiting.

"How do you know when they will come?" he asked.

"We know," Bera said simply in Sami.

Hans shook his head. "Is there a date by which they will be here?"

Bera smiled and said nothing.

"It is in the air," Marit tried to explain. "The deer feel it, and we feel it too. One day, they know it is time, and the journey starts. The winter air by the sea is damp and unpleasant."

"Why do they go then?"

"In the summer, the air here is too hot, and the bugs are very bad."

Hans nodded in strong agreement.

"The deer seek the sea breezes, and graze in the rocky cliffs of the fjords. When the snows come, we tie up the sleighs and make the trek back here, where they can winter far from the winds and the dampness. They breed here, and birth in the spring. Just before the snows melt, the herds go back."

Hans still found it strange that the women knew when Jakob would be back. Marit could see it in his eyes. He nodded at her every word, but he did not understand.

"So they will be here today?" he asked.

"In a day or two, *Njukcha*. Not more." Bera spoke with authority, and Marit had nothing to add.

Njukcha. Swan. Since Bera had learned Hans also meant swan, she called him nothing else. Hans seemed to like it. It gave him a status within the family, to have his own name from Bera.

The herds did come back the next day, in the late morning, under a strong sun, perhaps one of the last days of full sunshine before the long winter. And with the herds came another surprise.

"Jan!" Marit exclaimed, seeing him leading his horse on his skis next to the herds.

Jakob was also on skis, out in front of the lead reindeer cow, bringing her up the lower meadow, the whole herd in tow.

Marit and Lidy prepared the gates to the pens and watched as several hundred deer came in and ambled around, frustrated that they could not roam as freely as before. There were so many. Marit noticed the markings carved into the ears. The Alrikssen herd was here too.

Jan came up next to Lidy and greeted her.

"You've grown," she said.

"Thank you. Hello, Marit."

"Has Jakob adopted you then?" Marit asked with a smile.

"Mr. Alrikssen is sick. He couldn't bring his own herd, and it was too much for me alone. Jakob brought both, and I was sent to help."

"Enough chatting," Lidy declared. "Come inside, Jan. You'll need some lunch. We can send Marit for your mother at Mrs. Nansen's place. She'll be eager to see you."

"Thank you, Mrs. Enoksen. Once the herds are settled, I'll have some lunch, and then go find my mother directly. But maybe we could come back and visit later this week." Jan looked squarely at Marit, who suddenly felt uncomfortable. There was something new in his eyes.

That evening, they sat in the *lávvu*, sipping spirits and swapping stories of the trek from the sea and the summer in Karasjok. Bera had made her famous gulash, and no one but Marit noticed that Hans was not there.

She rose finally, and slipped out the back flap of the tent. There was light in Hans' room. She walked over through the snow and looked in through the window. He was bent over a large map, staring. He did not notice her at first.

When he did look up from the map it was so suddenly that Marit was startled, and a little embarrassed. He motioned for her to come in, and after a moment she did.

He did not get up as she pulled the door open and stepped inside.

"What are you looking at?" she asked.

"It's a map of Europe."

"I've seen maps before. This one looks different."

"It is," Hans said. "It's a lot bigger. All this blue is ocean. Karasjok is so small, it's not even a dot on the map."

"What does it tell you, your map? Why do you stare at it?"

"It tells me the future," he said, forcing a smile.

"Are you a *noaide*?" Marit herself wasn't sure if she was in earnest or joking. He did seem to believe he could see the future in this map.

"Me? No. I'll leave the soothsaying to Babi. The map tells me the future in other ways."

"Show me," Marit said firmly. She came closer and stood over the map next to him.

"Well, it's very simple really. We are here," he pointed to the far northern part of Scandinavia, up by the North Cape. "My country, Germany, is here."

His finger slid down quite a ways toward the bottom of the map. "We have gone north, west, south, and east. In September, this country, Italy, which was our friend, decided not to fight with us anymore. Our enemies are moving forward from the south, and from the east." He moved his fingers further east showing Russia and the armies that were mustering there.

"Soon," he said, "more armies will come from across the sea and move from the west into Europe. Already, from this island, their planes destroy our factories and bomb our cities. There are many, many millions of them." He put his finger on England and it seemed very close to Norway.

He moved his left hand from the west and his right hand from the east, slowly coming together in the middle of the map. "They will crush Germany. It is only a matter of time."

"What about us, in Karasjok?" She looked at the map. Karasjok seemed very close to the island, and very close to the middle of all this fighting.

"Maybe they will go south. But if they decide otherwise, we too will be crushed."

"I do not think they will want to come here. It is too cold."

"The Russians are not afraid of the cold. They are not afraid of anything. And we have hurt them very badly. They will not stop until we are destroyed."

Marit looked at him intently, trying to understand. She could see the pain in his eyes again, like when he first arrived in Karasjok. It had been a long time since she had seen the pain so strongly.

"Did you hurt them, *Njukcha*?"

"Not the Russians, but others, yes."

"In Yugoslavia?"

"Yes."

"Like Donkey." Marit felt her neck become rigid. Her hands clasped the edge of the map table. Her fingers hurt.

"No. Not like Donkey. He is a monster, and I was never like him."

"Then how, *Njukcha*?"

"By doing nothing, when all around was evil."

"I don't understand."

"I help people build bridges and roads, or sometimes find the ones they are likely to destroy. I went with other soldiers to find people like the prisoners from the Serbian camp—partisans who killed German soldiers in Yugoslavia. We sought out men who lived in the forest and hurt my comrades. When we found them, we were to bring them here, to the camps. But not all of them made it here. Many times, other soldiers decided it would be easier just to kill them ... And I did not stop them."

Hans' eyes had become hard and impenetrable. He was no longer looking at the map. Marit felt a deep sinking in her heart. Like her,

Hans had the pain that comes from watching helplessly while people die. She placed a hand on Hans' shoulder, but he seemed not to notice. A tear ran slowly down one cheek, but he did not wipe it off. After a moment, she moved her hand away and started to leave.

"Marit," Hans said suddenly.

"Yes?"

"I will go to the military hospital tomorrow, in Skoganvarre."

Skoganvarre. Across the *vidda* toward the fjord. She had never been to the other side of the *vidda*.

"I have a friend there that was with me in Yugoslavia. When I came here, he went to Russia. He is very hurt. Will you come with me to see him? It will only take a day."

"I'll ask Lidy."

*　*　*

"I'm surprised Lidy let you come."

"I am too. It makes me a little nervous."

"Why?"

"Lidy always has a plan."

"A plan?"

Marit wanted to say that perhaps Lidy found it convenient to have Marit out of the house, but it sounded conspiratorial and paranoid. Still, Marit had already learned to trust her feelings. They rarely betrayed her.

"Just a feeling. And why are we going to Skoganvarre?" Marit said.

"He is a very dear friend. I know him from before Yugoslavia, in Bavaria. We joined the army together. He was an engineer. He got me into his division, even if I didn't have the right schooling. And he helped me get out of the division when they were transferred to the Russian Front. I got news yesterday that he was transferred to Skoganvarre."

"Is he very hurt?"

"I think so."

They were riding in the reindeer sleigh, and coming into Karasjok.

"I have a surprise for you," Hans said.

"A surprise?"

"*Ja.*"

He was clearly proud of himself, like a child with a secret, eager to blurt it out, but waiting til the last possible moment for greatest effect. Hans steered the sleigh down the main road and brought it to a halt in front of the schoolhouse. There were several Germans standing there. One walked over and saluted Hans.

"*Alles in Ordnung?*" Hans asked him.

"*Jawohl, mein Kommandant.*"

Hans stepped out of the sleigh and helped Marit down. It was 9:30 and the sun was rising in the eastern sky. It was surprisingly warm, and Marit felt the anticipation of the surprise growing with every passing moment.

"So, what is it?"

"Well, we cannot go to Skoganvarre in a sleigh and be back by tonight."

Neither she nor Lidy had thought of that. It seemed far, but Hans had said they would be back by late evening. That was enough for them.

Hans walked over to the wall of the schoolhouse and brought forward a large motorcycle.

"My lady, this will be your carriage for today."

Marit's eyes widened. She had seen the motorcycles move in and around the town many times since the Germans had arrived in Karasjok. Bera called them *boazodiesel*: 'diesel-reindeer'. Marit had wanted to ride one from the first day she saw one.

Hans put his sack into the leather bags strapped to either side of the rear wheel. He straddled the cycle and kicked down hard to start it up.

"What did you have to trade for a day on this?" Marit yelled loudly in Sami, as the diesel engine came awake with a roar. Hans just smiled. He put on his military helmet and gestured for her to come sit behind him on the machine. He pulled a pair of goggles out of his breast pocket and passed them to Marit, who put them on without question.

She wasn't sure where to put her arms, until she realized that if she was to stay on the motorcycle, she had little choice but to wrap them firmly around Hans.

"Hold on!" Hans turned the accelerator downward as he kicked the cycle into gear, and they roared up the street toward the bridge and across the Karasjokka.

The ride to Skoganvarre was one Marit was sure she would remember for the rest of her life. She had never travelled so quickly before. The bright snow disappeared at breakneck speed to either side of the motorcycle as they raced down the road that ran across the *vidda*. The sun was higher now, and the shadows of the trees were short. The *vidda* had lost its forbidding aspect and was instead a long plain that seemed flatter at high speed. Hans was master of the plain, and on the motorcycle they would cover more land in a few hours than Jakob and Andarás did in several days. The ground was nicely frozen, although the sun melted parts of the road. After an hour or so of riding, Hans stopped as they reached a crest that offered a view of the surrounding valleys.

"From here on, the land changes," he said, gesturing to the rolling hills ahead and the mountains in the distance. Marit had never seen mountains so high. "We are leaving the *vidda* and coming into the lake country that lies at the head of the fjord. Skoganvarre is down there, along the river. Another twenty minutes or so."

"Why is the hospital in Skoganvarre?"

"It is hard to find in the forests and difficult to get planes there. The patients land in Lakselv and drive twenty miles to the hospital. It is safe there. It will never be bombed."

The mention of bombing left Marit a little intimidated. Sitting on the diesel-deer, racing across the only world she had known all in the space of an hour, the war suddenly seemed much closer, and much more dangerous. It was exciting and scary all at once, and she was happy to have Hans there to show it to her.

"Is it a big hospital?"

"Yes. The biggest field hospital I know or have heard of."

"Where do they come from, the patients?"

"From the Eastern Front. The war with Russia."

"Is it so close?"

"Yes."

They rode on, the engine now sounding more like a purr than a roar to Marit, who held Hans firmly around the waist and watched the scenery roll by. It had changed a lot. The road was not straight, but wound its way along a valley floor, following and sometimes crossing a little river. The forests were tall here, and occasionally they saw reindeer, either in the forest to the side of the road, or on a lake, crossing in the distance.

Suddenly, Marit heard the purring soften, and knew that they were close. They came to a turn off the road and a large red-and-white pole blocked their way.

Hans reached into his pocket and pulled out a paper that he showed the guard, who nodded and lifted the pole so that they could pass. They motored slowly down the road and over a little bridge. In the forest around them, buildings began to appear. There were dozens of them. Hans drove on until they came to a large field where many cars and trucks were parked. He drove to the far end of the field and stopped the motorcycle.

"This is it."

It was not what Marit expected a hospital to look like.

"Where are all the patients?"

"This is a field hospital. The buildings are spread throughout the forest, so they cannot be seen from above. There are thousands of patients here."

Hans walked with Marit over to the edge of the field where the vehicles were parked and consulted a large sign post. There were at least thirty markers on the post, indicating the infirmary, the mess hall, and many other places Marit did not recognize.

There were markers for other things too.

Berlin.

Moskau.

Paris.

München.

"*München*—2,932 km. That's where my family comes from. Or nearby, anyhow."

"Who counts these things?"

They walked quietly along a large path that ran through the open forest. In the distance, in a large clearing, were several very large buildings. They went inside the closest, and Marit listened as Hans tried to find the ward where his friend lay.

They walked down the rows, long narrow wards with beds to either side.

Dozens of beds.

Hundreds of beds.

On many floors.

Each bed had a man in it. There were bandaged heads, and limbs set in plaster. There were few smiles. The floor and walls reeked of antiseptic, but it was only a mask. Under the acrid smell of the cleanser, Marit sensed another more putrid odor.

Death.

It was the first time that Marit smelled it so clearly, but it was unmistakable, and oddly familiar. She recognized it like one knows a bad thing just before it happens, even if it has never happened before.

She knew.

Hans stopped suddenly in front of one of the beds. The man was sitting partly upright in his bed, looking at Hans. He spoke first.

"Bauer."

It was a statement. No joy. Just acknowledgement.

"Hermann ..." Hans said in a faint voice, failing to mask his shock.

The man's head was heavily bandaged, with blood seeping through the gauze in several places. The bandage came down to wrap his jaw as well, but his eyes spoke volumes. His left hand was missing, the arm coming out into space and stopping too suddenly, wrapped again in the white gauze.

"Didn't think I'd look so good, uh?"

Hans said nothing.

"It's a living hell out there. Hell. They say I'm lucky to be here. Lucky to be alive. Lucky ..."

They stared at one another in silence for a while. Marit stood a few feet back. She thought the man did not notice her until he gestured with raised eyebrows, as if to ask what she was doing there.

"Getting lonely in Karasjok?"

"Just a friend, Hermann."

"Sure. I had friends in the Ukraine too, before the front collapsed. Even dancing friends. She's pretty."

Marit blushed and turned away.

"So I guess you get to go home?" Hans said finally, trying to sound upbeat.

"Yes."

"They'll make you something for your hand, Hermann. You'll be working the farm again next spring."

Hermann said nothing. He looked left and right, and seemed to come to some sort of decision. With a quick gesture of his good hand, he pulled aside the bed sheet. Where his legs should have been, more white gauze, and two ugly stumps.

Hans sat down on the chair next to the bed and wept. Marit had never seen Hans cry. She wanted to say something, do something. His tears kept coming. Her feet seemed glued to the floor. Marit wanted to leave, but could not go without leaving Hans behind.

"*Genug davon.*" *Enough of that.* Hans lifted his teary-eyed face. Hermann's voice was bitter. "I don't need your pity. This is retribution, Hans. Payback."

"We didn't do anything." Hans was shaking his head.

"Exactly."

There was nothing to say. Marit sensed that Hans wanted to ask how Hermann had lost his legs, where his hand had gone, what he would do next, but there was only silence. There was blood dripping down Hermann's left cheek. An orderly came in and began to change the bandage. Marit finally found her feet and walked over to Hans, putting her hand on his arm. It woke him from his stupor and he stood. Hermann was staring into space. For him, Hans was already gone.

They stood together in silence in front of the bench at the front of the ward for a long time, not prepared to go back in, not quite ready to leave. It was 3 pm, and the sun was setting.

They should have been hungry, but Marit could think only of the two stumps and the smell of death.

It came to her, where she had smelled it before: in the pit, in Karasjok.

The leg.

The knee.

The shoe.

Marit wanted to ask what had happened in the forests of Serbia and Bosnia as Hans and Hermann tracked partisans for their Führer, but she couldn't.

And she didn't need to.
She had Arnfrid's pit.
She knew.

* * *

The motorcycle seemed quieter on the road back to Karasjok. Perhaps Hans was driving more slowly in the darkness. The light on the front of the cycle was a narrow tunnel cutting through the desolation. It was much colder, and in the darkness, the eeriness had returned. It was an ocean of darkness, and only the light beam offered any hope of salvation. It cut a stark path, and the road was swallowed up beneath them, but the darkness closed in again as soon as they passed.

Suddenly, Marit saw them.

She knew Hans was lost in thought, and wanted to be sure he could see too. She squeezed him very tightly. He slowed the cycle further, and turned his head back briefly. She squeezed him again and he slowed to a stop.

"What is it?" he shouted above the motor.

She didn't need to answer. He followed her eyes, and his head turned back to the night sky. Where moments earlier there were only stars, the sky came alive. He turned off the engine, as though he would be able to see better in the silence. Or perhaps it was to be reverent. It was indeed as though the Gods were parting the sky and stepping down.

Long streams of green and blue and yellow danced as they trickled down to earth. The sky was ablaze, drips of fire, molten but cold.

Blue fire.

Yellow fire.

A line arched from the north across the entire sky, over the road and down to the mountains that sat at the southern end of the *vidda*. From the line a cloud of blue and green began to rise and take on forms.

The forms changed before they had any real shape, and then they turned in a slow spiral that wrapped itself into a swirl that faded just as mysteriously as it had come. Another burst of light from the north, which ran in an exploding maze of lights all the way along the line.

"*Revontuli,*" Marit said. "Fox's Fire."

"Fox?"

"*Revontuli*. It means 'Fox's Fire' in Finnish. It's what my family calls these lights. We're Finnish Sami. There is an ancient legend that tells of how the fox was playing tricks on the bear. The bear eventually grew angry, and lit his tail on fire, and as he runs across the sky, he leaves his sparks everywhere for us to see ... There is another story about fox making porridge for his children, and the smoke coming out of the chimney changes into a thousand different colors. But I always liked the bear story myself."

"*Revontuli*. I like that," said Hans.

They watched in silence for a long time, but the air had changed. The darkness had been lifted by the magic of the Fox, so that when the lights stopped dancing, and Hans started the motor again, they drove of across the *vidda* riding a wave of light that shone through the dark night, and left them both serene.

CHAPTER 13

Karasjok, December 1943

EVERY YEAR, BEFORE THE WINTER SOLSTICE, the merchants came. In years past, they had always gone past Karasjok to a village on the way to Kautokeino where they set up their tents and sold and bought for several days.

The war changed many things. The Russians did not come to Vadsø in the Tana fjord anymore, so that the Vadsø merchants had less to sell. And many in the Karasjokka valley had less money with which to buy. But in Karasjok itself, the Germans had money, and so the fair moved to Karasjok.

Erik Larssen convinced the local merchants to drape streamers along the storefronts in the neighborhood around the old school, and some of the Sami elders carved an ice sculpture down by the riverbank where the sleighs arrived in town. It was a giant raven, with its wings partially spread, but the beak was so long and its outstretched wings so threatening that most felt it was probably a dragon of some sort. Milly's little brother said it was a harpy, even though it was clearly male. The Germans liked it very much, but the carvers only smiled in response to the praise. Along the river bank and on the small road that led up into the village, there were little kiosks with wares from the merchants and local artisans: woolen cloth, Sami jewelry, knives, axes, even little toys carved from reindeer antlers.

Not to be outdone, the Germans—many of whom were in fact Austrian or Bavarian—set up a small marketplace of their own. They set up a little pine hut in front of the barracks, decorated with fresh-cut pines boughs and pinecones wrapped in red ribbon. The hut was large enough to have openings on three sides and slanted tables were set up to display a few Bavarian things the soldiers had come by: small toy tops carved of wood, candles made with scented wax, and a few ornate figurines for a Nativity Scene. In the hut, every afternoon and evening, Arnfrid sold a dark wine mixed with rum and spices that one of the officers had taught her how to make. Many of the Sami liked it a lot, and there was much rejoicing in and around the village.

The highlight of the market fair was the reindeer race. It was not as flamboyant or popular as the great spring races in Kautokeino, but there were riders from most of the Sami peoples of the Finnmark. Johan Tor, the winner from last spring in Kautokeino was there, and so were some of the better riders of the Finnish Sami clans.

On December 21st, the morning of the race, the riders came early into town. The moon was nearly full, and in the cloudless sky, it shone almost like the sun, its light reflected many times over in the white, white snow that covered everything.

Marit watched them assemble near the bridge. The moon was still high in the sky, and would not set until midday. By then, the sky would take on that pale twilight quality. It was the period when one missed the summer sun the most. It was not quite dark, but not yet light, and would not be light again for many months. And yet, for an hour or so, in the middle of the day, it seemed that if the world could only turn a little on its side, or stretch a little north or south, the light would pierce through the hills around the town and shine its golden rays on the People of the Reindeer.

"Where will they run?" asked Hans, seeing the impatience of the riders as the last sleighs pulled up. There were a dozen riders now, a good turnout.

"They will walk the deer down the river to Rito-njargga," she said. *Near the old Serbian camp,* she heard herself thinking. "About a mile downstream. There they will line up and race straight back to the village. All together. Just one race. In Kautokeino, the races last for days and there are heats and eliminations, but here there is just one race. Winner takes all."

The reindeer were moving down the river already. They passed in front of Hans and Marit, who marveled at their harnesses. Each reindeer had its own colored harness, matching the tunic of the rider.

Jan was racing this year, and he looked splendid in his deep blue tunic, with its bright red-and-yellow trim. His reindeer had an ornately carved leather harness covered in tiny bells that jingled with every step. Over the head of the reindeer, Jan had placed a small hood that covered the ears but let the antlers come through. It matched the blanket on the deer's back, and Jan's own tunic. He was proud of the hood, his own invention. It gave his deer a supernatural quality as the animal blew steam out of its nostrils around the mask.

"Good luck!" Hans shouted to Jan. Jan smiled back at Marit and waved to them both.

As he came by, he threw something to Marit, who caught it.

"What's that?" Hans asked.

"I'm not sure." She looked at it more closely. "Looks like his rabbit's foot." It was indeed a rabbit's foot, tied to a sinew of reindeer skin so that it could be worn as a necklace for luck.

"Hold it for me!" Jan shouted over his shoulder and he shook the reins and moved his sleigh forward, quickly passing out of sight as the other riders came by.

Lidy and Bera stood a few feet away. Marit noticed the rabbit's foot did not escape Lidy's attention.

Milly stood fifty feet downstream with several other girls from the village. Marit raised her hand a little in response to her wave. Milly beckoned for Marit and Hans to join them, but Marit was embarrassed to find she didn't want to. She looked the other way, leaning slightly against Hans' shoulder.

Erik Larssen was tying a paper streamer across the river between two poles about thirty feet apart. This would be the finish line. Several hundred people had gathered to either side of the track that led to the streamer. The race was about to start.

Marit heard the rifle shot that meant they were off. It was only a mile. The racers were already storming forward and would soon be there. In the weak light, it was impossible to tell who was in the lead. The thundering of the hooves grew louder and louder, and two riders were clearly ahead of the others. In a moment they passed by at breakneck speed. Marit grew excited as she saw who led the race. Jan and Johan Tor raced antler to antler down the narrow finish stretch, with the other sleighs closely behind, squeezing each other as they struggled to find space in the last few hundred feet. The two sleighs raced closer and closer, until it seemed that the reindeer from each of the sleighs were actually locking antlers. Jan was yelling at the top of his lungs and whipping the reins up and down. Johan Tor said nothing, but he held a long whip over his head and it cracked sharply in the right ear of his reindeer. The whole sleigh moved sharply to the left and nudged against Jan, who pulled slightly back to keep his sleigh from going off the course.

Johan Tor's sleigh broke the streamer and carried on up the river to circle under the bridge and come back towards the cheering crowd. Jan, only a pace or two behind Johan Tor at the finish line, turned more quickly and pulled his sleigh over to one side. As he pulled up to the crowd, he leaped off the sleigh, beaming. To see his face, you would never think he had lost the race.

"Second place! Next year, the race is mine!"

Widow Nansen and Mr. Dahlstrøm had gone over with Jan's mother to congratulate him. Marit and Hans worked their way over too. It was a good race.

"Congratulations, Jan," said Marit as she handed him his rabbit's foot.

"No. Keep it."

"But I didn't bring you luck. You finished second."

"Keep it. Next time I'll finish first." He winked at her, as his mother kissed his cheek.

Hans had gone over to harness their own sleighs—one behind each of the two reindeer the four of them had taken from the farm to the village. They were heading back to eat before it was late. Marit had promised Hans a surprise that afternoon.

Lidy came over with Babi. Both were frowning.

"What's wrong?" Marit asked.

"Mr. Upsahl. He shot a bear last night."

Hans looked towards Marit. He had become quite dependent on her cultural translations. "Is this bad?"

"Very bad."

"Aren't bears dangerous?"

"Sometimes. They are the strongest of the animals of the wild. Almost a god. Bears protect the Sami people. Remember, we don't hunt bears except in very special circumstances. It must be prepared, and the gods must agree. Mr. Upsahl is Norwegian. He doesn't believe in Sami traditions. But still, it is a bad omen for the village." Marit thought of Hans' gun and the day he had almost shot a bear.

They climbed into their sleighs and started down the river along the path the races had taken only a few minutes before. Several other sleighs were taking the same path ahead and behind them.

"Everybody's going home," Hans called out to Marit from behind her on the sleigh.

"It's winter solstice. It's not as important as when the sun comes back, but it's still a big event. Every family has their own traditions."

"What are ours?" Hans said.

Ours. She liked that. "That's the surprise," she smiled to herself, hoping he would hear it in her voice as he sat behind her on the sleigh.

Back at the farm, they ate in silence. Babi in particular seemed distant and preoccupied. Marit gestured to Hans to get dressed for the cold, and the two of them went outside while Lidy and Babi prepared things in the house.

"Where are we going?"

"To the Spirit House."

Hans seemed to accept this, and followed along as they attached the sleigh to the reindeer once again. Only one sleigh this time.

"Is it far?" he said after they finished.

"No. On the island where the Karasjokka flows into the Tana. There is a huge boulder there, and some rocks. These big rocks are special to us. We call them *sieide*. A very long time ago, my ancestors built a hut in the ground, with a fire pit. It is right up against the boulder. In times past, the ancestors sacrificed animals there."

Hans listened in silence, apparently unsure of what to say.

"It is a very sacred place. We go every winter solstice to celebrate the beginning of the end of the long night, and ..." Marit hesitated a moment, wondering whether she should say more. "It is a great honor to be invited there. Lidy and Bera argued long into the night yesterday over whether you should be allowed to come. Lidy likes you, but you are a German."

"What did Babi say?"

"Babi said you are part of the family, and that she wanted you to be there for the vision."

"The vision?"

"That is why we are going. Babi will tell us what the future holds."

"With her crystal ball?"

"She is not a gypsy, and you should not doubt her. What you will see is very sacred to us. You mustn't tell anyone. What Babi does is forbidden."

"I didn't mean to be mocking. I would never hurt Babi."

Marit knew it to be true, but felt unease inside of her, like a cloud masking the sun for a moment.

"What do you Nazis care about Babi, anyway?" Marit said, letting her feelings show a little too much.

"I'm not a Nazi."

"You fight for your Führer."

"I fight for my country. If we don't fight, we won't have one anymore. It doesn't mean I believe in everything the party says."

The sleigh was properly set up, and Babi came out of the house and took her place inside of it. Marit decided to let things rest with Hans. Babi held Hans' hands together in her own as she stepped onto the sleigh, and he helped her sit down. She looked deep into his eyes, and Marit could see that Hans liked this. Lidy gave Babi a knapsack that she placed in her lap, and sat down behind Babi as the sleigh headed off towards the river.

"And us?" Hans said.

"We go on skis. It's really not that far."

Marit walked over to the barn and came out with skis for both of them, which they strapped on. Marit realized she had never seen Hans ski before. He smiled at her in the dim light of the winter day, and turned to set off after the sleigh, but one ski caught the other and he fell head first into the snow.

"Maybe I should lead the way," Marit said, suppressing a smile.

Hans stood up and brushed off the snow.

"Ladies first."

Marit blazed a straight trail down the lower meadow and out over the river. It was easier for Hans to follow in her tracks, and once they reached the river, Hans found his stride across the flat open spaces. She could almost forget that they were going to the Spirit House. The stars shone brightly in the moonless sky, and the dim light from the stars and the sun that lay hidden beyond the horizon just out of sight still reflected in the snow covered wonderland, leaving an impression of grandeur and majesty. She sensed their togetherness more than ever in the desolation of the frozen riverbed.

They skied along the river for about thirty minutes before they came to the small island.

"Stay in my tracks here," Marit said. "The waters of the Tana are swifter and there are places where the ice is not strong." She needn't worry. Hans had not stepped from her tracks since leaving the farm at Holga-njargga.

The island was not more than two acres large, and very flat, except for the massive boulder in the middle. It was at least 15 feet high and could be seen even at a distance amongst the sparse vegetation of alder and birch. There was smoke and a soft orange glow coming from the roof of the hut that lay up against the boulder. Outside, there were already several reindeer, and a few sleighs.

"Jacob, Andarás. Lidy and Babi of course. Probably Old Man Jacobsen too. Maybe a few others from the village ..." Marit let her voice trail off.

"Old Man Jacobsen?"

"What we say about him being not quite alive and not quite dead? Sami believe that spirits speak more clearly to elders. They're like a bridge. He is always there when Babi has her visions."

Marit brought her index finger to her lips and looked Hans squarely in the eye before turning to the door of the hut and stepping inside. The roof was low, but not as low as one might expect, since the hut was sunk into the ground. They walked down a few steps, Hans bending over a bit so as not to hit his head.

The single round room was about twelve feet across. The walls of the hut were not mud but thin logs of alder, tightly woven together by cords. On the earthen ground, at the far end, up against the rock, a large fire burned strongly. Around it sat about a dozen Sami, mostly elders from the village. Old Man Jacobsen nodded at Marit and Hans as they came in. Babi was in the middle of the circle, next to the fire. She was dressed in a long flowing robe that had many of the colors of the Karasjok tunic, but in a different pattern. The colored lines ran not just around the neck and along the hem at the base of the dress, but also vertically along the front. It was quite beautiful.

The fire was crackling loudly, and a few of the Sami mumbled softly to each other in low voices that Marit could not make out. Old Man Jacobsen motioned for Hans to come sit in the circle next to him. Hans seemed to hesitate.

"Go," Marit told him. "It is an honor to sit next to him. He is the oldest human spirit here."

Hans sat down on the floor, on which they had spread reindeer hides over dried grasses. It was not as uncomfortable as it looked. Old Man Jacobsen smiled broadly, revealing his toothless gums above his sunken chin. Marit sat down behind Hans, just outside the circle. Lidy was near the fire, and she put another large log onto it.

"They're going to start," Marit said softly in Hans' ear.

Babi began a *joik*, but it was unlike the *joiks* Marit heard the rest of the year. It was a deeper, darker *joik*. It was rhythmic, and entrancing, and several of the elders started to hum along, mumbling the words so that they could not be clearly made out, but the rhythm was clear. From under a stool, Lidy pulled out the drum and laid it at Babi's feet. It was about two-and-half feet long, and maybe a foot wide. Marit had only seen it a few times herself, and each time she noticed new things about it. Today, she noticed the flames that ran along the bottom edge in a jagged pattern. The ink that had painted them on the reindeer hide seemed darker and redder than she remembered. She could see that Hans too was intrigued by the drum. His body tensed a little, and his eyes widened. She leaned a little closer to whisper in his ear.

"It is the *noaide* drum. Babi uses it to tell us what she sees."

Hans nodded slowly.

The drum was covered in runic markings, mostly drawn pictures representing houses and churches and little stick figurines—the Gods of the Sami. There were crosses too, and symbols to represent other sacred beings like the evil *Stallo* and the Alder Man. In the center of the drum was the sun, and around the edges the stars and moon. Lidy handed Babi the drum hammer, a small stick with a reindeer-bone head. Softly at first, then more insistently, Babi began to beat the drum to the rhythm of the *joik*.

Along the bottom edge of the drum, fastened loosely by strands of reindeer hide, small bones and metal rings hung down. Babi picked them up now one by one and placed them on the surface of the drum, and she watched them jump to the rhythm of her beating.

Marit smelled a new smell in the hut. It was not the smoke from before. It was a lavender odor, and it smelled like spring flowers in the sun after the rain. Behind it she could also smell some pine, drifting in the smoke of the fire.

Out of the corner of her eye, Marit could see Lidy, mixing herbs and grasses and tossing them in large clumps into the fire. But the attention was not focused on Lidy. Everyone's eyes were fixed on Babi, who mixed some dried mushrooms together with some aqua vita, and drank these even as she beat her drum. Another glass of strong spirit was circulating amongst the elders, and Hans took a generous gulp. Marit took the glass from Hans and finished it, and passed it back to Lidy to be filled again.

Babi beat down faster and faster on the drum, and the chanting of the elders grew louder.

"Do not say anything, no matter what happens, and do not get up," Marit told Hans.

Babi was beating at a frenetic pace and chanting herself very loudly. The little objects tied to the base of the drum bounced along its surface from rune to rune.

Suddenly, she stopped beating, and turned to the fire. In the smoke of the fire, figures and shapes rose up, in several different colors—red, blue, green. The elders stopped chanting too, and only Babi kept singing the *joik*, again and again, as she stumbled in front of the fire, watching the shapes and colors.

It seemed for a moment that she could not breathe. She grabbed at her throat and stopped singing altogether, and everyone watched in silence as Babi stumbled backward and fell to the ground on her back, her eyes wide open in a look of horror.

Hans made a move forward but Old Man Jacobsen's hand came down firmly on his crossed legs and held him in place. Lidy rose from the back of the hut and placed a damp cloth on Babi's brow, and dabbed her cheeks and neck. No one said anything. Outside, the wind had begun to howl. It had been some time already since they came into the hut. It was in fact difficult to know exactly how long. Time seemed to pass strangely.

Marit stared at Babi, waiting for her to come back. They waited while Lidy washed Babi's face again, and loosened the top of her tunic. Finally, after a long silence, Babi coughed loudly and sat up with a jerk. Lidy turned her body around so that she faced the circle, with her back to the fire, and she spoke.

"There were large clouds, dark clouds of brown and red, like blackflies filling the sky ... They came from the east and filled the valleys in an endless stream of death and destruction ... Out of the clouds came fire, and death. Only the woods were spared ... A lamb stood in the middle of the fire, and the fire burned around him, but did not burn him. The lamb was brown, but his heart was white, and he drank from the river and was one with the land ... The wave of fire swept across and the people were gone, the town was gone. Only the lamb stood, high above the town, watching, waiting ... The brown cloud was washed away to the sea and disappeared, and the red cloud swirled eastward and rained drops of blood across the land ..."

Babi paused a long while, and everyone wondered whether she was finished. She closed her eyes, and swallowed hard. "The lamb was gone and everywhere was death and loss."

Marit watched with envy as Lidy lifted Babi's head and lay it softly in her lap, stroking the old hairs away from her face and dabbing her brow again with the cloth. It was a rare moment of tenderness from Lidy, and Marit could not resist wishing it was for her instead of for her grandmother.

Babi was asleep, and in the circle, the elders exchanged worried glances and unpleasant frowns. Babi had shown them a vision, but no one in the hut wanted to partake in the future she offered them.

They stayed for many hours at the Spirit House, saying little, and drinking, while Babi slept. Eventually, Old Man Jacobsen got up to leave and one by one the elders streamed out, following him. Soon it was just Andarás, Jakob and the women with Hans. Hans and Andarás helped Babi back to the sleigh while Lidy and Jakob put out the fire and picked up inside the hut.

The outdoor air woke Babi, and she was smiling again, and less preoccupied.

"Ride with me to the farm," she said to Hans.

"But the skis ..." Hans hesitated, but Lidy and Marit looked at him reproachfully.

"Lidy will ski back with Marit," Bera said.

They rode along the river, the reindeer trotting softly on newly fallen snow. It was very quiet, except for the breathing of the deer and the rhythmic trotting of the hooves.

"You know what I saw," Babi said. "You have seen it too ... Not in a vision. You are not a *noaide*. But you have seen it nonetheless."

Hans said nothing.

"You must be ready for what will come," she went on. "You mustn't be afraid. And you must do what you must do. It is in your heart."

She was finished talking. Hans did not have a chance to answer. There was a finality in her voice that did not brook dissent or questions. Before long, they were back at the farm. Babi went inside to light the woodstove again. As Hans put the reindeer in the pen, and put the harness away in the barn, he heard hooves approaching, from the Blood Road, not the river. A horse, not a reindeer.

"Captain!"

The younger officer saluted as he dismounted in the courtyard.

"A telegram, sir. The Sturmbannführer said I should bring it to you tonight. It is personal."

When Marit returned, Hans was in the kitchen. Babi was knitting by the woodstove. The telegram sat on the table in front of Hans, the envelope torn into small pieces.

"What is it?" Marit asked. Hans was shaking. His hands trembled. "What is it?"

"Hermann ... It's Hermann."

"Is he worse?"

"He was supposed to ship out today, to be home for Christmas."

Marit waited for Hans to finish. She knew what he would say. She picked at the pieces of the envelope, staring away from him, wishing her ears could change what she was about to hear. The fresh air of the starry night was already forgotten. She was instantly back in the hospital in Skoganvarre, overcome by the rancid, inescapable odor. And in every cot was a man with two stubs and no sheet to cover them.

"He hung himself last night. Over the edge of his bed."

CHAPTER 14

Karasjok, February 1944

THE SAMI ALWAYS MARK THE RETURN of the sun with festivities. Even if at first the appearance is very brief, the arrival is like that of a promised bride. Her engagement party lasts many days and is punctuated by bonfires, dancing and general merrymaking. This year was no different, and even Babi's dark vision from December seemed forgotten.

The sun had been back for a few weeks now, and showed up for more than an hour every day. Hans marveled at how different the land looked in the sunlight, and how accustomed he had become to the vast darkness, how his eyes adapted to every shadow and how his ears became sensitive to every distant noise. Suddenly, in the sun, he was blinded, and he needed time to readjust.

Marit stood with Hans behind the barracks. The children still used the yard as a playground, even if there had been no school now for almost four years.

"I think you will like this game," Marit said to him, as the children gathered in a corner and began taking things out of a large bag.

"What is it?"

"You'll see."

The eldest boy, perhaps not quite twelve, had taken out a large set of reindeer antlers. They were quite majestic, probably belonging to a seven or eight-year old buck. They were several feet across. He placed them playfully on his head, and spun round quickly, like a bull in a ring. He snorted loudly, and blew so that a puff of steam came out of his mouth into the cold winter air.

"Catch me! Catch me! Catch me, young *stallos!*" he shouted to his friends.

"What's a *stallo?*" Hans asked.

"Shhhh. It's a troll. A big forest monster. Remember? I told you when we saw Old Man Jacobsen. Watch."

The other boys took small lassos out of the bag. One each. As the tall boy ran across the yard from left to right, the three other boys threw their lassos, trying to ring the antlers and catch the "deer".

Hans started to laugh.

"I don't think I've ever seen anything like it. A Sami version of Buffalo Bill, performed by kids."

"Who's Buffalo Bill?" Marit asked.

"Shhhh." Hans teased Marit. "A big American troll that herded buffalo for the showhalls and fairgrounds of Europe."

They watched a few more minutes and applauded loudly when one of the boys finally caught his deer. The eldest boy fell to the ground and rolled in a circle as the younger boy threw himself on him, putting snow down his tunic and over his face.

"Kids!" Marit said.

"Hhmm." Hans grabbed a handful of snow and tried to put it down Marit's back.

"Noooo." She ran along the side of the barracks and came out in the main street of Karasjok.

Hans dropped the snow and sidled up beside her.

"I have a surprise for you and your grandmother tonight."

"Not Lidy?"

"Oh, an even bigger surprise for Lidy, if she agrees."

"Are you ready to go back now? To the farm?"

"You go ahead. Take the sleigh. I have more business here. But you can tell Babi and Lidy to put on nice dresses for tonight. After dinner, I'll show you the surprise."

Marit tried to contain her excitement as she rode back to the farm behind the reindeer on her little sleigh. The path along the river was wide and easy. She could let her thoughts wander, but they always wandered back to the same place. Hans was always opening her world to new things. He seemed so curious to learn about Sami life, and Sami customs, but most of their discussion seemed to turn to the other world, the broader world that Hans had seen. He didn't live in it, he explained. He lived in a world like hers—small and closed. But between the two, in Germany and France and throughout Europe, there was another world. A bigger world. With cities and newspapers, and traffic and planes and a thousand other things that Marit could not even imagine.

That night, Lidy and Babi put on their formal dress and waited for Hans to come back.

"I don't think this is a good idea. What does he want to do?" Lidy asked.

"I don't know. He just said the biggest surprise was for you." Babi smiled as she watched Marit try to manipulate her mother into liking the surprise.

"I still don't like it."

"Then why did you get dressed up?" Babi asked.

"Not for Hans. I have a surprise for the two of you as well." She could hardly keep her words in. She seemed determined to have the last laugh after all.

Marit and Bera looked at each other and then at Lidy. Marit wanted to say something, but Hans came in and the discussion stopped.

"I'm late. I'm sorry." He was carrying a large box and a bag on top of the box.

"Let me help you," Marit said.

She took the bag and set it on the table. She could see it contained several of the records he played at Mr. Dahlstrøm's.

"It's a gramophone. A small portable one."

"Looks pretty big to me," Lidy said.

"Sit down and eat, *Njukcha*. You must be hungry."

"It's alright, Babi. I ate at the barracks."

He took off his coat and revealed his dress uniform. He looked very sharp, like a foreign prince or a nobleman, not a soldier.

"I have some new records. Waltzes from Vienna. By Strauss. He's Austrian. I'm going to teach you to waltz, Lidy."

"You'll do no such thing."

"I'm not sure Babi wants to try, so maybe I should ask Marit instead."

Marit tried to conceal her excitement. It was quickly dashed as Lidy stood up.

"I will try one of your dances, Hans. And then I will have something to show you. We are expecting some visitors tonight."

"Great," said Hans. "The more the merrier."

Hans set the first record on the turntable and connected the small horn to the gramophone's needle arm.

"Listen to the music, Lidy. Hear it call to you. Na na na na na, na na, na na. Na na na na na, na na, na na. One two three, one two three, one two three. Can you hear it?"

"I can hear it."

"Can you hear the rhythm? One two three? One two three?"

"Yes."

"Good." He stepped toward her and stretched his arms out. "Come stand next to me, and I will show you how to follow the rhythm."

Babi and Marit chuckled softly as Lidy took an uncomfortable step toward Hans, and stretched her arms out to meet his.

"This is crazy," she said after a few steps. "I can't dance."

"I'll try, Hans."

"Alright, Marit."

Lidy sat down, flushed. Despite her objections, she seemed to be enjoying herself.

"Put your right hand into my left hand like this," he said taking her hand. "Now put your other hand in my back." He did the same to her and pulled her very close. Babi chuckled loudly, and Lidy pretended not to notice.

"Now, when I step forward, you step backward. And then you forward when I go backward. Always with the music. Always one two three."

They started moving across the living room floor, one two three, one two three.

"Relax, Marit. Let me guide you. Just follow my lead and the rhythm of the music. She closed her eyes and found it actually became easier for a moment. One two three, one two three.

"Yes, yes. That's it. One two three, one two three. Na na na na na, na na, na na. Na na na na na, na na, na na."

The music was very fast now. The end was nearing. It was over, and the record spun around and around making a loud noise that shattered the reverie.

"Very good, Marit. We can try again."

There was a knocking at the door. Jakob and Andarás stepped in, shaking off the snow.

"Jakob!" Hans called out. "I'm teaching your niece to dance."

"Good. She'll need it for the party."

"Party?"

"Yes."

Behind Andarás, the door opened again, and people began to come in: Mrs. Erikssen, Old Widow Nansen, Milly and her mother…

Marit looked to Babi, who seemed unfazed.

"What's going on, Babi?"

"Ask your mother, child. But I think you must know as well as I do."

Marit saw Milly standing next to Lidy. She rocked a little on her feet and kept giggling, but Lidy didn't seem to mind. A few of the Erikssens' close friends came in, and finally, at the very end of the line, Jan. They had begun to sing a *joik*. It was a *joik* that Marit knew, although she had not heard it often. It was the engagement *joik*.

Hans was humming along, oblivious to the meaning of the party. He pulled up a chair and sat next to Babi.

"These are Jan's closest friends and family. Normally his father should be here, of course. Everything is changing with the old ways. Not even an uncle to represent poor Jan." Babi shook her head slowly.

"Represent him for what?" Hans asked.

"To present his case to Marit's father, or Lidy in this case. This is why they sing the engagement *joik*. Jan is proposing to Marit."

Hans sank down in his chair. Across the room, Marit caught his eye. He seemed paler suddenly, but Marit could not be sure she was not just imagining it. The music was too loud; the air was too hot. She felt ill. Very ill. She had been fine when she was waltzing. Now that she had stopped, the world had begun to spin, and it was not slowing down.

"Marit!" Hans cried out, as she crashed to the floor. "Marit! Are you alright?"

He was hovering above her, holding her head off the floor. The singing had stopped. They were a circle of faces, all around Hans, who held her head. Lidy kneeled down beside him and took her head from him.

"I think she had better get some rest."

"But the proposal?" Jan protested.

"If it is a good proposal," Babi said, "it can wait for another time. When Marit is able to receive it."

Lidy glared at Babi. Jan and his family slowly shuffled out the door, gone as quickly as they had come. Andarás and Jakob sat by the fire with Babi and Hans.

"So is Marit engaged?" Hans asked.

Jakob pondered this for some time before starting to answer. "There was no father to propose for Jan, and no father to accept for Marit ... We didn't sing all the *joik*. We didn't agree on what Jan would bring to the marriage. In fact, we didn't really discuss what we wanted to agree on. We didn't even have time to drink. No, I don't think she's engaged."

Babi grinned as she looked into the fire. "Not yet," she said. "Not yet."

Chapter 15

THE CHURCH WAS NOT WHAT MARIT HAD EXPECTED. It was modern, but built with old materials. The walls were stone, three feet thick. The windows were intricate stained glass. There were three large windows on each side, a few feet across and perhaps fifteen feet high. Each window had its own theme. Three quarters of the way down the aisle, high above the parishioners, was a massive Jesus carved in pine.

They must have used a solid trunk for the body, and hoisted it with a crane. His feet were two feet long. He stood, larger than life, hung on a cross beam from the rafters, with his arms outstretched, reaching down to earth. His open palms were even larger proportionally than the rest of the carving.

The altar captured Marit's attention. Or rather the picture behind it. The altar itself was a large stone slab, open to all sides, not fenced off like in Karasjok. Behind the altar, a massive mosaic covered the entire wall. Its bright colors and strange shapes created a fragmented impression that left one a little broken. As she looked more closely, she could see the Virgin Mary, holding her bleeding son, her own eyes tearful, and his arms dropping to the floor.

The contrast with the risen Jesus in the rafters was striking. Marit knew this mosaic from somewhere else. The other image was more traditional: a painting, representative not abstract. It was a painting from the church in Karasjok. Blues and greens made up the

Madonna's features with twisted glass or broken stones around her eyes—they all conveyed a great sadness. Her body lay limp on the chair, her son limp in her arms, their courage sapped and their spirits spent.

The church began to fill up. Johannes gestured for her to sit, but instead of sitting next to her, he crossed the aisle. Just like the old days in Karasjok: women on the left, men on the right.

She sat down and turned to the closest of the windows. The morning sun streaming through gave each shard of glass its designated hue. The effect was a dazzling display of color, yet the overall impression was still of sadness. It was Joseph and Mary's flight to Egypt. Mary perched upon the donkey's back, her child cradled carefully in her arms, but her shoulders drooped and her eyes were again very small. Joseph, instead of leading the animal, sat to one side, looking away, perhaps looking back from whence they came, or perhaps only lost in thought.

The other windows all had a similar style, but each was executed along a separate theme. The next closest window to her was all about the flight from Egypt. Moses led the Jews of Egypt across the Red Sea, and the armies of Pharaoh were drowning in their wake. The Jews in the window were tall and blond, and the pursuing Egyptians wore Russian-styled headdresses that looked anything but pharaonic. To Marit, the scene depicted instead the retreat of the 20th Mountain Brigade of the Wehrmacht across Lappland from Finland, so many years ago. She remembered one woman telling of the troops streaming by her house, which was on the main road from Lakselv to Hammerfest. They kept coming, an endless line, day and night for over six days: 200,000 Germans and 60,000 Russian prisoners.

Marit had not sat through a Catholic mass in a very long time. For the first years in California, she had gone to a Catholic church. With time, though, the service saddened her, until she found she would cry every time she came to communion. She felt broken, and the act of sharing the body and blood of Christ, instead of healing her wound, ripped it open every time, until one day she decided she did not want to go any more. She simply could not bear the proximity of Christ and the self-acceptance he demanded of her.

The Bavarian priest had Hans' accent, and she enjoyed the musical tone of the words. Marit let the droning voice lull her into a gentle trance, bringing her back to better days, on the banks of the Karasjokka, sunny days spent with Hans and Star. Sitting a few feet back from the monumental Jesus, she felt as though his arms were outstretched to her. His giant hand was reaching down, and in a moment would lift her up and out of her broken state.

This Bavarian mass bore a striking resemblance to the Lutheran service in Karasjok, except there was no translator here. In Karasjok, the mass was given in Norwegian and translated line by line into Sami for the people to understand. Here, everyone was German.

Except Marit, of course.

She felt the eyes of the parish bearing down on her, although she could not catch them watching. They recited the creed together, and out of the corner of her eyes, she could see them looking at her, but when she turned to check, they all looked forward. Only Johannes followed an opposite rhythm, looking to her when she sought to catch his eye, and smiling a reassuring grin.

Despite the uncomfortable stares, Marit breathed a sigh of relief. She had come to find Hans. Here he was. In the bodies of the villagers, she could make out his large frame. In the finely crafted stained glass work of the church, she could divine his refinement. Even in the open palms of the oversized saviour she found his generosity and goodness.

"You survived a Bavarian mass," Johannes said after church.

"I hadn't realized they were dangerous."

"Oh, yes. Even deadly. This priest is particularly boring. We lost several ladies last year."

He chuckled, trying to put her at ease.

"Was he boring today?" Marit asked.

"No. Boorish."

"Really?"

"He lectured on the indivisibility of marriage. What God has put together, man cannot put asunder."

"You don't agree?"

"Marit, I believe in life. And sometimes, life sees things differently. We all want life to be black and white, but all around us are shades of gray. Love in particular is not black or white, Marit. We don't always choose. Sometimes love chooses for us."

Marit smiled broadly. "Are all Bavarians so charming, or did I stumble upon the only two?" They reached the door to the old age home. It was in a modern building next to the local pub. Marit remembered Hans' fondness for beer. Johannes caught her smile and guessed her thoughts. "You're right. We had quite a few beers here these last years. I'm sure it kept him going to know that friends could always enjoy a nice drink with him, even if he wasn't at home anymore."

"Take me inside, Johannes," Marit asked of him. "I want to see where Hans lived."

Inside the home, Marit's comfortable feeling left her immediately. It was a sterile, institutional place. The main entry felt very much like a clinic. Marit tried to repress the wave of sadness that washed over her at the thought that this is where Hans had ended his days, he who cared so much for others. The bright watercolors of alpine scenes on the walls had pastures with too much lime in them, and the skies were not a deep enough blue.

A nurse greeted them and took them up to Hans' room.

"Will you be clearing out his things?" she asked.

"We're just visiting," Johannes told her. "But we will speak with Hermann. He will come soon."

"Why doesn't he come?" Marit asked.

"Hermann and Hans were very different people. I think they loved each other, but it is difficult for Hermann. He judges so much."

Entering the room was like entering a time capsule. The cold institutional feeling was gone. Here, Hans had recreated his own little world. She felt her legs weaken beneath her. As she sat on the bed, she noticed with some relief that Johannes was gone. He had stepped back into the hallway and left her here with her thoughts.

The room was small but comfortable. Besides the bed she was sitting on, there was a small writing table set up under the window, which looked out over the mountain. A little to the side, a dresser had a large collection of photographs on it. In the far corner, a small table had a hot plate to warm simple things, and a cupboard on the wall probably held a few dishes. The private bathroom was through a door a little to the left of the one she'd come through.

The furniture had probably come from the farm. It was antique Bavarian: a large pine bed and sturdy country style chest and table.

It struck Marit how similar this room was to Hans' room on the farm in the Finnmark, so many years ago.

She walked over to the writing desk and lifted the lid.

Some paper, some ink, a few pens.

It did not seem that Hans was writing much these last days.

She turned her attention to the dresser top. There were several pictures set up there, but her gaze lingered on one that she did recognize, with some surprise.

It was a snapshot of her own farm: Holga-njargga. She remembered the day it was taken. The army photographer had come to pick up Hans for a tour of duty, and Hans had asked him to take a picture of the farm with his camera, and another picture of Marit with her mother and grandmother.

Bera had protested, but the photo was taken.

Where was that one?

The farm was exactly as she had known it. The picture was taken from just outside the feed barn, looking down past the small house towards the river in the distance. It was early summer, and in her memory, the grass was very green. There were no reindeer, or other animals.

The laundry was on the line, blowing softly in the wind.

It almost moved across the crisp black-and-white photograph.

The sky seemed smaller than she remembered. Perhaps it was the lens of the camera that could not capture it, or the angle of the shot. It was the sky that she remembered most from the farm: a huge, deep sky that could swallow everything.

And the river, of course.

The other pictures were of his German children: Hermann and two girls. There was a picture of his farmhouse in Traundorf, and another of him with his wife. She looked away as she saw it, not so much that it bothered her—she knew he had married. It was more the sense that here, without Hans' consent or knowledge, she was intruding somehow on something very private. Something he had chosen after her, and she was perhaps never meant to know.

She paused again and thought to herself how ridiculous she was being. Hans was dead, after all, and had actually asked her to come.

She picked up the photo. His wife was a beautiful woman, or at least had been. The photo was taken when they were very young.

It was the Hans she remembered. He could scarcely have been much older, and he had that same carefree happy look that had first seduced her. You saw it best in his eyes: eyes that love life, eyes that *are* life. Even in the photograph, they seemed to sparkle.

Marit set the photograph down on the dresser top and opened the top drawer. It wasn't filled with clothes, but an assortment of knick-knacks. Even a Sami carving of a reindeer pulling a sleigh. She didn't recognize it, and it surprised her. *Had she forgotten it, or had she never seen it?*

Next to the carving was an old letter, addressed to Mrs. Bauer, Dorfstrasse 29, Traundorf. It was postmarked July 1942. It was mailed from Karasjok.

Marit sat down on the bed and pulled the letter out of the envelope. The paper was yellowed, but not brittle. She unfolded the letter and immediately recognized Hans' applied hand writing. She had always loved it. His letters were straight and strong and his words finished with neat swirls. She found her glasses in her pocket and put them on.

Karasjok, Norway, 29 July, 1942

Dear Mother,

We landed several days ago in the far north of Norway, in a region called Porsangerfjord. From the head of the fjord, it is a few hours' drive to the North Cape, though I was unable to go myself. There is light all day and all night, and the people seem never to want to sleep, hiking and going about their business sometimes even late at "night". I left almost immediately for my posting, a small village a few hours' drive south across a desolate moor the locals call the vidda. *It is overgrown with stunted birch and aspen, gnarled by the wind and the winter cold. From a distance everything seems barren and rocky, but as you drive into the* vidda, *you see that the trees are in fact taller than a man, and the landscape is not flat but broken by small ravines and hillocks, so that to wander into this wasteland is a certain death sentence for any but those intimately familiar with its paths. It looks dry and parched in many places, but in the ravines are marshy patches where the mosquitoes thrive, making it necessary to wear a net over my military helmet. This is the land of the "People of the Reindeer", nomadic herders that are amongst Europe's last indigenous peoples. The Sami, they call themselves, although we have always called them Lapps. Those that have left nomadic life make up most of the population in this part of Norway; they live much as we do in Bavaria, on farms and in small villages in valleys and along rivers. They wear their traditional dress, dark tunics, with bright borders that are distinct in every part of the country. They are close to the land, and understand it better than Norwegians do. I am eager to learn from them the secrets of this mysterious and beautiful place.*

The narrow road south comes to an end in a valley a sixty miles from the fjord. One drives off the plateau and suddenly a lush valley opens at your feet. The village, Karasjok, is named for the river that runs through it, the Karasjokka, a wide, meandering river that sparkles in the summer sunlight. It runs emerald green in the village, and to either side of it, the low banks are full of long, yellow grasses. On the hills around the village, there are tall pines, not unlike our own Bavarian forests. The Yugoslav partisans have been placed in a camp on the north shore of the river, just outside of the town. I have not seen it yet, but I am told they are well taken care of. The town itself is on the south bank over a straight and narrow bridge, and is the end of the road. I was told it was a place of some 1200 people, but most of these are actually on farms in and around the valley, so that the village itself is hardly a few dusty streets around the church and the school. The church is all wood, whitewashed with red trim and a dark red roof, and its steeple can be seen for miles up and down the river. Twenty or thirty old wooden houses painted in bright yellow and green and purple and blue are clustered together on the bank that juts out into the water in a bend where the bridge crosses, with many long boats pulled up along the bank. It is clear that the local people travel along the river as their highway. Indeed, I came on the bus from Lakselv and there were only Germans with me. The villagers are linked instead to Kautokeino upriver, and the villages along the Tana River valley downstream.

I have been billeted with a family that lives on the river bank a few miles downstream from the town. This way I will be close to the worksite, where we will build the road to Finland. Once it is finished, I will stay on to ensure the border is secure and help with the organization of the Führer's plans for this beautiful region. It is far away from our beloved Bavaria, but it is in many ways very similar, and I am glad to be here and not with my comrades in arms, pushing towards Moscow ...

Marit set the letter down and let her eyes close. The letter continued but she found reading Hans' words difficult. It was as though he was speaking again, and when she read each word she could hear his voice, in his lilting Bavarian accent, speaking each syllable distinctly and smiling with eyes all the while.

"Marit?" Johannes stepped slowly into the room. "Are you finished?"

"Yes, Johannes. I think it is time to go back to the hotel."

*   *   *

Yes?

Is this Hans?

Yes.

It's Marit.

Really? Marit? I thought I recognized your voice, even in English, but I cannot believe it. I have dreamed it many times, but it wasn't like this.

Hello, Hans.

Hello, Marit.

My granddaughter found your number for me on the computer.

It's funny that you are calling. I've been thinking of trying to find you too. I was wondering if you were still alive.

Not dead yet. Alt. Müde. Aber nicht Tot.

Silence. Not even a bird's call. Not even static on the line. He was in the same room as her. He could reach out and touch her. His voice surrounded her, swallowed her.

You have a granddaughter, Marit?

Yes. Jennifer. A daughter too.

I see.

They are very beautiful. They are blonde. Like you, she wanted to say.

I'm sick, Marit. That's why I was going to call.

But I called you.

I'd like to see you again.

See me? I live in California. Why am I calling? Why didn't you call me? Why have we waited sixty-nine years?

Do you remember that I said one day …

… that you would like to show me Traundorf? Yes. That was a long

time ago.

I would still like to show you Traundorf.

And here she was.

Alone, without Hans, without Mary or Jen, far from everything, with no way of finding anything, with no sign of why Hans waited so many years, and still did not try to find her.

If only there was a way back to Karasjok, a way back home.

But Karasjok too was gone.

There was no home.

Only emptiness.

Chapter 16

Karasjok, June 1944

THEY WERE RUNNING IN THE TALL GRASSES along the riverbank at the bottom of the lower meadow. The grasses are already waist high by mid-June.

"Not fair!" Hans cried out, thrashing at the grasses in his path. "Star is taking sides." The dog ran in his feet, slowing him down as he tried to catch up with Marit.

"You just aren't as fast, that's all," she yelled back at him, cutting up the meadow a bit to a spot that was dry and hot in the mid-afternoon sun. She let herself fall and turned on her back to watch Hans and Star arrive, breathless but smiling. Hans collapsed beside her. Neither said anything for a moment as they struggled to catch their breath.

They lay in the tall grass of the meadow, basking in the sun. The crickets were humming again.

"You are faster than a Bavarian foot soldier," Hans said matter-of-factly.

"On home ground with my dog as an ally. True. And you gave me a headstart back at the farm."

The snows of the previous weeks evaporated from their memories. Now it was hot again, and the light shone brightly.

In a few weeks, it would be midsummer night. She looked over at him, aware that he was watching her. He was going to say something. He seemed to hesitate. She looked away to help him find his words.

"Do you miss him?"

"Who?" Marit asked Hans.

"Jan."

"Jan? Why would I miss him?"

"Because he went back to the coast with Jakob and Andarás ... Maybe you wish he'd come back to propose again."

"I don't miss Jan." *And I don't want him to propose again...*

She lay on her back, staring up at the clouds that came together in big clumps and drifted apart again. Her stomach rose and fell with her nervous breathing. The run was already behind her, but she could not relax. Hans lay only a foot or two away, propped up on one arm, looking at her. When she turned to him, she couldn't quite see his eyes, because the sun was behind his head, making him a dark silhouette against the bright afternoon sky.

She turned back to the clouds, and tried to ignore his gaze. Her blouse was unbuttoned at the top, and the cleft between her breasts was evident. She knew he was looking at it. She couldn't look back, but didn't move away. It was a waiting game, though it was never clear who was cat and who was mouse.

"He courted you before leaving ..." Hans continued.

"Yes. I didn't see it at first. No one has ever courted me before."

"You weren't marrying age before."

"I'm not now."

"Aren't you?"

They both blushed at the question, the discussion having taken an uncomfortable turn. Hans felt he may have stepped over some unseen boundary. Marit knew she was old enough to marry now. Many of the girls in the village were married at sixteen, let alone seventeen.

"I want to finish school before I marry. I want to be a teacher."

"Mr. Dahlstrøm says you will make an excellent teacher."

"You've talked to Mr. Dahlstrøm about me?"

"Only in passing," Hans said, lying with a broad smile. It is okay to lie, Hans had once explained to her, if the lie is so obvious that everyone knows it is untrue. He plucked a long blade of grass and held it a few inches from Marit's face. He touched her nose with it, and her chin.

"Stop it! That tickles!"

"I'll do it more softly," he said in a whisper.

She closed her eyes, and he ran the blade slowly down her left cheek. It came to her chin and he let it slide off onto her neck and throat. He ran it back and forth a few times, and brought it down further, until it caressed the top of her breasts, and the space between them.

"Does that tickle too?" he asked.

She tried to take a deep breath, but she could hear herself shaking as she breathed inwards. She didn't dare talk. She lay very still.

He came closer and brought the blade of grass back up to her left cheek. He stroked it softly. He was very close now. She didn't dare open her eyes, but she could smell his breath on her forehead. He was only inches away from her.

She didn't move, not knowing what to wish for, afraid and excited all at once. Her mouth was partly open, and her breath came out of it in short, nervous gasps. His hand was in her hair, slowly pulling the locks away from her left cheek.

"Does it still tickle, Marit?"

"No," she said, almost under her breath.

His lips touched her forehead, and she clenched her eyes more tightly shut. They came down softly, first along her forehead, then her nose. They found her upper lip and lingered a moment.

"Marit, oh Marit. I cannot stay away, Marit."

He kissed her more firmly, his hands grasping her firmly on each side, stroking her arms and pulling her closer to him. She wanted to kiss him back. She felt her lips answering his, but her voice still resisted.

"Don't. Please, don't."

"What is it?" he said, pulling back far enough to look into her eyes. She opened them and pushed him a little further back.

"I can't. I just can't."

"I'm sorry, Marit. I thought ..."

She pulled away suddenly, leapt up, and ran back up the meadow as fast as she could.

"Marit! Marit! Come back."

He stood in the meadow just above the riverbank. She saw him over her shoulder as she ran. He didn't move. He gazed at her as she ran back to the farm, running his hands through his hair.

In the courtyard she pulled madly at the pump and brought up a bucket of ice cold water that she doused on her face and arms, washing away the scent of Hans, trying to wash away the desire to hold him, to be with him.

"Are you alright?" Lidy called from the kitchen window.

"I'm fine, Lidy!"

"Where's Hans?"

"I don't know."

"I thought he was with you."

"He isn't."

She buttoned up the top button of her smock and straightened her tunic. Star had followed her back up the hill, and went over to lie down in front of the barn. Marit too made her way towards the barn door. She pulled it open and went in out of the sun. From the barn, she could see Hans making his way up the meadow. Had he seen her go into the barn?

She wanted to leave again, but did not want Lidy to see her like this. She paced nervously.

She wanted to go to him.

To ask him to kiss her again.

To kiss him.

To be with him.

He was coming into the courtyard. He said something to Lidy, and then started towards the barn. Lidy closed the kitchen window.

Hans opened the large door and let himself in. He closed it without saying a word, and stood not twenty feet from Marit. He paused, perhaps to let his eyes adjust to the darker barn light. Marit could already see him clearly. She was breathing heavily. She wanted to say something, but nothing came to her. He was looking straight at her now.

"Why did you run?" Hans asked.

Marit had her tongue between her teeth. She bit down hard on it.

"Marit?"

He was walking toward her. If he came to her, she would not stop him. If he took four more steps, she would not stop him. Three more steps. He was walking slowly but without hesitation.

"Marit ..." he said, as he took another step.

She ran forward and kissed him strongly, holding his surprised head between her hands. In her excitement, she almost broke his neck.

She felt her own body tense and pushed back from him. He reached out to grab her, but she was as fleeting as a sparrow, dodging between his arms and running past him out of the barn, with Star right behind her.

"Marit!" he called. But she was already gone.

* * *

At dinner, Hans was somber. Marit did not dare to look up from her soup as they sat around the family table.

"Babi, Lidy. I have news," he said.

Marit looked up for the first time. He was not looking at her but at them, yet she knew the words were for her more than for anyone else.

"I'm leaving the house."

"You don't have to go," Marit exclaimed.

"Quiet, child!" Lidy said, annoyed.

"I do have to go," he said turning to her. "I wanted to tell you this afternoon by the river, but the sun was very hot and, well, it didn't seem the right time." Marit caught a gleam in Bera's eye, but ignored it. "Russia has launched a major new offensive against Finland. The Finns have retreated back dozens of kilometers. The High Command is redeploying the troops that were posted along the border to ensure we can better support the Finns."

"And to remind the Finns who their friends are, yes, *Njukcha?*" Babi smiled.

"Yes, Babi."

"When did you find out?" Lidy asked.

"Yesterday evening, when I went by the barracks. Many of the engineers are leaving too."

"They don't need engineers to fight the Russians," Lidy said.

"They do, actually. To figure out where mines go and to blow up bridges. To plan the retreat, if it comes to that." *Retreat. He said retreat.* "They even need engineer assistants like me."

Hans didn't need to leave to find the war. The war would come to Hans in Karasjok.

"Will you come back?" Marit asked.

"Yes. As soon as I can."

CHAPTER 17

Karasjok, September 1944

HARALD EDVARDSEN WAS CUTTING MEAT. Arnfrid was holding the paper. It was yesterday's paper from Tromsø. Even with the censorship, the news was bad for the Germans.

"Unilateral ceasefire with Russia. President Mannerheim to call for separate peace." Arnfrid read the news excitedly.

"Don't get too excited, Arnie. You know what it means," Harald said.

"Who's Mannerheim?" Milly asked, trying to follow.

"He's the new President of Finland. He's calling for peace with Russia," the butcher said plainly.

"So Hans will come home?" Marit asked.

"Home?" Arnfrid glared at Marit. "Home for Hans is a long way from here."

"Hans will be back, Marit, along with a lot of friends." The butcher cut aggressively into the meat, trying to pry off a leg from the carcass.

"I don't understand," Milly said.

"It's not that complicated, Milly. If the Finns sign peace with the Russians, the Germans have to leave. Their only way out is through here and along the coast to the north. They won't go out through Leningrad." Arnfrid was smiling nonetheless.

"So why are you so happy?"

"It's over for them now, don't you see? The Italians went to the Allies last year. The Americans just took Paris. Soon they will be in

Germany itself. It will be a few more weeks, a few more months, but the war will be over, and we will win." Arnfrid was beaming.

"I'm not sure we want to be with the last of the Germans as the Americans clean up. Isn't there another way they can go?" Marit asked. But she remembered the map from Hans' room. Hans had seen it already. She also remembered the vision. It loomed more ominously than ever.

"The Germans aren't stupid. They will also see it coming. They will seek peace before it is truly over." Harald was nodding to himself as he spoke, as though he wanted to convince himself it might be true.

Arnfrid stood up and started packing sausages into a bag. Since the closing of the Serbian camp, and the completion of the road, she was going further and further afield to help the enemies of Nazi Germany. There was a camp for Russians just before the border, where they quarried stone for the Finnish roads, and for the new railway they had started clearing through the tundra. She travelled by boat most of the way with the sausages, and then hiked up the hillside to the outskirts of the camp.

"I don't like that you're taking all these risks," Marit told Arnfrid. "You don't know the soldiers at the Russian camp, and the ones along the river have all changed since the spring."

"I won't let them starve."

"It's warm. Winter's late. You should wait until they really need it."

"Marit's right, Arnie," said Harald. "Maybe we should lay low for a while. Things are going to get difficult around here, very soon."

Arnfrid turned on her brother like a harpie. "Dammit, Harald, I think I've taken enough risks on my own not to have you tell me when it is 'safe' and when I should be careful."

"I'm sorry."

"We're scared, Arnfrid." Marit had said it, but Milly was nodding her head in violent agreement.

Arnfrid closed the pack abruptly and put on her jacket over her tunic. It was a long jacket, and its inside was black, so that she could turn it inside out and disappear into the night. Her bonnet too was lined with black. She didn't bother greeting them as she left. She stepped out of the shop and into the street, leaving her brother and the two girls to their worries.

"I don't like it," Milly said.

"You never did," Marit answered. "Come on. Help Mr. Edvardsen cut some steaks."

Milly took a knife from Harald Edvardsen's hand, and Marit noticed for the first time how Mr. Edvardsen's eyes lingered an extra moment, and how gingerly he offered the knife to Milly. Milly for her part only seemed to notice the knife, and began to slice the haunch of reindeer meat into thin steaks for the village.

Marit left them to their cutting, eager to see what other news the village knew. She found Mr. Dahlstrøm outside the barracks, not far from the river landing.

"Any news?" she asked.

"Of the armistice?" There was a twinkle in his eye. Did he know too that what she really wanted was news of Hans?

"Yes."

"Well, there has been a lot of talk, but so far, just the ceasefire. It won't be long though."

"How do you know?"

"Hans telegraphed the barracks this morning."

Marit's heart was racing.

She hadn't seen him since June. He had delayed and then cancelled his summer vacation. He had sent a postcard from Helsinki, and another from Ivalo in northern Finland.

Then nothing since August.

"He's coming back within a week," Mr. Dahlstrøm said.

"Really?"

"It's not good news, Marit. Not for Hans, and not for us. Hans has been advising the German Command in Finland on possible evacuation routes. The Finns will sign an armistice with the Russians. They are only delaying to give the Germans a little more time to get out. If Hans is coming back, it is because the discussions are over."

"Why is that bad?"

"The Russian Front. It's moving."

"To where?"

"To here, in part at least."

"But Hans said they would go south. They would race to Berlin. They wouldn't care about us."

"The Germans will have to be sure that they don't change their mind. They'll have to be doubly sure. They won't give them any choice."

"What do you mean?"

Mr. Dahlstrøm started to answer, but stopped mid-sentence. There was a commotion down by the riverbank.

"Let me go!" It was Arnfrid, shouting.

"Nein, mein Fräulein. Du hast sicher etwas für mich."

It was one of the new German soldiers from the barracks. He held Arnfrid's long blond hair in one hand, and her pack in the other.

"Let me go! I haven't done anything!"

Two other soldiers had approached now, and a small crowd was gathering. One of the soldiers opened the pack and pulled out some of the sausages.

"Ah ha! The Christmas tree decorator!" the other soldier said, laughing. "We've been looking for you."

They slammed her to the ground, making sure she could not run away. The other soldier ran toward the barracks, and a half dozen more soldiers came down to the river bank.

"Arnfrid's in trouble," Mr. Dahlstrøm said. "Go find her brother. Tell him to get out of here. Now."

Marit didn't want to leave, but there was very little time.

She ran back to the store and found Milly and Mr. Edvardsen still cutting up the steer.

"They've got her. They've found the sausages. They'll come here next."

"Damn. Damn, damn, damn," Harald said quickly. "Milly, go home and don't come out. If anyone asks, you were not here today. I don't think anyone saw you but Marit and Arnfrid, and neither will say anything. Go, now!"

Milly didn't hesitate. She turned and ran out the back door of the store.

Mr. Edvardsen reached into his pocket and pulled out a large key.

"There's a locker out by the cemetery, where we store supplies for burials. Under the tarps at the back, you'll find weapons and other things. The people of the village may need them. If it comes to it, we'll take our chances in the forests. We're not evacuating."

"Evacuating?" Marit wanted to understand, but there was no time. Mr. Edvardsen was frantically putting things into a small sack.

"Evacuating. You'll see. They won't have a choice. They'll suggest it first. But in the end, they'll want everyone out. They have to stop the Red Army. And we are in the way. You can trust Erik Larssen."

"Erik Larssen? The mayor?"

"Yes. I know we don't agree on a lot of things, but we've talked about this for a long time. On the important things, we both agree."

Marit stared at him. Precious seconds went by.

"Marit ... Please, take care of Milly. She's not bright, but her heart is in the right place. There's just so much about all this she doesn't understand. She needs you."

Marit ran out the back door and made her way around the backs of the houses to the river landing. She was glad she had come by boat. She would be back at the farm in twenty minutes, maybe half an hour. The farm didn't offer any added safety, but it felt safe.

She wanted to stay to see what might happen to Arnfrid, but she knew she could be of no help. If she stayed away, and Arnfrid did not talk, perhaps they would forget how they had worked together, and how she had befriended Arnfrid again these last months and years since the first time she saw Arnfrid hanging sausages for the Serbians.

In her pocket, she felt the wooden horse, the little trinket that never left her.

Be strong, Arnfrid.

CHAPTER 18

Karasjok, October 1944

IN THE VILLAGES IN THE SOUTH, there were stories of people who had been shot for helping the enemies of the Nazis. Many stories. The Nazis made examples of people, so that others were not tempted to help again. For several days in September, Marit thought they would all be summoned to the square in front of the school to watch the Germans shoot Arnfrid.

The truth turned out to be much more banal. She simply disappeared. The Germans did not say where she was sent. Her brother could not enquire after her. He himself had disappeared at much the same time, though the village whispers said he was on the *vidda*, waiting, watching, and ready to punish the Germans. Of Arnfrid, the village had nothing to say. Half the village thought she was herself a Nazi, or had slept with many anyhow. The other half was too afraid, given their own dealings with her, and what she might reveal, to even talk about it.

Arnfrid had simply vanished.

No public display of the prisoner. No renewed threats or reprisals. Nothing.

Hans stopped in at the farm as soon as he arrived in town, and brought his travel bag. He was going to stay for a time.

"They wanted me to stay in the barracks—there's room now that so many have moved out. But I convinced them I should be close to the border and to the road."

To Marit, it sounded like Hans was giving them excuses, not reasons.

"We're happy to have you back, Hans," Lidy said. "You can keep using the boat too."

"I won't be staying long. You've seen the order for the voluntary evacuation."

They all had. Germany and its Norwegian ally wanted to empty the Finnmark—everyone was asked to leave. It was just as Harald Edvardsen had predicted.

"Hans, they took Arnfrid Edvardsen, the butcher's sister, last week," Marit said, stepping closer to him.

"I heard." He looked away from her, towards the window.

"You know where she is … Is she alright?"

"I don't know. I only heard she was smuggling food to prisoners, and had been for some time. We used to call her the Christmas Lady in the barracks, because she would hang sausages from trees. She knew that would be dangerous. Prisoners are prisoners." Hans turned to look in Marit's eyes, but now she turned away from his glare.

"I have to help her, Hans." She spoke almost at a whisper, as much to herself as to anyone else.

"I don't think anyone can, Marit."

"You have to find out where she is."

Hans was silent.

"She won't have anywhere to come back to anyhow," Lidy said quietly.

"Your mother is right. Everyone is leaving. It will be done within a few weeks."

"We're not leaving, Hans." Marit crossed her arms across her chest, trying to look resolute.

"You have to leave," Hans insisted.

"We're staying," Marit said.

Bera was on a chair in front of the woodstove. It wasn't burning, but she looked into the box the way she would if it was. Her mind seemed elsewhere.

"The order is for voluntary evacuation, Hans. Marit and Bera think it would be better if we stayed," Lidy said, unsure herself of how strongly she felt about staying or leaving.

"The order is voluntary because they think people will listen. You don't want to stay."

Hans looked tired. His features were drawn and his skin was pale. His summer in Finland had not suited him. He was growing impatient. "If people do not leave voluntarily, they will be taken out. It is only a matter of time. If you leave now, it will be easier, for everybody. Surely you see that?"

"What happened to you?" Marit asked, stepping closer.

"What do you mean?"

"Where is the Hans who left us in June?"

"A lot has happened since June."

"Indeed."

"*Njukcha*," Babi said softly from the other side of the room. Everyone else became quiet. "*Njukcha*, if you think we should leave, then we will leave. But it will take us some time to get ready."

"Babi! We don't have to go," Marit pleaded.

Hans went to the door. "It's the right thing, Marit. You'll see. Listen to Babi."

He stormed out into the courtyard and set off for the landing at the riverbank. Star had risen to follow him, but the door closed behind him too quickly, and she was shut inside.

"So we're leaving?" Lidy asked Babi.

"You and Marit will have to leave. Hans knows it. The order will come. If not today, then soon. You need to be prepared."

"Babi, we're not leaving without you," Marit said, placing her hand on her grandmother's shoulder.

"I'm not such an old dog that I haven't any tricks. I will stay behind. There is much discussion in the village already about the evacuation. It is no secret that they will tell everyone to leave. We will be safe in the woods until Jakob and Andarás arrive with the herd."

"Babi, they might not come with the herd this year. There is talk that the Germans are seizing the herds along the coasts and slaughtering them for meat. Even if they do come, they will be evacuated too when they arrive."

Babi only stared more strongly into the firebox, lost in her thoughts.

Lidy went to the bedroom.

"Babi, please."

"Child, your mother needs you more than I do."
"You can't stay alone."
"I won't be alone."

*   *   *

In the village, much effort was made to give the impression that everything was continuing normally. Some overt preparations were made to show that people did indeed intend to evacuate. For those who knew the village well, however, the impression was quite different.

Marit noticed right away that half of the Upsahl's cows were missing. In the town, although the butcher's shop had been closed for weeks, the back door was unlocked and people came and went, fetching supplies. Night had returned for long hours since September already, and when the night fell, there was commotion around town. Marit spent a night at Milly's just to see what was going on.

"They're all staying," Milly said.

"All of them?"

"Pretty much. We're going, of course, and your family. The blacksmith's daughter who's pregnant. The priest and Mr. Dahlstrøm. Most of the Norwegians in fact. But everybody else is staying."

"How can you be sure?" Marit asked. It was strange for her to be asking Milly. It reinforced her sense that they were wrong to go. But Babi had been adamant. They were evacuating.

"Look," she said, drawing the curtain. In the alley, behind the house, Mr. Tomms was leading a horse drawn cart laden with hay. Further along, at the Albritsens, Marit could just make out their young boy packing saddle bags. "Have you ever seen such a frenzy of activity?"

"Where will they go?"

"Mr. Dahlstrøm told me the Sami elders have chosen a few places. There is a cave to the south near the marshes behind the big hill at Dilliavarre. There is another place where people used to hide on the other side of the lake at Gimisvarre. It's not as close, and you need to cross the river, but it is safe. There is a trail to the lake, and the Germans can't get across without a boat. It would take a week to carry a boat through from the village." Milly was excited. It almost looked like she wished she wasn't being evacuated.

"Milly, you can't tell anyone you know these things."

"I won't. No one thinks to ask me anyway."

The girls lay in their beds, listening to the village preparations.

"I can't believe the Germans do not see what is going on," Marit said as much to herself as to Milly.

"Maybe they do. Maybe they think people are getting ready to evacuate."

"Maybe."

"Have you seen much of Hans?"

"He's been very busy since getting back. I don't think he will stay long either."

"Is he evacuating with us?"

"I don't know."

"You like him, don't you?"

"Of course I do. He's been very nice with us."

"That's not what I mean."

Marit stared at the ceiling, as unsure of her own feelings as of her desire to share them with Milly.

"I've watched you with him for months, Marit. I'm not blind."

"It's different since he's been back."

"Is it?"

"He's changed."

"He's scared."

"We're all scared, Milly." But Marit realized that Milly was right. His tense looks, his frustrations and impatience. He was scared. *But of what?*

"Mother says the war will be here sooner than we think. She has a cousin in Kirkenes, up at the head of the Tana fjord, along the border. They've been bombed over a hundred times."

"No one is going to bomb Karasjok, Milly. There isn't anything here to bomb."

"Still, the war is coming. There's the Blood Road, and the bridge. The Germans will want to make sure the Russians don't come this way when we all leave."

Marit listened in amazement to Milly's reasoning. When did Milly become a war strategist?

"You seem to know a lot about all this, Milly."

"A little, I guess."

"You've seen him, haven't you?" Marit had figured it out.

"Who?"

"Who? Mr. Edvardsen, that's who! The Blood Road, the bridge. He told you they would mine them, didn't he?"

"Oh, Marit! Please. Don't tell anyone. They'll kill him, like they did Arnfrid."

"We don't know that they did any such thing. She's gone. That's all."

Marit tried to sound convincing, but in her own mind, as she said it, she had images of the pit behind the Serbian camp, and imagined Arnfrid half buried there.

"He's been hiding in the woods. He's helping to get things ready for the evacuation. It could come any day."

"Are you still leaving with us?"

"Yes. Harald said I had to. But we'll be back in the spring when everything is over. It won't be long. It may not last past Christmas."

CHAPTER 19

Karasjok, October 1944

MARIT LAY AWAKE, WIDE AWAKE, listening to the winds that howled down the valley. They rushed east, as thought to meet the fighting armies, but even this crushing force would do no more than slow the arrival of the men. For the last few nights, she heard the cannons. Hans called them the "Organs of Stalin": giant mortars that bombed Kirkenes, far to the north and east. But across the usually quiet barrens of the north, even at this distance she heard the shelling, a quiet rumble, like spring thunder, only constant and relentless.

The entire front was collapsing; the Germans had foreseen it long ago. It was this foresight that had brought Hans. And now, the chain of events that would take him away was set in motion.

She stared at the ceiling that she made out even in the darkness. She'd seen it her whole life. It was her world. Suddenly, violently, she hated it …

She could hear her mother and grandmother breathing regularly as they lay in their beds on the other side of the room. Outside, the wind howled louder, calling her. Calling her to him.

Her heart was racing as fast as the wind. Inside, she felt a longing, a pulling that was stronger than any reason, stronger than any sense of caution left inside of her.

Tomorrow, maybe the next day, he would be gone. He hardly slept now— a few hours between his patrols and work shifts, and often not at the farm. In the long autumn nights, they could see the fires burning to the east. The sky was lit with the burned houses of the Finns as the Germans retreated westward. Hans took naps where and when he could. But tonight, he was in his room again, maybe for the last time. He lay in his sheltered hut, one hundred feet away from Marit's bed.

She didn't decide to get up. She only realized after a moment that she wasn't looking at the ceiling, but had already begun to pull on her shoes under her covers. Her decision was *not* to stop herself, *not* to hold herself back any longer, and it was an easy one. The resolve had grown in her these last months. Suddenly unleashed, her desire to be with him was an irresistible current, carrying her forward at a frantic pace.

She left her bed, conscious of every breath her mother and grand-mother took. She crossed the room stealthily and pulled a coat on over her nightgown.

The door to the room had creaked since as far back as Marit could remember. It was the noise that told her that her father was finally coming to bed, or that her mother had arisen to milk the deer, or that something was wrong outside, and Bera was going to see what was amiss. Tonight, Marit wished with all her heart she could change the creak of that door. The creak sounded even louder since she was expecting it, dreading it. She passed through and closed the door behind her. She was carried by her excitement, and the fear that she may already be too late. He might rise now, tonight, to go off to join his men. He may be packing as she waits. He may even be gone.

She crossed the outer room as quietly as she could and let herself out of the door. She did not think of what her mother would think when the outer door opened. Maybe she slept soundly for once. It didn't matter. Marit was not turning back, and Lidy would not come to get her. She closed it tightly, and wrapped her coat around her. Even the October wind was bitter, and it whipped at her ankles and ran up her nightgown, leaving her frozen inside and out.

Across the courtyard, Hans' hut was lit. He was still there. A soft light, cutting around the edges of the door. She put her hand gently on the handle, and without more than a second's hesitation, pushed it down and stepped in.

Hans was sitting at his writing table. He turned as Marit came in. His body seemed startled, but his eyes were the same.

Reassuring, welcoming.

He stood up, but said nothing.

"I ..." Marit started, but could not speak. She stood firmly in the room, her back against the closed door. Resolute but immobile.

The door was shut, but the wind still howled from outside.

She let the coat fall slowly from her shoulders, and stood before him in her nightgown. Without taking his eyes from hers, he reached slowly over to the desk and turned the light down until it was almost out.

He blew softly down the chimney of the lamp. For a moment they were in total darkness, until their eyes adjusted to the starlit sky that came in through the window.

She could just make out a shadow, moving slowly forward in the darkness, but she could hear him too. He was only a few feet away now. She tried to take a step closer, but her fear kept her desire in check.

It had taken everything to come here, to close the door and stand firmly waiting. His hands reached out and touched her. Every part of her body was awake and alive, frozen in a panicked excitement.

She opened her mouth and willed herself to breathe. One breath at a time. Quickly in, then trembling as she tried to breathe out more slowly.

He was right against her now. His body touched hers. His chest touched the nipples of her breasts, which stood erect, pushing through her nightgown, and the touch sent a tingle through her body that folded her knees.

He caught her in a single movement as her knees buckled. His arm was already there, under her knees, holding her, and his other arm wrapped around her shoulders and upper body and together they lifted her even closer to him.

She could smell him. A strong, musty scent that she recognized from that day they had gone hiking, over a year ago. Even that first day alone together at Mr. Dahlstrøm's, she had sensed it. It was the same odor, but more of it. It was strong but attractive. It was Hans.

Her hands clasped his neck, and he carried her to his bed, and lay her down. Every part of her trembled, not from the cold, but the excited anticipation, and the fear.

His hands stroked her arms, and chest, and belly through her nightgown, saying *do not be afraid* in a thousand little ways, but he himself said nothing. She could just make out his breathing, matching hers, quickly in, and slowly out.

He stopped touching her and stood up. His hands quickly undid his shirt buttons and belt buckle, letting his trousers fall to the floor. He lay down beside her, and her hands instinctively reached out to touch his chest. Her small fingers ran across it, stroking it. It was soft and warm and sent a wave of warmth through her own body, from her arm to her belly, from head to toe.

He leaned closer, letting his lips come slowly onto hers, and, gently pressing against them, moving a little, sliding along her mouth, kissing her softly with just the very tip of his being. Gradually, she kissed him back, unsure at first, then more ardently, as she was drawn into him by the aura of warmth he projected around her.

As he kissed her, his hand ran down her leg and found her skin under the gown. It ran back up, pulling the edge of the gown with it. And down again. It stroked the outside of her leg, opening a fire within her. It ran higher, and down again, higher, and down again, until her breathing was so fast she felt sure she was going to pass out.

She was surprised she was not shy to let his hands run over her. She did not feel naked. She felt whole, and more alive than ever before. It was exhilarating to touch him, and be touched by him. To hold him. To be so close to him. He let his shirt fall to the ground, all the while kissing her even more strongly. He sat up suddenly and lifted her nightgown upwards, first over her legs, then up further until he could pull it over her head, and she lay completely naked before him in the darkness. She was hot and cold all at once, trembling out of nervousness, little goose bumps on her chest and arms.

He was on top of her now, moving his whole body up and down along hers, running his skin against hers. His hands reached down and slid his own underwear off, and the two of them lay trembling together, slowly rubbing against each other, his body each time sliding closer to the point where he would come inside of her.

He was there, just outside of her, with her in every way, and then, in a moment of tension-breaking pain he pushed himself inside. Every muscle in Marit's body tensed and released and tensed again, and she gasped for breath, unable to find it for more than a second, gasping again. She wanted to scream out but his fingers were in her mouth, holding her lower jaw, pulling on it. She bit him, almost as though the teeth belonged to someone else. There was her body, and there was her spirit, and the explosion inside of her had ripped the two apart. She felt him closer, then further and close again, like waves on a beach, or the soft melody of Babi's *joiks* that rose and fell, repeated yet each time a little different, a little stronger, a slightly larger wave. She thought she would never catch her breath when suddenly it stopped.

He collapsed inside of her, on top of her. She closed her eyes tightly and tried to take hold of the feeling inside, to feel the sparks that drifted in the air around the explosion that was over but not forgotten. It was retreating, but was still very present, like a series of smaller explosions, each wave getting softer, and feeling a little more distant. *Like the ripplets from the water crawlers*, she thought to herself. A hundred thousand water crawlers rippling in her insides, sending little waves across her body.

She wanted him to start again, as her own breathing subsided. She held him close to her as with a second set of imaginary arms she grasped beyond him at the retreating waves of pleasure. She heard his breathing and let it reassure her, as a song can lull a child or a stroking hand brings serenity.

They lay together for a long time, neither saying anything. His body was drenched in sweat, as was hers, but it was no longer only sweat. She was wet with him, inside and out, and the feeling felt strange and foreign. He rolled softly to one side and suddenly they were two people again, not one, and she was cold.

She wanted to talk, but there were no words. He seemed asleep, if that was possible, but when she reached over to touch his chest, she saw that he was only breathing softly, and his hand came back to touch her belly and hold her protectively. He ran his fingers slowly through the hair between her legs and twirled the ends in little circles, until inside she came awake again, and wondered if he was not going to come inside.

"I love you, Marit," he said almost inaudibly in German. "*Ich liebe Dich.*"

It came out as a confession, whispered into the air with a hope that it would float to her ears and be heard, but only a hope.

Marit reached with her right hand and touched his cheek, and ran the back of her hand along it, until a finger found the corner of his mouth, and she ran the finger along his bottom lip, and then his top lip.

She wanted to tell him she loved him too, or that she had always loved him, from the first day at Mr. Dahlstrøm's. She wanted to say they would be together forever, that she would leave everything for him, do anything for him.

"I'm leaving in the morning," he said.

I know, she wanted to say, but again, there were no words. Instead she lay down, snuggling up closer to him, and stared through the darkness at the boards in the ceiling. She could just make out the lines of the grain in the moonlight. Knotted pine. It was grey and splintered. Old wood, with many stories. She did not care that she should not be there. She did not want to lose even a moment of these last minutes. Tonight, they were together. Tomorrow, the world would be another place. Hans' breathing became shallower, and she felt his hand become limp and he drifted off into sleep.

Sleep, sweet Hans. Rest.

She held his large hand in hers. His fingers were strong. They were hands that knew work. She moved the hand slowly across her belly, pretending to herself that he was still awake.

From the holes in the knotted pine, she imagined little eyes peering down on her through the ceiling: the eyes of a fox, curious to see who had stolen his fire and who enjoyed such pleasure. Marit smiled back at him, confident in Hans' arms.

Mischievous, jealous fox.

CHAPTER 20

Karasjok, October 1944

HANS WAS GONE. She hadn't slept. Not more than a moment anyhow. One instant he was asleep, his broad arms wrapped safely around her; the next she was alone. She must have dozed off in the early hours of the morning.

It was dark, but already late. She could see that light would come soon. She could hear Lidy at the well in the courtyard.

She sat up quickly and found her nightgown in a pile on the floor. The bed was damp, and she felt cold inside.

Where was Hans?

She pulled the nightgown over her head.

Her coat was neatly folded over Hans' writing chair. Her reindeer boots were lined up side by side next to the chair.

She put both on, aware that the noise at the pump had stopped.

On the desk was Hans' copy of the Habanera, some other records, and a very short note. She picked up the little piece of paper and read Hans' delicate writing: "Goodbye, dear Marit … please take care of yourself." That was all. Not a letter, not a real goodbye.

Nothing.

Marit shivered.

She set the records down and put the note into her coat pocket.

Stepping out into the courtyard, she could see Lidy watching her from the kitchen window. Lidy's eyes held a strange mixture of reproach and fear.

Marit walked straight across the courtyard and stepped into the house. Bera was sipping tea at the kitchen table. Lidy stood at the washbasin, her hands tightly gripping a washcloth. Neither spoke.

Marit walked across the room to the bedroom door, never lifting her eyes. She reached the door, opened it, and went inside. As the door closed behind her, she felt the first tears welling up inside of her. She tried to swallow them down, but they came up more quickly, choking her, until she was once again gasping for breath, not from excitement but for fear of drowning.

The door creaked.

"Hans gave me this when he left this morning." Lidy was standing in the doorway, holding a sheet of printed paper. She was trembling, but Marit felt there was as much fear as anger in her gesture.

Marit stopped crying and turned to her mother, who stepped forward and put the paper down on the bed.

"It's the mandatory evacuation order. An edict from Hitler. They are burning the Finnmark."

"Did Hans know?"

"Yes. They found out yesterday. That's why he was packing. He's being sent to Finland to meet up with the retreating army. We'll be gone before he's back."

"When do we have to leave?"

"Today."

"Today?"

Marit wiped the rest of the tears from her cheeks.

"Are you alright, Marit?"

"I'm surprised, that's all."

"I mean …"

"I'm fine."

"Marit, we haven't much time. Some of the elders came by yesterday. Many of the villagers are staying behind, in the woods on the north shore, and in the marshes to the south. Most left last night already. Babi's going with them."

Marit stared blankly into space. It was all happening too quickly.

Hans.

Hans leaving.

Lidy leaving.

Babi staying.

"But it's mandatory," Marit said. "This says they'll shoot anyone who stays behind."

"That's why you and I are leaving."

Lidy turned and went back to the washbasin. Bera was still sipping her tea.

She was in a rocking chair, and it moved slowly back and forth on the wooden floor. She wasn't saying anything, but Marit could hear her softly humming an old *joik*. It was familiar but she couldn't place it at first. She stepped into the room to better hear her grandmother. Babi set her cup on the table and rocked more swiftly. From the corner of her eye, she winked to Marit. She started singing the *joik* again, first softly, but with a growing voice. Marit recognized it now. It was called Great Circle …

"The Wind is blowing
A road we all can follow;
Let it wrap itself around my soul,
And carry me away
Change is coming,
Old ways are bending;
Oh Gods of my fathers, bring solace to my heart.
The Great Circle turns
To the beating of the drum.
Oh little ones, oh crying child,
What world do I leave behind for you?
Oh Wind of the endless night,
Can you call back Mother sun?
I am not afraid of darkness,
Only of the void within the hearts of men.
In my soul I hear you River.
You awaken to Sun's call.
Your waters never tarry, like Wind that always blows.
Endless Circle, run by Gods of old,
Gods of my fathers, Gods of my child.
Change is coming, but my heart is always the same."

Chapter 21

Karasjok, November 1944

THEY GATHERED AT THE BACK SIDE OF THE CHURCH, near the main road that ran by the schoolhouse and the town building. Marit clutched her sack tightly, afraid that everyone there could see what was inside.

You will need this, Babi had said. *You are the* noaide *now.*

Marit didn't have to open the sack to see what Babi had wrapped in a woolen cloth and carefully tucked along the back of the bag. Its oval shape could be distinctly felt. She was the *noaide* now.

Marit looked around to find those she thought she might see. There weren't very many. The Germans had parked a dozen trucks along the road. They wouldn't need half of them. Marit didn't recognize the German soldiers who mulled around the trucks. They were young and new, and looked scared. Like the first ones that came, in the beginning, Marit thought. Right here. A few hundred feet from where she stood now. Where she might never stand again.

Hans wasn't anywhere to be seen. She had thought he would be here, to be sure they were in the trucks, but she had thought a lot of things.

"Marit Enoksen, Adventuress Extraordinaire, off on a new adventure."

"Very funny, Milly."

Milly set her own bag down and looked around. Her parents were a few feet behind her.

Milly's mother stepped forward and bowed slightly to Marit and her mother. "Hello, Marit. Hello, Lidy."

She didn't ask where Bera was. She didn't need to. No one said anything about those that were not there, but the tension in the air made it clear that they were not far from anyone's thoughts. Marit wondered if the Germans would be upset that so few had answered the call to evacuate, and what they might do. She knew from her meeting with the mayor, when she gave him the key that the mayor would not be here. Mr. Edvardsen had gone into the woods weeks ago. But the other notables: the storekeeper, the blacksmith, the merchants, the undertaker ... Not one stood in the little field in front of the church.

Milly's parents were here, and her little brother Sven, along with the minister, the schoolmaster and some of the farming families from in and around the village.

That was it.

Marit looked down and noticed a bandage on Milly's left foot.

"What did you do?" Marit asked.

Milly blushed. She looked left and right.

"I wanted to stay behind too. I tried to jump out of my window last night."

"And you sprained your ankle."

"It's a long way down."

"You might have noticed that before you jumped."

"I landed on my bag."

"Ah."

"Anyway, I'm pretty sure Harald would have been upset."

"Me too."

Marit shook her head. If even Milly had tried to stay behind, surely Bera was wrong about Marit needing to leave. *Why did she need to go, when so many risked everything to stay, when Bera herself would spend the winter in the woods in a tent or cave?*

Your path lies elsewhere. Take care of your mother, Babi had said. It felt strange to leave behind the place she knew best when it needed her most.

The soldiers eyed each of the bags as the evacuees climbed into the trucks: one 40 lbs bag each. In a few cases, they opened the bags and took out things that seemed valuable. The young boy who helped Marit into the truck didn't take her knapsack. He just held her hand as she climbed up into the vehicle and settle in on one of the benches.

They fit into three trucks—a little less than thirty per truck, with a single guard in the back, and a driver in the front.

It was dark when the engines started, but not late yet. The days were very short already. It was probably five o'clock when the trucks pulled onto the road and over the narrow bridge, slowly working their way up the steep hill on the north side of the river and out of the valley, onto the *vidda*.

In the dark, Marit could not see much of the village. She guessed at where the main buildings were, struggling to make them out. Already on the bridge the church steeple had faded into the anthracite sky.

There were no stars, no hint of moonlight, no snow covered fields or buildings.

Only darkness.

As they reached the far end of the bridge, Marit thought she could see Hans in a group of officers, watching the trucks drive by. There were three of them, and one stepped away from the others as the trucks rolled past. His black silhouette disappeared against the darkened landscape as the truck rushed by, and his face had not been visible. Maybe it wasn't him at all.

The trip across the *vidda* was very different from her last one. There were no blinding lights, or beautiful stars. There were no strange shadows. There was just blackness. It started just outside the canvas-covered truck, and seemed to go on forever, or go nowhere at all.

A void.

The truck was slower than the motorcycle, but bounced more, and it was hard to sit still or talk. They rode in silence, letting the sputtering of the engine punctuate their journey. It was more than an hour, but they arrived, in the evening, in Skoganvarre. The trucks for the evacuation only took them as far as the military hospital. It was still at least fifteen miles to the head of the fjord where they would be put onto the ships and sent south. The German soldiers at the hospital got them out of the trucks, and set them on their way. They each lifted their bags and started down the road.

All that they could take with them fit into small bags and suitcases.

All that would be left of their lives as they were scattered across Norway to create a barren wasteland to keep the Red Army at bay ...

Marit fit all her own things into her knapsack, and in her right hand she carried Milly's suitcase.

"How's your foot?" Marit asked.

Milly frowned. "Still very sore. It's bruised and sprained, but not broken." Marit didn't say she would find it hard to walk the fifteen miles. It was where they were going, and she had to walk it. She tried to set a steady pace that Milly could keep but that did not have them falling too far behind the others.

Lidy walked beside them in silence, Milly's parents and brother a few steps behind. They made an odd group, the six of them, but since Milly and Marit were inseparable, the three adults were becoming friends as well. Sven could be a poster child for the evacuees, humming a ditty and kicking the rocks gleefully as they marched along the road. The ten-year old had never left Karasjok, let alone gone off on an adventure like this.

No one spoke about those that had stayed behind, even if it was clear that that was what was foremost on everyone's mind. Marit wasn't sure anymore what to hope for. If the snows did not come soon, Jakob and Andarás could not come to Karasjok and help Bera. But the late snows also meant more time to get ready for the winter. A winter without shelter was deadly, and the men of the village who had found refuge in the hills around the village and on the islands in the lakes of the *vidda* would need time to build huts and store food for themselves and the animals.

Marit looked first ahead and then behind.

Mr. Dahlstrøm.

The Johanssen girls and their parents.

The blacksmith's daughter, who was pregnant. The blacksmith himself was not there, nor was his wife or any of their younger kids. They said her baby was a German baby, so she could go with the Germans …

There were several farmers from the upper valley that she recognized from church but didn't know well.

The Upsahls.

It was surprising how few had come. Mostly women and children. Less than a hundred, not one man in ten from the village.

They were joined on the road now by others from other towns along the road to Lakselv. Skoganvarre was evacuated as well, and its inhabitants were strewn along the road, making their slow way towards the sea.

CHAPTER 22

Porsangerfjord, November 1944

THE VILLAGE WAS TYPICAL OF COASTAL NORWAY. It amazed Marit to see how different it was from every village or town she had ever seen.

The houses were clustered around a small bay, with a second ring scattered up the hillside in every direction. The pink and green and blue and red houses shone even more brightly in the morning light because of their colors.

Those who had walked more quickly were already sitting on the docks in the sun, warming up. It had been cold through the night, but the walking had helped. Milly's foot was much worse, but she'd walked the fifteen miles and was hobbling down the hill toward the municipal wharf. There were several hundred people there, and a dozen well-armed German soldiers inspecting bags and checking papers.

The boat that would take them away from the Finnmark lay at the dock. It was a small merchant vessel: the Karl Arp. She was old and ungainly. Her fittings were for cargo, not people. Marit wondered how so many of them would fit unto such a small ship.

"How long is the trip to Tromsø?" Marit asked Lidy.

"It's only a day or so. It's not that far. If the boat goes directly, and we leave soon."

Lidy had made the trip with Marit's father, many years ago, to visit Uncle Tomas in Tromsø.

"Can we stay with Tomas?" Marit asked Lidy.

"I don't know. I hope so. We're family."

They walked down the wharf, next to the old vessel. It was even older than Marit had first thought. The paint along the hull was peeling, showing rust in many places.

The baggage was piled in a large mound near the front of the ship. A merchantman grouped the bags into smaller piles wrapped up in a net that could be lifted aboard. The little crane at the bow picked up the first of the nets. People shuffled along the dockside and began to line up near the gangway. It would probably be hours before they could board, but the first in would have the best places. Lidy sidled over to the queue and took a place. Milly and her parents were still at the beginning of the wharf.

"I'll get Milly," Marit offered.

Marit was surprised to find how well her mother embraced the changes. She exhibited little discomfort with this much bigger world so different from their home. Her assuredness gave Marit a sense of security, a sense of comfort.

Milly was sitting on the edge of the wharf, looking out into the bay. Her brother, a few feet further down, threw little rocks into the fjord and watched as they splashed into the clear water.

"Where will they take us?" she asked Marit.

"Away."

Marit wondered what away meant even as she said it. This town was already so different from home. What would Tromsø be like? Would they be able to stay there? Lidy had said that the evacuation orders were for southern Norway. Tromsø was only a transfer point. Neither Lidy nor Marit's father had ever been south.

Milly was transfixed by the wind on the waves. Outside of the bay, there were little whitecaps that made a pretty pattern on the surface of the sea. Soon, they would be out there, in the fjord, making their way to the ocean.

"I'm afraid, Marit. Maybe I should have stayed behind. It seems more dangerous to be leaving in the end."

Marit wanted to say something reassuring, but found no words. *What could she say?* She knew nothing of the world beyond the Finnmark, nothing of the people they would find there.

"Come on," she said instead. "Let's get your parents and go find Lidy. We should stick together."

The wait to get onto the Karl Arp lasted all morning, but the sky cleared and the warm sun improved their mood. The hours passed uneventfully as they watched the line behind them grow. Some of the arrivals came by foot. Others were being trucked in. Marit had been able to speak to the sailor loading the baggage, who said they were to leave today.

Sometime after noon, they opened the gangway and let people go aboard and down into the hold. Perhaps it was silly to be in a hurry to be locked inside the hold, but Lidy convinced them it would be best to find their spot before things became too crowded. They came down into the dark and chose a corner set apart from the main area, behind a ladder that led to another compartment of the ship.

It took longer than expected to load the ship. The hold became progressively more crowded, until it was hard to move around, and harder still to breathe. Before long, the decision to sit far from the hatch proved unwise. The air turned stale, and the smell of so many hundreds of people locked into the small hold became stifling.

Marit had kept her bag with her, and on the advice of the sailor, had found some dried fish and cakes in the village. They had some bread from the farm. They huddled behind the ladder, the six of them, Milly's mother nervously massaging Milly's ankle.

After what seemed an eternity, the boat began to move. Mercifully, the sailors left the hatch open. As they moved out into the fjord, the wind made its way down into the hold and renewed some of the air. There were no portals, and only a little light came in from the deck. Soon however, the boat began to rock on the swells, as they washed across her port side. Almost immediately, Milly's mother felt queasy. As several others in the hold became seasick, the stench in the cargo hold became overpowering.

Sometime in the evening, they left the fjord. They could feel it in the way the boat behaved. It pulled more strongly against its own engines. The steel hull rang out each time a wave crashed into the side, and the rolling worsened.

People clung as best they could to whatever they found.

A loop of rope in the floor of the hold.

A ladder.

A crate.

Other people.

About the same time, the sailors closed the hatch. The setting sun left them in total darkness hours earlier, but now whatever fresh air that had wafted in from the hatch was blocked. Despite the cold outside, it was becoming warm in the hold. The eerie quiet was only interrupted by babies' cries and the groaning of the ship itself as it stretched and pulled through the turbulent waters.

No one slept that night, making it the second night without rest. The warm stale air and the lack of sleep left their bodies sweaty and drained. In the morning, the waters calmed somewhat, although the wind picked up. The sailors opened the hold and let in some light. Some water cups appeared from above and those closest to the hatch shared with a few others. Marit considered pushing over to get some for Milly and Lidy, but quickly abandoned the idea. The crush of people around the hatch formed an impassable wall, and she risked being crushed herself.

After a while the darkness returned, and Marit found it harder and harder to keep track of time. Were they near Tromsø already? She could only hear the pull of the engine, feel the roll of the ship, and wonder what might come next. She tried not to concentrate on how slowly the voyage progressed. She thought instead of brighter days — of picnics along the Karasjokka, of boat trips to the Tana fjord, of reindeer races, of her hikes with Hans.

Hans.

Where was Hans? Where was Babi? How could she have left them?

The rocking of the boat must have put her to sleep. Or perhaps the odor in the hold put her into a trance. In any event, it was Milly who shook her awake. She noticed the silence first. The constant throbbing of the engines had ended.

"We're here!"

"Here?"

"Tromsø, I think. They're unloading."

They were indeed unloading. Marit forced her eyes open. Lidy's head was in her lap. She too had fallen asleep. Milly's parents and Sven were already standing, pushing towards the opening in the distance.

"We can wait a few more minutes, Milly. We will all get out eventually."

Lidy opened her eyes.

"We're here, Lidy."

She lifted her head, surprised to be in her daughter's lap. For a moment, she smiled, and Marit smiled back. Marit could not remember the last time they had shared such a moment. It passed quickly, as Milly stood and Lidy too. Milly took her little brother's hand and helped him over to the ladder out of the hold.

About half of the people in the hold had left. Some were still asleep on the floor of the hold. Some simply were not moving.

CHAPTER 23

Tromsø, November 1944

THEY EMERGED FROM THE HOLD, awash in the morning sun. The fresh, cool air brought Marit back to herself instantly, and even Milly perked up notably. They walked down the gangway and came out on the docks. Tromsø was a big town. Bigger now with all these refugees.

"Uncle Tomas says there are 30,000 people living here," Lidy said.

"That doesn't include the Germans, and there seem to be a lot of them," Marit added, pointing to the dozens of soldiers that lingered along the docksides, watching the refugees unload.

"Or the refugees," Milly pointed out. "There were over a thousand just on our boat."

Marit stood at wharf's edge and peered over into the water. It was crystal clear and went down at least thirty feet. The bottom gleamed in the sunlight. She could clearly make out every rock and plant. There was a large purple starfish stuck to the largest rock, and a metal barrel a little further out.

"What are you looking at?" Milly asked.

"The starfish."

"What's that?"

"There. On the bottom. On that rock. It has arms like a star."

"Stars aren't purple. And I don't think they have arms. How do you know about starfish?"

"Hans told me."

Lidy and Milly's parents had already started up the street. One block up from the docks was the Storgata, or "Big Way". For Marit and her mother, for Milly and her parents, the Storgata was like a grand boulevard. To the other side were shops stories high, and hotels with elaborate chandeliers and huge reception halls. The street was more crowded than even the busiest market days in Karasjok, and perhaps more surprising, it was paved with small stones so that you could walk without muddying your feet. They wandered in the morning sun watching people go about their business, alone in the crowd of people, stunned and amazed, like fish out of water.

"What do we do now?" Milly asked.

"We need to go to the Refugee Adminstration—Storgata 55." Lidy was already heading down the street in the right direction. Nothing seemed to faze her.

Number 55 was a simple-looking two-story house. The line in front of the door ran several hundred feet up the street. Lidy found the end of it and started her long wait. In the end, the line moved more quickly than expected. Inside the building, there were several desks with clerks registering people. Lidy took her documents out of her bag, and Marit's as well.

"Point of origin?" asked the clerk.

"Karasjok."

"You'll be relocated to Trondheim. For now, anyway. There are families there that will take you in."

"I have family here in Tromsø. We'd like to stay."

"Everyone would like to stay. Do you know how many people have come through Tromsø this week alone?" The clerk wasn't waiting for an answer. "Nine thousand. Nine thousand people. By the end of the month, it might be as many as forty thousand. You can't stay. There isn't room."

"We have family."

"If you know of people that have room in their house in the town, you must tell us. We can register their rooms."

"We can work. My daughter and I."

"Work?"

"We're nurses," Lidy lied.

"There's no profession listed on your documents."

"We're Sami. The documents are old."

"We could use some nurses at the hospital that speak Sami. Some of the refugees haven't travelled well."

"We don't need a place to stay," Lidy repeated. Marit listened in amazement, as her mother lied to the clerk again.

"Who will you live with?"

"My brother-in-law. Sjøgata 50."

"Your brother-in-law? Where is your husband?"

"I'm a widow."

"I see."

Marit watched the face of the Lutheran clerk. She clearly wanted to know whether Lidy's brother-in-law was married, but was hesitant to delve too deeply into this. The clerk looked past them at the line that stretched out into the street, and must have decided she had already spent a lot of time with Lidy and Marit.

"Very well, Mrs. Enoksen. You and your daughter can stay with your brother-in-law. I need a letter from him tomorrow morning stating he has room in his house and that you can stay with him. You'll report to the hospital this afternoon."

"Thank you."

"Mrs. Enoksen... You'll probably find that the hospital here is bigger than you're used to. Don't be afraid to ask if you're having trouble. It may take a few days, but they will make nurses out of you. They really need help." The clerk looked at Lidy. Behind her stern demeanor, Marit could see that she did not believe Lidy's lies. She was drawing lines in the sand. Lidy's lie just moved the line a little.

Milly and her parents weren't as lucky. With no reason to stay in Tromsø, they were shipping out to Trondheim in less than a week. In the meantime, they would board in the local school up the hill from the Storgata. Marit and Lidy left them to get settled, and went up the Storgata, looking for Sjøgata 50.

Sjøgata, meaning "Ocean Way", turned out to be a small street that ran off of the Storgata for a distance before running parallel along the seaside. They had gone past 50 before they found the street, so they walked back down a few blocks. It was on a hillside, about a block from the harbor. There was a dirt trail that led down to the water directly opposite the house. The house itself was painted a bright red. It was narrow, but had a back yard. It was actually quaint. Marit liked it right away.

"When did you last see Uncle Tomas?" Marit asked her mother.

"At your father's funeral."

"Oh."

"He'll be happy enough to see us."

They walked up a few steps to the front door and rang the bell loudly several times. It was a little past noon by now, and people were coming home for lunch.

"What does Uncle Tomas do?" Marit asked as they waited on the front steps.

"He has a fishing boat."

The door opened and an old lady stood in the doorway.

"Good afternoon," Lidy said in her best Norwegian. "Is Mr. Enoksen in?"

"He is not."

"May we come in?"

"On what business?"

Lidy looked at Marit and back at the old lady. She wasn't comfortable talking on the steps. She'd hoped to see Tomas.

"I'm Tomas' sister-in-law, and this is my daughter, Marit."

"Well, say so then! I didn't know Mr. Enoksen was ever married. Come in, come in from the street." She stepped back and motioned for them to follow her in through the narrow doorway.

"He wasn't married," Lidy corrected quickly. "I was. To his brother."

"Oh. I see." She was taking their coats, and eyeing their bags with some suspicion. "Will you be staying for dinner?" she finally asked.

"We'd love to," Lidy answered, accepting the unoffered invitation. "When will Mr. Enoksen be back?"

"Any time now. The market will be closing in another half hour, and he'll need to wash up, but he'll be back for lunch. You can discuss dinner with him," she said sternly, clearly wondering whether she'd done well to let them in.

Lidy and Marit sat together in the living room, looking out the only window down the little trail to the sea. The view left them breathless. The house was small, but seemed comfortable. The old lady apparently was a maid, but it wasn't clear whether she lived with Tomas or somewhere else. They were both startled from their reverie by the front door slamming shut and a deep, booming voice.

"Margret? What are these bags? What are you up to?"

Lidy rose and stepped forward into the hallway.

"Hello, Tomas."

"Lord Almighty. Lidy! You haven't changed much." He smiled broadly, and Marit breathed an audible sigh of relief.

"You're still charming, Tomas. I know I'm a lot older than fifteen years ago."

"Has it been that long? I'm sorry he's gone, Lidy."

"It was a long time ago."

"Yes."

"This is Marit, Tomas. Your niece."

"Good afternoon, sir."

"Don't sir me. Tomas is fine. Hope you have your father's good sense."

Margret had reappeared in the hallway. "Shall I prepare some extra plates for the lunch table, sir?"

"Of course, girl. And hurry up! I'm famished." Despite his gruff tone, Marit liked him right away. Here was someone who did not beat around the bush –and didn't mind calling an old woman 'girl' when she was silly.

"We've come with the other evacuees," Lidy started.

"Suppose you want to stay in my house, eh?"

"Well..."

"I know what's going on. And I know you haven't a place to go. Everyone's talking about it. Damn fool's work – burning the Finnmark! They expect 100,000 refugees."

"We really don't have anywhere else to go."

"You do, actually. They're relocating everyone south. May take a few days, but they've promised to ship everyone somewhere."

"We would like to stay," Marit said, looking her uncle in the eyes.

"Well you do have your father's bluntness, I'll give you that."

"We don't have any other family."

"Haven't had me for the last fifteen years either. Anyhow, of course you can stay. Lidy's probably already told them you would anyhow, haven't you, Lidy? Think that I forget? You haven't changed. But you can stay. I need the company, and they'll end up putting me up with strangers if I don't say yes, so I might as well ..."

Marit forgot herself a moment as she wrapped her arms around her uncle and hugged him tightly. She thought Lidy would scold her, but when she let go, her uncle was beaming and Lidy smiled too.

"Thank you, Tomas," Lidy said. In her own way, she might as well have been hugging him. His eyes flashed a quick acknowledgment and he set off to make arrangements for their stay.

He came down a few minutes later and they sat down to eat.

Lunch was delicious—a fish soup and some beef tongue served with a spicy red sauce that Marit did not recognize.

Tomas found some humor in Lidy's story about being nurses. Many of the evacuees arrived hungry and sick. The hospital was overflowing, even though Tromsø itself had not actually been bombed.

That afternoon, Lidy and Marit walked up the hill to the hospital, about twenty minutes from Uncle Tomas' house. The view from the front door of the hospital was worth the climb itself. You could not really see the sea from Tromsø, but you could clearly see the channel that separated the island from the mainland. And across the channel, a mountain rose from sea level to at least 1800 feet. It was a wall of ice and snow, and even in the pale November light seemed to glow as it watched over the town.

"Your father showed me this mountain when he took me to Tromsø to meet his parents," Lidy said as they stood looking at it.

"Really?"

"It always scared me a bit. He said there is a troll that lives inside of it: an old and ugly *Stallo*. One day, the *Stallo* heard another voice, and was surprised to find that he was not alone. In that smaller mountain over there," she pointed, "was another troll. Guri was her name. A lady troll. She hounded him, and annoyed him, begging him to marry her. One day, he was so tired of her pleading, he went away on a holiday, far to the south. He stayed away for a thousand years. But after a time, he came to miss the lady troll, with all her warts. He even missed her nagging. He came back and married her, and brought his tropical island back too, and parked it right in front of the mountain so he could see it every day." Lidy was lost in her memory of that moment, looking out over the channel at the mountain, so many years ago.

"Was that my father's way of being romantic?" Marit asked sarcastically.

"I suppose maybe it was. He wasn't very romantic. But he loved me nonetheless, in his way."

Marit felt warm inside, despite the cold November air. The story of the thousand-year wait that was eventually rewarded made her smile. There was fresh snow crunching under their feet as they walked the rest of the way to the hospital entrance, and Marit listened between every crunch, hoping her mother might say one word more.

Inside the hospital, Lidy and Marit found it was not hard to be put to work. They were quickly set to changing bedding, and interpreting for the other nurses and doctors who did not speak any Sami. Most of the Sami there suffered from dehydration, exhaustion or hypothermia. None of them were from Karasjok, but they all told similar stories of leaving on a day's notice, with only a few belongings.

For the most part, the villages in the interior fled to the hills and lakes of the *vidda*. For the coastal Sami, the story was different. Most of the villagers were evacuated by boat or by road. And they were still arriving. The roads were thick with refugees. Further inland, some of the refugees had seen the first divisions of the retreating army. Marit struggled as she listened to these stories. Somewhere out there was Hans, forced to destroy her homeland and maybe to track down her own family and friends, guilty of staying behind. She wished he could be here in Tromsø instead of with the Wehrmacht.

She closed her eyes, and imagined him here, in the hospital. It was very real. Eerily real. He *was* here. She opened her eyes again and saw only an empty bed.

Lidy and Marit worked into the evening and night, finally leaving long after dinner. They would earn their time in Tromsø, of that neither had any doubt.

* * *

Marit sat in the bedroom upstairs, keenly aware of every sound in the small house. She wanted to rest after a long day at the hospital. It was only her second day, but already it felt like an eternity since they had arrived. An eternity since leaving Hans and Karasjok.

Her Uncle Tomas was in the living room downstairs, talking with Lidy. Their voices were not loud enough to make out entire sentences, but a general drone rose up to Marit, and the occasional word.

Russians.
Germans.
Refugees.
Sadness.

Marit stared out the small window that looked down the little alley opposite the house out over the outer docks of the little port village. Night came early. The sun had set around 3:30, and with the hills around Tromsø, it was dark by 4:00. She could make out a lantern on one of the fish processing buildings down by the dockside, and then nothing but blackness beyond. Somewhere out in all the darkness, Hans was alone too. Or not alone. With the Germans, wreaking havoc on the countryside and laying mines to keep the Russians out.

Fire.
Heathen.
Karasjok.
Babi.

Marit reached under her bed and pulled out the knapsack Babi had given her when they left. It was her own knapsack, and Lidy had thought nothing of it, but Babi had packed the bag and placed it delicately in Marit's hands. She felt the oval shape right away, and had wanted to speak, but Babi's eyes warned against it.

Marit opened the knapsack fully now and lay it on the bed. She gingerly pulled out the long oval drum and placed it on her pillow. Inside the bag, she found a half dozen small packages wrapped in butcher's paper: Babi's herbs and mushrooms. There were no labels on the packages. She would have to tell by color and taste what was what.

Marit stared longingly at the drum. She had never used it, but Babi had showed her how. Babi had coached her through the beginning phases of the trance, so that she could let her inner spirits guide her until she found the greater spirits that would take control. The drum wasn't necessary. It was a tool like any other. A comforting tool to help find the greater spirits. And to inspire those that watched. The *noaide* could beat the ground or walls or even rocks. The beating could be reproduced in other ways, like by singing a well-known *joik*. It was the herbs and mushrooms that put the *noaide* into the trance, and the rhythm of the beating.

Marit studied the symbols on the drum. She stopped on the left when her finger touched the church. She felt a pulling within her. The fingers of her other hand wandered to the licking flames of fire that rounded one of the edges of the drum. She wanted to connect the two, but knew she was letting her own mind connect things. She needed to let go.

She set the drum down again, knowing she could not beat it without attracting the attention Lidy and Tomas. She paused a moment to be sure they were still in discussion.

Sickness.

Hospitals.

Germans.

Boat.

She willingly closed them off and turned toward the bags that lay on the bed. Two of the packets seemed a little familiar, and their wrapping showed signs of frequent use. She opened the first. It was the scented dry grass that grew on the riverbank that Babi harvested every spring when it first flowered, and carefully wrapped away to ensure it would keep its scent. Sometimes she would throw some on the fire in the *lávvu*, and the whole tent would take on a smell of spring sweetness.

She turned to the second package. It was odorless. Inside, she found a large quantity of dried mushrooms, broken into little chunks small enough that they were almost powdered. This is what she was looking for, but she had no idea how much to take. The mushrooms were fatal if ingested, and *noaides* built up a slow tolerance to them over time. If she took too little, she would not feel any effect. If she took too much, she could kill herself.

She had watched Babi take them many times. Babi always mixed them with spirit water like Aqua Vita or at least some rum. She didn't dare go down to her Uncle's alcohol cabinet. Marit went over to the water basin and poured herself a small glass from the pitcher. Coming back to the bed, she delicately put a pinch full of the powder into the water and stirred it with her finger. It dissolved nicely and she sipped slowly at the rim of the glass.

Still blocking out the conversation from below, she began to gently hum an old *joik*—one of the ones she knew best. It was a simple song about a girl who does not want to go to bed, until her parents threaten her with many different punishments. It was perfect because the worlds were very simple and came back again and again with each new threatened punishment. She hummed it a little more loudly and tapped her hand on her thigh, drinking down the rest of the glass.

She let her mind wander, trying to steer it towards Hans, but not to steer it too strongly. Downstairs, the conversation suddenly seemed louder, and began to pull against her wandering. She could see Lidy and Tomas in the living room, sipping their tea and could almost make out every word they spoke. She reached down with her damp finger and thrust it into the mushrooms and then into her mouth, sucking off whatever had stuck to the finger.

She pulled back from the living room and was wandering again, floating now, floating higher, not on a river, but in the air. It was light, not dark, and she could see for miles and miles.

She was Raven, flying high over the *vidda*, seeking, seeking.

There.

She could see it in the distance.

She had never seen it from above, but she knew.

It was Karasjok.

She could see it all at once in the distance and up close. The bridge that crossed the river was a jumble of metal pieces in front of her eyes, and the river ran under it in many different directions all at once.

She could see the houses, but not as one sees a map or a picture. She could see all of the houses at once. Pink. Green. Blue. Old Widow Nansen's house. Mr. Dahlstrøm's room. The gramophone. The schoolhouse. The Germans.

Everything.

All at once.

She tried to pull back.

She was the Raven, high in the sky. Karasjok was below her. This time she tried to see it in separate pieces. One house at a time.

Then she smelled it. An acrid burning smell. It was a fire, but not the fire of a *lávvu* or a midsummer night festival. It was a house. Or two. It was everything. It was hot. Her wings ached and her eyes cried in the smoke. She swooped down, trying at once to get closer and not be inside of the fire.

Distance.

Distance.

In the middle of the fire was the church. Its steeple was distorted. It was twice as high as it should be, and the door was wide open, twice as large as she knew it to be. There in the door stood Babi, slightly bent over, leaning on a walking stick and holding her hand defiantly in front of her.

And there too was Hans. He stood side by side with another German whom Marit could not see clearly. Behind them stood a dozen or more Germans, in their ugly metal hats, with funny packs on their backs, holding long sticks of fire like the ones she had heard about from other refugees.

Hans and the German officer were shouting, partly at Babi, partly at each other. The other Germans stood like wolves watching two males circling a dead animal, unsure of whom to listen to, unsure who would win the kill.

Babi said nothing. Babi did not move. The flames were licking everywhere. Every building was burning, and in the middle of it all, the church stood taller than ever, perhaps three times its normal height.

The smoke was getting stronger and it was harder and harder for Marit to see. Hans was yelling. The other Germans were yelling too now, all of their faces blurring together. She looked at Hans, but saw Babi with her sharp, glassy eyes, and Marit's head was spinning, spinning.

The smoke was too strong and she could only cough and cry, coughing harder and harder until she began to fall toward the fire on the ground. She could hear gunshots, but her eyes were blinded. Another shot rang out, and more yelling. Something held back her wings, and the harder she flapped them, the harder they held back. She tried to call out to Hans, but her lungs were scorched and the fire seemed to be inside of them. Only the coughing kept the flames from burning out her insides.

They were binding her wings so tightly now, that she fell like a lead ball to the burnt, smoldering ground.

Everything was blackness.

* * *

Marit woke to the cold dampness of a towel wiping her brow.

"She's coming to," Lidy called to Tomas.

"Lord Jesus! Your bloody witchcraft has almost killed her."

"Marit, can you hear me?"

Marit opened her eyes slowly. She could not move her head. Lidy was bearing down on her. Her features were blurred, but she could clearly recognize her mother. She could not see Tomas, but he must be somewhere in the room.

"Marit, can you speak?" He was on the other side. One on each side.

She was lying on her bed. She was vaguely aware of blood on her dress, and on the sheets.

"The doctor is coming, Marit. He's been here once already. You ate too many of the mushrooms. You've been vomiting and spitting blood." Lidy said it without judgment. She had seen her own mother recovering too many times from the trance to judge. "Are you okay, Marit?"

"Yes," Marit said hoarsely. She closed her eyes, and her head felt better. She tried her voice again. "I saw them."

"Who?" Lidy asked.

"Babi, and Hans."

"Was it the future?" Lidy asked again.

"No, the present, or the past. It was last night."

"Witchcraft." Tomas spat out the word. "This is pagan worship, Lidy."

Lidy eyed Tomas cautiously. Lidy had never practiced the *noaide* arts. She didn't have the gift like her mother and grandfather. But she had seen it work too many times to dismiss it outright.

"What else did you see?"

"Karasjok." Her voice cracked. "It's gone."

"Gone?"

"All gone. Everything but the church. Burned to the ground by the Germans. The bridge is in pieces in the riverbed. There is nothing left." Tears were flowing from Marit's eyes, but she seemed strangely disconnected from them. It was as though her body was crying and mourning the village, but her spirit was still not quite back.

"They can't have burned everything." Tomas was shaking his head. "What about Babi?"

"I don't know. She was there. She was in front of the church. She was holding back the Germans."

"Bera? Lidy, this is nonsense. The girl's had a dream. I'm getting the doctor now." He left the room, and both Lidy and Marit breathed a sigh of relief.

"Search your heart, child. Is Babi alright?"

"Hans. He's hurt. But he's alive. He's coming. He's coming here."

"And Babi?"

"She's okay."

Marit closed her eyes. Suddenly her spirit was at one with her body, and the pain in her head and limbs and chest was acute. She wanted to cough again, but couldn't. Her chest was heavy, as though Hans and Babi and the rest of the village were sitting on her. She took as deep a breath as she could, and let her body fall back into sleep.

* * *

"You need fresh air. You need to get away from all this Sami witchcraft. Remember, child, you are half Norwegian too." Uncle Tomas was lecturing. He meant well, but he rambled. It had taken almost a week, but he had coaxed Marit and Lidy out of the house, away from the hospital, for a picnic on the fish boat. A fish boat was the last thing Marit wanted right now. She had been queasy most of the week, still reeling from her overdose of the mushrooms.

"Come up to the bridge and look out over the water." They were standing in the pilothouse of his little fishing trawler. Tomas was lucky enough to be able to continue to fish. He had a license from the government, and hadn't lost his boat to the Germans yet.

"Here," he said. "Hold the wheel. Now, keep her steady while I check on your land-loving mother."

Lidy was on the aft deck, staring out over the water. She was pale, but not ill yet.

"I thought the cruise was supposed to make us feel better."

"I thought it would. We're almost there. Here, have some tea." He handed her a steaming mug and climbed back up the few steps to where Marit steered the boat.

"Where are we going?"

"On a picnic."

"I know. But we could have walked. Why did you take us here?"

"You need the air, and there's something you should see."

"Ah-ha."

They were rounding the south end of the island, coming into the channel that ran into the fjords behind Tromsø.

"Bring the boat to starboard," Tomas called.

"Starboard?"

"Turn right, child!"

She turned slowly right and straightened again.

"More."

She turned the boat until she had rounded the tip of the island and was heading back along the far shore.

Then she saw it.

At first it was like a tree, only there were no trees that tall here. It looked like it was planted on top of the small island in the distance, but it was much too large. It was a boat. Except that it was too big to be a boat. It was a very big boat. Marit had only seen a few boats in the harbor since arriving in Tromsø. Some fish boats. Even a troop transport boat. There was also the boat they'd taken from Porsangerfjord. This boat dwarfed them all. It was a ship.

"The Tirpitz," Tomas said mysteriously.

"The Tirpitz?"

"Admiral Tirpitz. It's the largest battleship ever built. The pride of the Nazi fleet."

"What's it doing here?"

"Hiding. It was badly damaged earlier in the war. The engine is ruined. They had to tow it here. I think they are trying to sink it in the shallow waters to use its guns." He pointed to the massive double guns mounted on the bow deck, and to other large guns further aft.

"I didn't think they could bring her this far into the fjords, but they did. They have started flooding her lower decks. They want to make a battery out of her."

"A battery?"

"Guns. Boom! Boom! No plane will come near Tromsø with her permanently beached here. If they succeed in beaching her in the shallow water, she will be unsinkable."

Tomas reached over and slowed the engines.

"What are you doing?"

"We can't go closer. See the small craft around her? And the nets marked by the buoys? We have strict orders to stay out of the bay."

"So why are we here?"

"To picnic, until we're told to leave. We'll anchor off the shore here, across from the little island. It's still a fair distance. We can picnic and maybe not be enough of a nuisance to be noticed and told to go away."

"Why?"

"I come as often as I can. We need to know as much as we can before the Nazis have her so firmly on the bottom that she cannot be sunk."

"We?"

"Quiet, child. There are many things it is better you do not know."

Tomas gave her a wink and took on a mysterious look that she was slowly becoming accustomed to. He slowed the engine further still and she idled gently into a little bay opposite the huge battleship. Even from this distance, she dwarfed the island behind her, the top of her tower well above the hill behind her. She was at least 600 feet long, and 150 feet high at the tower.

Marit let the anchor out and Tomas cut the engine. They were alone in the silence of the bay.

Over the water, the sounds travelled well. They could make out instructions being yelled out in German. Not every word, but the tone, and a few words. There were men on the deck of the Tirpitz, cleaning the decks, painting the railings. In the water they could make out the soft chugging of little engines of the small craft that patrolled the bay, when they turned their sterns to Tomas' fish boat. Otherwise, the loudest sounds were the birds that scavenged the beach a few hundred feet away.

Lidy took out the lunch and set it up on the aft deck, using the footlocker that held Tomas' tools as the table. Around it Tomas set out three folding chairs. It was cool in the November air, but the sun was out. It was almost noon, and the light was good for this time of year.

Marit was the first to hear them. It was like a distant buzzing sound. Not the buzzing of bees, which Marit knew well. A different buzzing. A droning that grew louder, and louder. It came from the hills to the south. It was high in the sky. Marit peered upwards, and saw five flecks against the bright morning light. Five small flecks, growing with every passing second as the buzzing grew louder. The flecks were spots already, and still growing. They were in a line, a broad line. Far behind them, five more flecks appeared, and still the noise grew louder.

A new noise rang out across the bay. A siren, and yelling. A lot of yelling. Ironically, now that so many were yelling, it was much harder to hear what anyone said. The occasional voice that had floated across the still bay was replaced by the wailing siren and indiscriminate shouts and the little ants on the Tirpitz' deck scurried about in a frenzy.

"Oh! Lord!" Lidy cried.

"Lancaster bombers. Quite a few by the looks of it," Tomas said coldly.

"Are we safe?" Marit asked.

"As safe as we can be. They're not looking to bomb us. We're at least a half mile away. I'd like to think the English have better aim than that. Anyhow, there is nowhere to go. Just wait, and trust we will be okay."

"Will they sink her?"

"They certainly mean to."

Tomas looked to the sky. There was now a long line of bombers on the horizon. They were coming in waves of five. Marit counted at least four waves, and they were still coming.

The batteries on the far side of the island came alive. They shot high into the air, and explosions went off around the planes as they shot up flak to try to bring down the bombers. The first wave passed over and each plane dropped a single, massive bomb. The water around the Tirpitz exploded on a series of geysers as the bombs hit the water and sent columns of water fifty feet into the air.

"They missed!" Marit shouted. The noise from the planes was deafening, and the huge bombs were now falling in rapid sequence, raising water columns and shaking the earth where they struck the island.

The second wave was already there, and still they could see more waves coming behind. It looked like six waves in all, and a few planes behind the last wave—32 planes.

Maybe more.

Suddenly the air was filled with the shrieks of men.

There was smoke in the air above the ship. A first bomb had hit its mark. Yelling replaced the shrieks. A second bomb hit, and a third, in close succession, all near the port bow of the great ship.

"She's taking on water."

"How can you tell?"

"I can hear it."

Marit listened closely. There was a slow groaning noise.

"The metal is twisting. The bulkheads are breaking. She's going to sink, and sink fast."

More bombs were still falling, but most seemed to land in the water between the Tirpitz and the fish boat. The water columns made for a beautiful show, but in the background, the cries of men grew louder. It was harder to see the ship now, her bow totally shrouded in smoke. The bridge still towered over the scene. It was difficult to believe that the stoic tower that rose above the decks was part of the same whole with the havoc below.

Then it happened.

The groaning grew louder and something seemed to snap. The tower lurched towards them and the entire hull turned turtle.

"God save them," Tomas muttered under his breath.

The drone of the planes had faded. The roaring fire from the ship was extinguished. A giant wave rushed towards them, and past them.

Marit could make out little heads in the water. The screams of individual sailors floated across the bay. German screams. Painful screams.

"They'll freeze to death," Marit said. "We have to help them."

"They'll swim to shore. We have to get out of here. Lift the anchor."

Marit ran forward to turn the anchor winch. Tomas had already started the engine and pulled forward slowly to release the tension on the anchor chain. The engine of the small fish boat seemed to roar in the sudden calm of the bay, and it served to mask the shouts of the hundreds of sailors.

Marit closed her eyes, but she could not close her ears. Even when the boat had rounded the island and was in the channel on the way back to Tromsø, she could hear them. She was too far away, and the only noises were the beckoning seagulls, but she heard them nonetheless. Indistinct cries from across the water.

Painful, plaintive cries.

CHAPTER 24

Tromsø, December 1944

SUNDAY MORNING, MARIT WOKE WITH A START.

"He's here."

"What?" Lidy asked from her bed across the room.

"He's here. Hans."

"What do you mean?"

"I know it."

"The army is still retreating. It may be weeks before they all get to Tromsø."

"I saw him last night. In a dream. He's hurt. I have to go see him." She was sitting up already, pulling on her clothes.

"See him where?"

"In the hospital, of course."

"It's Sunday. You don't work. We're going to church."

"I'm going to the hospital. Now." She stood up quickly and sat down again just as fast. She was holding her stomach.

"What's wrong, Marit?"

"Nothing."

"What's wrong?"

"I'm a little dizzy, that's all. I got up too quickly." She started to get up more slowly, and ran suddenly to the washbasin. She plunged her head into it as she began to vomit.

"Good Lord! Have you had more of the mushrooms? Is this how you know about Hans?!"

Marit didn't answer. Lidy came over and put a washcloth into the jug of water. She ran it over Marit's neck.

"Sit down, Marit. Did you take more of Babi's powder?"

"No. Of course not. I'm just feeling a little sick."

Lidy sat down next to Marit. "Hans will come to Tromsø soon enough. When he does, he will come find us here. He can look at the registry to see where we went."

"He's here. I'll see him today."

Lidy's tone switched from empathy to reproach. "You are stubborn. It won't bring him back you know. Even if he is here. He's an officer in the Wehrmacht. He'll be shipped to Germany. Will you follow him there?"

"If I have to."

"Damn it, child. Your life is here, and in Karasjok when this war is over. I need you. Babi needs you."

"I love him."

"You don't know what love is."

Marit rose silently and wiped her face with another damp cloth. She put on her shoes, and lifted the dirty basin to take it downstairs.

"You're sick. You shouldn't be up. Where are going?" Lidy asked.

"To the hospital."

It was much colder than the previous days. The light dusting of snow had blown away, but the wind was bitter and the temperature had dropped well below freezing. Marit could not help thinking of the soldiers on the road towards Tromsø, and the evacuees who were still coming into the town every day. She thought also of those left behind, in the woods, in caves. In this cold, the ground would soon be frozen solid. If they had not finished digging the foundations for their huts, they would not have a warm winter. *How many would die because they chose to stay behind? How many had forgotten too much of the old ways to be safe through the long, dark night?*

From the hill at the front of the hospital, Marit could see a large ship at dock. There were German soldiers all around the ship. It had a large red cross painted on the smoke stack. Hans had come in this ship. She was sure of it. He came last night. He was somewhere in the hospital.

At the front desk, she saw Marin, one of the nicer clerks.

"Good morning, Marit. Are you working today?"

"No Marin. I'm looking for a friend. Have they registered the men that came in last night?"

"Off the ship? No. Not yet. They're all Germans anyhow. Evacuees from the east."

"From Porsanger?"

"Maybe. The east anyway. Some of the badly wounded, and some officers being shipped home to Germany. You have German friends?"

"Yes."

Marin eyed Marit suspiciously. "They're on level three. Most of them anyhow. Those that were really in bad shape are in the ICU." She must have noticed Marit's puzzled expression. She added: "Intensive Care Unit."

Marit walked down the long hall to the stairs and made her way up to level three. The ward had been mostly empty the day before. She should have known they were expecting people. They never announced when the soldiers were coming, but the hospital always knew.

She walked down the main aisle of the ward, looking up and down at the beds. She found him about halfway down on the right, sitting on his bed, staring into space.

"Hans?"

He seemed changed. He looked older. Sad.

"Hans?"

"Hhhmm? Marit!" His eyes brightened for a moment, but he turned away when she stepped nearer to hold him.

"Hans? What's wrong?"

He struggled to find his words. He clearly wanted to speak, but he said nothing. His hands rested on his crutches, and he looked up at Marit, and down again. Marit sat down on the bed opposite his.

Marit reached forward and placed her hands on top of his. She wanted to ask him again; she was asking again, even if no words passed between them. She waited. Surely he would speak.

"Marit, I'm so happy to see you."

"I knew you were here. I dreamed it last night. I could see you getting off the boat."

"You dream many things." He was so sad. She wanted to reach inside of him and rip out his sadness. Or fill him so full of happiness that he could not possibly be sad anymore. Her own heart beat strongly. She was content just to be here with him, to have her hands touching his.

"Hans, I know about the village."

He looked at her, perplexed.

"How can you know? How could you imagine?" His voice trailed off ... "I'm so sorry, Marit. So ..."

It was the tone of his confession in his bed that night, *Ich liebe Dich*. Instead of joy and marvel at the moment, it was the heavy voice of regret, almost before it was spoken. The same tone. *Es tut mir leid. Es tut mir so leid.*

"Hans, it doesn't matter what happened. You're here. And you're safe. Everything will be better."

"I want to tell you, Marit. I have to."

"Alright."

"I was the senior officer from the detachment at Karasjok. Most of the others you knew had already shipped out. It began just after you left with the evacuees by truck for Skoganvarre." Hans paused briefly, organizing his thoughts.

"They began streaming into the village from the Border Road. Thousands and thousands of them. You never saw so many soldiers, ragged, and exhausted. They were hungry, and defeated. Their eyes were hollow and their hearts sullen."

Marit looked at Hans as he spoke, and realized he might be describing himself.

"For almost five days they came, walking day and night. When one group rested, another was on the road, creating the illusion of a constant stream of lost souls. It was warm, and the officers wanted them out of Finland and out of the Finnmark before the cold came."

"On the morning of November 6th, another group came into the village. This group was of another type. They rode in cars and tanks. They were battle-hardened SS—some Norwegians from the Skandinavia Korps, but mostly Germans. Their eyes were hollow too, but not from defeat. Their eyes showed only the hunger of destruction. They opened unto a void that could never be filled, no matter how much wanton pain they caused. They ran across the countryside like one of the waves from Revelations, a fiery wave of destruction that left nothing alive in its wake. They burned the farm that first morning, and every other building between the border and the village, and those past the village along the south bank of the Karasjokka."

"Later that evening, the order came to burn the village. Everything. And blow up the bridge. The last of the evacuees had crossed the Karasjokka. It was over."

Hans' voice cracked a little, and he stared at the ground as he talked. She wanted to look into his eyes, and tell him she forgave him, but he could not look up.

"I headed a troop along the western side, moving house by house along the river. We doused each home with petrol first, then lit it with the flame throwers. The entire night sky was ablaze in a hellish light. It was as bright as day, but felt oppressively dark. Many of the men took pleasure in the burning. They ran from house to house, screaming and laughing, drunk with the excitement of destruction. At times, along the edge of the village, I thought I could see the eyes of those who stayed behind, watching us from behind a tree or a little ridge, angry and helpless."

"We converged at last on the church. It was one of the last buildings to burn before the river crossing. We agreed it would be easiest to burn the church from the inside with the flame throwers. We were running out of petrol, and needed more for the cars to leave again. I walked forward, a little sick at the thought of burning even the church ..." Hans cried as he spoke now, and it was harder and harder for Marit to make out the words. She was floating back to the village again in her dream. She was the Raven. She could see him coming up to the church. She was here, and there also. One, but apart, in separate places, different times.

"When we got to the church door, it was already wide open. Babi stood there in the doorframe, leaning with one arm on a walking stick, her other arm raised in defiance. She didn't say anything. She just stood there, her gaze locked on me."

"I told her we had come to burn the church. I heard her voice in my head. 'You won't burn the church, Hans.' That was all she said. 'You won't burn the church.' For a moment I thought she was right. Why did it need to burn too? Why could we not just leave, and never return? I wanted to listen. I wanted to obey. Then he appeared."

"Donkey ..." said Marit. She could see him now, through the smoke. She could make out his ugly features, and his balding head. His big ears. He was the officer Hans had sparred with. It amazed her that she had not seen him before, in the dream. Her own mind somehow had blocked him out. There he was now, even before Hans had spoken his name.

"Yes, Donkey. He came with the SS men that had been at the Front. Because he knew Karasjok, they had him leading a group of troops on the other side of the village. He took out his gun. His men were behind him, eager to burn the church. He called Babi a witch, and he raised his gun to shoot her." Hans' hand went down to his leg and held it a moment. Marit let her hand follow his, and rested it on the injured leg.

"I grabbed his arm, and he shot my leg, and then my knee. I hit him in the face with my elbow. I think he would have shot me in the chest, but another shot rang out from behind. Old Man Jacobsen was there, with a rifle. He came out of nowhere. He shot Donkey in the neck, just under the helmet. He fell forward into my arms, limp and lifeless."

"The other troops were so shocked, they turned away from me. They ... they burned Old Man Jacobsen. Like a torch. They could not miss him. They were hardly twelve feet away. He didn't scream. I can still see his face through the flames, staring out at me, as though he didn't know he was on fire. Babi watched the whole thing without moving. The fire in the village was now so hot, I thought for sure the church would burn without us lighting it. It was hard to breathe, and soon, we would not get across the bridge to safety. The path to the bridge was in danger of being cut off. I told the troops to retreat across the river. Somehow, they listened. I turned to get Babi out of the church, but she was gone and the door was closed. I ran down to where Old Man Jacobsen had been, and there was only scorched earth. Just ground. No charred body. No bones."

"Somehow I limped down the road to the bridge and made it across before the order was given to blow it up. We climbed into the trucks and drove towards Skoganvarre, the night as bright as day as the village and camp burned around us."

"I waited days for one of the men to challenge me about Donkey. He had his own set of enemies, I guess. No one has said anything since then. Officially, Donkey was lost during the burning."

Marit stared at Hans, her Hans, who had burned her childhood home and that of every person she had ever known or loved. She tried to hate him, but felt only compassion. It was his unbearable pain and sadness that made Marit turn away.

"Forgive me," he said. "And ask Babi to forgive me."

"You saved Babi, and the church. You don't need forgiveness. You did what you could."

"So much evil, so much death and destruction...for what? For whom?"

"It is meant to be. He has a reason."

"What reason can He possibly have, that he lets the Good suffer and rewards evil?"

Marit held his hands tightly. She squeezed them. She kissed his forehead, but he had finished speaking, and she felt him slipping away. He retreated back into the shell he had been in since that night in Karasjok.

"Rest, Hans. Rest."

She lay him down in the bed, and unfolded a cover to put over him. She sat down next to him, listening to the bells that began to ring out from the church on Storgata, a few blocks below. She could feel the bell swinging, back and forth. Back and forth. Hans lay motionless, looking upwards. Tears formed in the corners of his eyes, but he said nothing. Marit took his hand, his large, strong hand, and put it in her lap.

Chapter 25

Tromsø, Christmas 1944

"WALK SLOWLY," MARIT SCOLDED HIM.

"I'm trying to. You keep walking quickly." Hans was using his crutches while Marit tried to steady him on the icy hill.

"Don't fall."

"I won't. Are you sure it's okay with your uncle, that I come for Christmas?"

"He suggested it."

"Really?"

"Well, no. But he said it would be alright."

"Anyhow, he won't be there."

"He won't?"

"It's a surprise. You'll see."

They were already in the Sjøgata.

"It's pretty down here," Hans said. "I like Tromsø."

"It's big," Marit said.

"It's small. You should see Munich."

"You told me you lived in a village like Karasjok."

"I do. But Munich is nearby. I'd like to show you Traundorf. It's very much like Karasjok, and very different too." Hans was quiet again.

"What's wrong?"

"Like Karasjok was, I wanted to say."

"You promised to be happier for Christmas."

"I did."

"So keep your promise!"

"So many promises," Hans said.

They came to the house, which Lidy had decorated with several candle lanterns and wreaths of pine boughs with pine cones.

"Come on," Marit said. "Let's get inside."

Margret opened the door for them and eyed Hans suspiciously.

"He's a troll, Margret. He'll eat you!" Marit told Margret, making her eyes bulge out from her face and puffing up her cheeks.

"Marit Enoksen, God scold you for your arrogance!" Margret mumbled to herself, as she retreated to the living room. Hans and Marit took off their coats and followed her into the room.

Lidy was cutting paper. There were several long chains of the colored paper glued together on the table in front of her, and little baskets in green and red and yellow, filled with nuts. In the middle of the room was a tree that almost touched the ceiling. It was decorated with streamers of white-and-gold paper and long, white candles.

"You're just in time. Quickly, help me put the baskets and chains in the tree. Hello, Hans."

"Hello, Lidy. Nice to see you too. What's the rush?" Hans asked as he took a streamer and wrapped it around the nearest part of the tree.

"The *julenisse* is coming!" Marit said.

"*Julenisse*?"

"The Christmas gnome. He brings the gifts, and sticks and coal for bad kids."

"I know what I'm getting," Hans muttered.

Marit jabbed him in the ribs and he dropped his hands to defend himself, almost falling over without his crutches. "Yes, I know. My promise."

There was a loud knock at the door. Three knocks.

"Here he is," Marit said, running out to open the door.

"I can't believe your mother put me up to this," Tomas said from the doorstep. He was in a red outfit, with a bright red cap. He carried a large burlap sack over his shoulder and looked very grumpy.

"Shhh. You're the *julenisse*."

"We're both too old for this."

"The *julenisse* is very old," she said, kissing his cheek. "Come in, *julenisse*, come in. What have you brought us? No tricks, I hope …"

"No tricks. Just gifts." He stepped into the living room and came face to face with Hans. "Merry Christmas," he said in his gruff *julenisse* voice.

"Merry Christmas. Thank you for letting me come."

"So what have I got in this bag?" He reached in and pulled out a series of packages. He looked them over and gave one each to Marit, Lidy and Margret. He set a fourth package down on an empty chair.

"That's for Uncle Tomas. I'm sorry, Hans. I haven't one here for you."

"Yes, you do," Marit said, poking his oversized belly.

He reached in again and pulled out a small package.

"I guess I do."

He reached over to the table and took two of the small chocolate balls that sat on a plate. There was a large glass of rum next to the plate, and he drank it down all at once.

"You treat the *julenisse* well. Merry Christmas to all, and a happy New Year." He grabbed his sack, slung it over his shoulder and disappeared outside.

They took their gifts and sat down to open them up. Marit found a beautiful sweater. Lidy had a woolen scarf. Margret had a bottle of scotch whiskey, probably worth a fortune. Hans' gift sat unopened on his lap.

"I didn't bring you anything. I'm sorry."

"You brought us you! Now open your gift." Marit watched in anticipation. Hans was removing the paper a layer at a time. She held her breath as he came to the last layer.

It was a large leather belt, with a giant silver buckle. It was ornately etched with little drawings of reindeer and runes. It looked a little like Babi's runic drum.

"I've never seen any belt so nicely made." He was smiling. His hand ran softly over the surface of the runes.

Lidy glared at Marit, stood up, and left the room. Tomas came in as she left.

"What was that about?" he asked.

"Hans' gift," Marit said. "She's upset. It belonged to her father, Babi's husband. Babi gave it to me many years ago." Marit could feel Babi sitting next to her, humming. *For your husband, when the day comes*, she had said. *When the day comes.*

Marit went over and gave her uncle a big hug. "Thank you for these beautiful gifts."

"Ah, not me. The *julenisse.*" He opened his own package and found a bottle of rum that he set on the table next to his glass. "Come, I can smell dinner."

Lidy had recovered her composure and was setting the meal on the dining room table. There was a large plate of *pinnekjott*, a sort of smoked, salted, dried lamb. There was a bowl of mashed rutabaga, and generous helpings of rice pudding.

Uncle Tomas poured each of them a large glass of red wine and sat down at the head of the table.

"Lord, we pray for those who are less fortunate, for those who have lost everything, and for those who are alone tonight. God bless this holy meal, and those that gather together to share it in humble adoration of His holy name!"

"Amen," they said in unison.

Chapter 26

Tromsø, January 1945

"YOU LOOK TERRIBLE," TOMAS SAID, passing the herring and bread across the table.

"Thank you," Marit answered.

"I mean it. Lidy, she looks terrible. She should be back in bed. You're pale. Margret says you've been sick again."

"It's not the mushrooms. I promise."

"Well that's good. Enough witchcraft in my house. If they find out you have one of those drums ..."

"You promised not to talk about it anymore, Uncle Tomas."

"Alright. But I think you should stay home." He took a long sip of his coffee. He seemed to be choosing his words.

"Not today, uncle. I have to go today."

"Did he talk to you yesterday?" Lidy asked.

"Not a word."

"Well, maybe you should stop visiting him?" Tomas suggested.

"Maybe," Marit said.

"The war will be over by spring, Marit. And he'll be gone before that. Tell her, Lidy. They're shipping officers back to Germany, and the healthy soldiers too."

"Marit knows, Tomas."

"Then why does she keep seeing him?"

"I'm going with him. Back to Germany."

"You'll do no such thing." Tomas slammed his cup on the table so that the coffee spilled over. He stood up and turned to her in anger.

"You can go to the hospital today, but if you get any sicker, you'll be staying right here." He didn't wait for an answer. He turned again and left the room.

"You've spoiled your uncle's Sunday, the one day he isn't up before dawn on the fish boat."

Marit rose to leave.

"Where are you going? Can't you see he's right?"

She found her long, woolen coat in the hallway and let herself out the front door.

Hans was doing better. Much better. He didn't say much these last days, but he'd started hobbling around the hospital on his crutches again. He'd been down into town three times since the Christmas trip. If he still slept at the hospital, it was because there wasn't another bed in Tromsø. He'd be released soon and sent back to Germany. They had to make their plans. She walked briskly along the path up the hill to the hospital. They had a week, maybe two, before Hans was shipped back. He didn't know where to yet, but probably not to his own division, which was still in Norway. He would be reassigned, somewhere far from the front because of his leg.

Maybe back to Bavaria.

She could go there and live with his parents until he came home. The irony amused her. She could see herself sitting in the kitchen, telling stories of Karasjok, and Hans meeting a bear. His father would dance with her, just as Hans had, and catch her if she started to fall. He would teach her to know music, like he had taught Hans and like her own father might have taught her, if he had not died.

"Good morning, Marin!" Marit called out to the nurse at the front desk.

"He's up and about. And he's looking for you!" she answered.

"Really?"

"Yes. He came down a half hour ago. I said you weren't working today, but that you'd be by after breakfast, as usual. He went back up to pack, I think."

Marit raced down the hall and up the three flights of stairs. Hans faced the bed, his back to the room. He was stuffing a few clothes into his green duffle bag.

"Running off?" she asked from behind as she got to his bed.

"Not doing much running for a while, I think," he said without turning around.

"I thought they said you had another week with us?"

"Army thinks differently. The leg is not that bad. I can walk with the crutches. There's a ship sailing tomorrow. It sails for Kiel. I'm to be on that ship."

"Can't you delay?"

"No."

"What about after Kiel? Where will you go?"

"Black Forest, I think. Near Bavaria."

"Hans, I want to come with you."

He stared at her blankly.

"Hans? Talk to me, Hans!"

"I'm sorry, Marit. I'm not going home. I'm reassigned to a fighting unit."

"A fighting unit? You can't fight. You can hardly walk!"

"I can still fight better than many that are drafted. You can't come where I'm going. You need to be here, with Lidy, and then in Karasjok, when this is over."

"Karasjok? What is left for me in Karasjok?"

"I'm sorry, Marit, I didn't want to burn it."

"But you'd have me go back to rebuild it? Alone?"

"You have Lidy and Babi. Germany needs me."

"I need you. What has happened to you?"

"I've wanted to say this for a long time."

"Then why didn't you, instead of letting me fill in all the missing words? Do you think it's easy? Talking alone for weeks and weeks while you feel sorry for yourself?"

"I can't go with you to Karasjok. They'll shoot me as a deserter, and they'll shoot me for burning the Finnmark after the war is over. And you cannot come to Germany."

"Why not?"

"Lidy and Babi need you."

"That's for me to decide."

"Everything's bombed there. There's no food. It's war, Marit. You don't know what it is like. It isn't Tromsø. People are sleeping in tents and bombed-out houses. There's nothing to eat. You don't know war. You live in a fairy tale."

"You live with me in one. I don't want to be without you. Not again."

"You cannot come."

"I can and I will."

"I don't want you to."

Marit looked at him, startled.

"I mean, I want better for you. You can't come to Germany."

Marit turned and stormed down the passageway between the beds.

"Marit! Marit!"

She could hear him behind her, hobbling on his crutches. She blocked the sound from her ears. *I don't want you to. I don't want you to.*

She ran out the front door of the hospital and into the cold, her coat open and the wind rushing against her face and neck. She chased his words from her thoughts until she heard only her heart beat. But behind the beating she heard the shrieks from the sailors in the water. In the dirt roads of Tromsø she saw the hands and feet of the prisoners coming out of Arnfrid's pit, and from the houses to either side of the street she smelled the flames that engulfed Karasjok and the world she had once cherished as home.

*   *   *

Hans stood at the door of the small house on the Sjøgata. Marit saw him from the window in the bedroom upstairs. He looked tall even from above. She kept a little back from the window, to be sure he did not see her.

"Hello, Lidy," he said.

"Hello, Hans. I'm glad you're feeling better."

"I've come to see Marit."

Marit strained her ears to hear his words. They drifted out into the street and were almost lost amongst the other sounds. Lidy's voice was soft, and it was hard to hear her too.

"I'm sorry, Hans. Marit is out."

"When will she be back?"

"I'm not sure, Hans. Maybe it would be better if she came to see you."

"I know she's here, Lidy," Hans began. Lidy said nothing. "I saw her at the hospital, not half an hour ago. She ran off, upset. Am I unwelcome here, Lidy?"

"No, Hans. Of course not. It's just the neighbors. You know. Marit can't have German callers. And the burnings. It isn't easy for us either. I'm sure you understand."

"I do."

"I'll tell Marit you came."

"Why won't she come out?"

"Leave her alone, Hans. It's better for everybody."

"I will. I'm leaving, Lidy. My ship sails in the morning. I came to say goodbye."

"Marit told me. Well, goodbye then."

"I'm sorry, Lidy. I'm sorry the war had to come to Karasjok."

"You brought the war. We didn't ask for it. Go away."

Lidy shut the door. Hans peered through the glass, apparently oblivious to Marit as she looked down from above. He raised his hand to knock at the glass, thought better of it and left.

Marit felt her strength waning. Her legs felt heavy. She wanted to go back to bed, but she could only lean against the wall. She was going to be sick again. She wanted to call to him. She wanted to go to him. She was dizzy just from standing at the window. Lidy's footsteps rang out in the staircase.

"Get away from the window, child." It was Lidy, in the hallway. Her footsteps were rushed.

"I'm not at the window," she lied.

Lidy came into the room. "Get back into bed."

"I want to see him."

"He doesn't want to see you."

"Why did he come then?"

"He came to say goodbye. He's leaving Tromsø for good, just like I said he would."

"He won't leave. He can't. Not without me."

"You're not going anywhere." Lidy guided Marit back into bed and tucked the covers down around her.

"You didn't tell him, did you?"

"That you're sick, no."

"Good."

"I've sent for the doctor."

"No. I'll be fine."

"You're not fine. Your body is on fire. You're vomiting. You're pale. The doctor is coming by this afternoon. He should be here soon."

"I don't need a doctor."

"But …"

"I'm pregnant, Lidy."

"What?"

"You knew. That last night at the farm. You knew of course. Babi knew. You both knew."

"Are you sure?"

"I haven't had the bleeding since last October. I'm pregnant."

"Why didn't you say anything?"

"What would you have me say?"

"So this is why you've been so sick. I can't believe you didn't tell us. We've been so worried about you. You only care about yourself, and about your silly love story."

"I couldn't tell you."

"Yes, you could have, if you weren't so selfish. Hans doesn't know either. You were afraid he would see. That's why you don't want to see him. You thought he might guess."

"I saw Hans at the hospital. I didn't want to see him again because I could not stand to see him as he is now, a shadow of his former self."

"What shadow? He's better. He's sorry, and sad. But he is much better. He looks very much like when he arrived. A little less love-struck, maybe."

"Do you *want* me to see him?"

"No."

The doorbell rang downstairs.

He's back, Marit thought.

Her heart raced. She sat down on the bed, trying to think of what to say. This was her chance to be sure he would take her to Germany. He came back to apologize. Marit sat down on the bed, trying to compose her thoughts.

"It's the doctor, Mrs. Enoksen," the maid said, poking her head into the room. "Shall I let him upstairs?"

"I don't need a doctor," Marit said.

Lidy nodded to Margret. "I want you to see him, especially if you are pregnant. And you aren't in any position to refuse me."

Marit's heart sank. She wondered if indeed she should see the doctor, and before she could make up her mind, he was standing in the doorway. He stepped in and bowed slightly to Lidy and Marit.

"Doctor."

"Madam. Madam. I'm told you are feeling ill. Dizzy. Feverish."

He stepped closer and sat down on the bed next to Marit, putting his hand to her forehead.

"I'm pregnant," Marit said.

"I see. Well, that would account for some of your symptoms. Not the fever," he said, taking his hand off of her forehead. "You're very pale. How do you feel?"

"Partly dead."

"Mostly alive still?" The doctor smiled at her and took her wrist.

"Partly alive," Marit said, smiling back.

He listened to her heartbeat and took her pulse. "You'll be alright. Get some rest and I'll check on you again in a few days." He stood up and walked toward the door. "May I see you, madam?" he said to Lidy.

Marit strained her ears to hear them in the hallway. They spoke in very low voices. In a few moments, Lidy was back.

"So?" Marit asked.

"So you've got a high fever. Maybe some sort of flu. The doctor said it's going around. And you're definitely pregnant."

"Did he hear the heart beat?"

"No. It's too early. But the sickness. The dizziness. The feebleness. This is not just the flu."

"So he doesn't know if the baby is alright?"

"It's too early to tell."

"That's not what he was whispering to you."

"He wanted to know if the father is German."

"Did you tell him?"

"Yes."

"And?"

"He says you need to rest. It can be dangerous for you and the baby, this flu."

"And?"

"He wanted to know if you wanted to keep the baby."

Marit jumped up from the bed and threw herself toward her mother, her arms flailing.

"Get out! Get out!" she yelled, as her mother grabbed each of her arms.

"I only asked him what was possible."

"Get out!" Marit said, retreating to the bed in tears. "Get out!"

*   *   *

A bell rang in her sleep. She opened an eye and heard it again. She had been in bed a long time. The sun had set, so it was impossible to know if it was early afternoon or already evening. The doorbell rang again. Why did no one answer?

Marit put on her housecoat and went down to the door. Perhaps Margret had gone out and forgotten her keys. The house was in any event empty. The bell rang again.

Marit turned the lock and opened the door wide. Hans stood in the doorway, his eyes red, his hand shaking.

"Hans?"

He stepped forward and held her tightly in his arms. She felt her body swoon, and her legs give way a little. He smelled of whiskey.

"Marit … I'm so sorry for this morning."

"Shhhhh …" She put her finger to his lips. His eyes glanced back and forth, suddenly aware perhaps that he was holding her in the open doorway.

Marit took a step backward and brought him into the house. She closed the door and he stood in the hallway, looking at her, his mouth half open.

Her fever was gone. She had dreamed again and again of all the things she would tell him, but her anger left with the fever, and she was speechless. Hans' touch made her heart race and brought color back to her face. She could feel the blood rushing. Without a word, she took his hand and turned, pulling him slowly down the darkened hall to the staircase, leading him slowly up the stairs.

When they got to her room, she paused a moment, not to hesitate, but to listen one last time for the others. The only noises came from the distant street, or further away, in the port.

She pulled him into the empty room and shut the door behind him. His coat still had a dusting of snow and she brushed it aside before pulling it off his shoulders. It fell in a heap on the ground, a half moon keeping him close to her, keeping him from stepping away.

The lamps from the street cast long shadows in the room, and with her fingers she could make out a large grin on Hans' face. His arms came alive now, and he untied the strap on her housecoat. Marit took his crutches and leaned them against the door behind him.

He hobbled with her over to the bed, and lay down first. She could see he was shaking, either from excitement or nervousness.

She wondered if it was alright, to be close with the baby inside, but trusted her body, which wanted only to be close to him again. She lifted her nightgown over her head and stood naked before him in the halflight. She could see the shadowy patterns that the flickering lamps made across her chest and belly, and she laughed. He reached up, naked too now, and pulled her down on top of him in a passionate embrace that sent shivers up and down her legs and back until she shook as he did.

As he came closer, though, something inside of her tightened, and she could feel part of herself running away. Her thoughts drifted from Hans to the child within her, barely formed, tiny and vulnerable. Hans' touch suddenly felt rougher, his grip on her buttocks too tight, his rhythmic groaning not one with her. Not with her at all. He was just barely inside of her, and as he pushed further, he seemed to push her further away, until she wanted only for him to stop. And he did, collapsing exhausted.

Perhaps he sensed her distance, though she tried to hide it by stroking his chest. He seemed asleep, but his breathing was too shallow. She looked around the room for some sign of the fox again, but the house in Tromsø was very different. She saw only her mother's bed across the room, some of Lidy's clothes stacked on a dresser. Her hand stroked Hans again, wanting to pull him in closer, but he was already so very far away.

*   *   *

Sometime later, they must have fallen asleep. She lay beneath the covers, wrapped in his arms, his chest heaving slowly beneath her. It was the sound of the front door closing loudly that brought her from her sleep. It wasn't Tomas. He would have called out. It was probably Lidy, back from errands or the hospital.

She snuck quietly out of the bed and found some clothes in a drawer. She dressed and quickly tossed her nightgown and housecoat under the bed. She put Hans' clothes over the back of the chair and crept out of the room, careful not to wake him. In the hallway she could hear Lidy coming up the stairs.

"Are you up, my dear?" she asked.

"Yes," Marit answered in whisper.

"Why is everything so quiet?"

"Hans came back. I let him sleep here. He's exhausted, and he leaves tomorrow."

"You let him sleep …"

"Shhhhh … you'll wake him," Marit said, ignoring her mother's accusing tone.

Lidy was carrying a lamp and some matches to light the others.

"You're looking much better," she said. "Your color is back." She hesitated a moment, and then added: "you've been sitting with him."

"Yes."

"In the dark."

"I watched him sleep."

Marit took the matches from her mother.

"I'll light the lamps. Perhaps you should start dinner. Margret has been out all afternoon."

"So you've been alone?"

Marit pretended not to notice.

"Hans is staying for dinner, mother, and for the night. I can sleep in the living room on the sofa."

"Or in your bed again, if it makes you feel better. But he's leaving tomorrow. And he's leaving for good."

Lidy turned back down the stairs in a triumphant gesture that ran through her gait and posture. Although she longed to call out that Lidy was wrong, Marit said nothing.

* * *

Hans was still asleep when Lidy called Marit to dinner. Margret served warm cod and some pickled vegetables. Uncle Tomas was out with some of his sailor friends and wasn't expected back until late.

They ate in silence, unable to share their very different thoughts, or so Marit imagined. She knew that Lidy knew she had shared Hans' bed again. Her mother played a waiting game, and seemed likely to win, which enraged Marit all the more. Margret said nothing of her afternoon activities, and Marit was thankful for it, as it allowed her to avoid lying again about what she had been doing.

The silence ran through the entire house, so that when Hans walked ever so softly down the steps from the bedroom, it was impossible not to hear the boards creak.

Marit jumped up from the table and ran to the staircase. He was dressed in his overcoat, his crutches under his left arm as he grasped the banister in his right hand.

"Just like that?" Marit asked.

"I have to check into the boarding house."

"You can stay here."

"They are waiting for me there."

"You weren't as cold when I let you in from the snow this afternoon."

"Marit," he started, as though he had a great litany inside to get out.

"Yes?" she cut him off. "What, Hans? Did you get what you came for? And now you are leaving again?"

"No."

"You aren't leaving?"

"I'm sorry, Marit. You know I love you," he added in a soft voice, so that only she could hear it.

"Then take me with you." Her voice was more pleading than she meant it to be. It came out faster than she wanted, a plaintive cry marked by frustration or even despair.

He started walking down the stairs again, working his way past her and to the front door. She stood waiting for him to turn around, to say he would stay. She stood immobile while he opened the door and let himself out into the night. By the time she recovered enough to go to the door, he was gone, lost somewhere in the patchwork of light and shadow the oil lamps created along the Sjøgata.

* * *

Marit stood along the wind-swept pier, her body tired from the long wait. She stood back from the barbed wire fence, with a clear view to the ship at dock. *How long had she stood here, waiting for a glimpse of him? Two hours? Three?*

The guard at the gate into the port was not letting anyone that was not military personnel into the compound. She tried to leave Hans a message, but the guard said he had already gone inside. He was at the officer's mess. A few hundred feet away. Already outside of her grasp.

Several of the wounded officers were boarding the ship. Judging from the increased activity around the boat, it would sail soon. Stevedores were moving the last cargo onto the ship by crane. People were making their way up the gangway, and waving to comrades still on the dock.

There was a light at the corner of the fence, and Marit stood almost directly under it.

One of the soldiers was hobbling up the gangway on crutches.

It was him.

It had to be him.

The duffle bag was slung around his midrift. He looked left and right as he worked his way up the steep walkway.

He must see me.

She waved, but he didn't wave back.

She waved again.

The soldier was on the deck, and someone was helping him with his bag.

They were lifting the gangway.

"Hans! Hans!" she waved again, as the ship's whistle blew. "Hans!"

Why didn't he wave back? Couldn't he hear her?

It was hard to see the deck. The boat was just beyond the lights, and higher up. The shadows played tricks on the eyes.

The man with the crutches was leaning against the rail. As the ship slipped away from the dock, it came towards her. She saw him more clearly. It wasn't Hans at all. He stood like Hans. Tall, erect. He was smoking a cigarette, and his hair was light brown.

"Hans!" she screamed in desperation. She sank to her knees. He wasn't on the deck. Maybe he was already in his berth. The ship's whistle sounded again, and its smokestack spit loudly.

Marit kneeled on the edge of the pier and watched as the ship slowly put out into the channel. Her body wavered. Her head spun. The water was coal black. The light from the lamppost shone down and closed the surface to her eyes. Hans was there. In the water, his face was shining back, his features broken by the wake left as the ship passed. She wanted to plunge in after him. She wanted to wrap herself in the icy mantle of the fjord's waters and be swallowed whole.

Somehow, she pulled herself away from the side of the pier.

The sea was calm again, and Marit heard the ship's large engines pounding the pistons up and down as she picked up steam and headed out of the small harbor. She was already several hundred feet away, and gaining speed. As the ship moved further into the distance, Marit's legs collapsed beneath her. She lay crumpled on the ground, cold and exhausted.

A minute later, the boat was gone, along with Hans and several hundred other young German men, returning to a homeland they still hoped to defend, leaving behind a land they had once came to as conquerors. There were few others on the pier. Mostly men from the 20th division, stacking supplies for the next transport.

Marit felt her eyes well up again, and she turned her eyes away from the cold water and the sinister abyss it promised to open for her.

She got up and made her way back towards the Storgata, where she could wander the long street and lose herself in other thoughts.

But there were no other thoughts.

There was only the emptiness.

The Storgata was crowded, so crowded she thought she could not breathe again. The contrast between her own inner void and the masses pressing against her was too much. She left the street and found her way higher into the town, up the unpaved roads that ran up to the top of the island. She wandered from house to house in the dark streets, peering into windows and wondering who lived in each house and how happy they were. She wanted to go anywhere but back to her uncle's home, back to the reproachful eyes of Lidy and dank squalor of the too-crowded townhouse.

She let her body lead her through the narrow back streets of Tromsø, unsure of where she was going and where she had been. It was late at night when she finally found her way back to number 50

Sjøgata. The small light still burned at the door, but all the other lights in the street were out. She lifted the glass of the lantern and blew softly on the candle, keenly aware of the waste her long walk had induced. It was certainly her uncle who left the candle lit. Yet it was Lidy who sat in the downstairs sitting room, feigning to read. It was Lidy who spoke as she came in the door, and stared, tears welling in her eyes as she tried to say something, anything.

"Are you alright?" Lidy asked.

Marit felt Lidy's hand on her forehead and, to her surprise, she found it hot. Very hot.

Marit nodded slowly. Her lower lip quivered. For the first time in many years, Marit wanted to reach out and be held by her mother. Had Lidy lifted a hand or taken a step forward, she would have gladly fallen into her arms. But Lidy only looked forward.

"It's better he's gone. They're all going. We'll be back in Karasjok before summer, and we can rebuild again. You look pale, Marit. You're cold as ice. I told you not to go out. Go to bed, and I'll bring you some tea."

Lidy felt like a stranger to Marit. Marit turned quickly and walked up the stairs, trying not to run. She did not even have the privacy of her own room, but maybe she had a few minutes to get undressed and under her covers before her mother came up to bed.

She stripped quickly and put her long gown over her head and shoulders. Her skin was wet with sweat despite the cold. She felt strange, both hot and cold all at once. Her skin was cold to touch, even under her own frozen hands. The house itself was cold. There wasn't enough coal and there would be no more before the next winter, Uncle Tomas was sure of that. He used it sparingly, and let the house get very cold at night.

The cold numbed her feelings and gave her the strength not to break down and sob. Still, as she lay on her bed, her head deep in her pillow, waiting for sleep to come, the tears dripped down her cheeks one after the other and into the hard cotton.

Lidy came into the room, carrying a cup of tea. She sat on the bed next to Marit, who pretended to be asleep.

"Marit? Marit?"

She set the tea down and took a cloth to wipe Marit's face. "Marit, you're so cold." She took a blanket from her own bed, and put it over

Marit's cover. Still, under the covers, Marit shivered. She kept her eyes tightly shut, and said nothing, wishing with all her body that her mother would go away. Lidy put her warm hand to Marit's brow a few more times, then got up, turned off the kerosene lamp, and let herself out of the room.

Marit tried to choke back the tears. She felt her body shake under the effort, and she struggled to control herself. The emptiness inside clawed at her, and ripped her open until only the crying offered some relief. Eventually, the tears too stopped. She lay in her bed, staring at the ceiling. In the room below, she could hear voices. Uncle Tomas. Lidy. But she could not hear what they said. It was just a low mumble that reminded her that she could not be alone, and that she could not be with Hans.

CHAPTER 27

Traundorf, 4 July, 2013

MARIT PULLED THE CORD ON THE BELL, and it rang loudly. She smiled at the thought that the whole village here would know she was coming to visit with a bell like this. Norway was clearly more protestant. People kept things to themselves, and did not want others to know about their visits or their habits.

Secrets.

The large door with the beautiful hinges opened suddenly. Hermann stood in the doorframe.

"Thank you for sending for me," Marit said, breaking the silence.

"Come in."

He walked a few feet and turned up a few steps to go into a sitting room. The walls were covered in carved wood, and the furnishings were comfortable. The corner was occupied by a Franklin fireplace.

"It's American," Hermann offered. "I chose it myself."

He gestured for her to sit and she did. His eyes looked tired and he still seemed only partially decided to speak with her.

"I'm sorry about the other day," he said.

"It's alright."

"I knew you were coming. I promised my father I would speak with you."

"I see."

"It was harder than I thought. I didn't think I would be upset. It was all so long ago. I guess I was mostly upset with my father."

Marit looked at him. His hands were trembling.

He looked into Marit's eyes. "What do you want?"

"I came to find Hans."

"You knew he was dead."

"Yes."

"So what do you want?"

"I'm not sure."

She wanted to say more, but she wasn't sure what else there was to say. She didn't really know what she was looking for. Just finding Hermann and being here in the farmhouse was already something.

Hermann stood up and walked around the room, putting his hands into his pockets and taking them out again. Finally, he pulled out a cigarette and lit it without saying anything. After a moment, he stuck out his hand and offered her one as well. She shook her head.

"Your father helped my family a lot during the war, Hermann."

"Did he?"

"Did he ever speak of the war with you?"

"No. Sometimes of the campaign in Yugoslavia. Of Norway, he said almost nothing."

"But you know who I am."

"Yes. My mother told me, many years ago."

"Your mother?"

"Yes." He hesitated, sucking in strongly on his cigarette and exhaling slowly. The gesture reminded Marit of Old Man Jacobsen smoking the pipe, so many years ago. "And I spoke with him about it in the last days, before he died."

"I see."

"Mrs. Enoksen ..."

"Please call me Marit."

"Mrs. Enoksen, I loved my father dearly. We did not always see eye-to-eye, but I loved him nonetheless."

"I did too." She paused a moment to gather her thoughts. "He lived with us—my mother and grandmother and I, for over a year. He saved my grandmother, and risked his own life to do it."

"He never spoke to me of her. He never wanted to go there."

"He seemed very happy."

"It was the war. How could he have been happy? He was happiest in Bavaria, at home, with his family."

Hermann turned abruptly at this and walked to a cupboard on the wall, which he opened. He took out a large envelope and set it on the table. Marit could see he was still deciding whether or not he would tell her something.

"Is this for me?" she asked, after a silence.

"Yes. He wanted you to have this. He made me promise to give it to you when you came."

Marit looked at the package.

"It has some letters in it, and a few other things," Hermann said simply.

Marit looked at Hermann but he said nothing. It was as though the envelope would speak for itself. She took the envelope into her hands and stood up to leave. Along the wall, near the fireplace, there was a small table with several picture frames. The largest was a picture of Hans. He was in full uniform, as she had seen him earlier in the war, before the harder times. He stood next to a tall, beautiful woman. They were both smiling, and held between them a young boy in baptismal robes.

Marit's heart stopped. She tried to find her words, but could hardly breathe. He was in his Wehrmacht uniform. This was not a picture from after the war.

"Are you alright?" Hermann asked sincerely.

"It's you," she finally managed.

"Yes, of course. It's my baptism. My father and mother were married during his leave after the Yugoslavia campaign. I was born in April 1942, just before my father was transferred to Norway. That's one of the reasons he was sent north. He spoke some Serbian. He was to set up the prisoner-of-war camp there."

Marit felt dizzy. She looked for a seat, a wall, anything.

"Mrs. Enoksen!"

She opened her eyes again. Hermann was holding her. They were both on the floor. Maybe there was something of Hans in him after all.

"I'm alright," she said.

"You fainted."

"I'm alright. I have low blood pressure. I'm sorry to have troubled you with these old stories."

She sat up.

"You need rest. I'll take you back to the hotel."

"I'm fine. I can walk."

She stood slowly. The envelope was on the floor, like a rock between them. They both looked at it. Marit turned away first, and started towards the door.

"What about the envelope?" He picked it up and took a step towards her.

She hesitated.

"You didn't know, did you? About my mother?" Hermann said looking straight at her.

"No. I mean yes, maybe, inside. I never really wanted to think it would matter."

"Take the envelope. Too many years have gone by, and too many secrets have been kept. Father is dead. He wanted you to have it."

She took the package reluctantly.

"I'm sorry, Marit. I thought you knew. I thought he told you."

"He did, Hermann, in his own way. We never used a lot of words. But I knew he had to come back to Bavaria."

The door to the farmhouse closed one last time, revealing the beautiful hinges that grew from the frame like vines over a building, wrestling the door shut and keeping it that way.

Locked in time.

In the street, the birds that flitted from the bushes on either side did not hold the same charm as before. They seemed to mock her with their chirping as they flitted back and forth from one side of the street to the other. Even the sun, which she was warm and welcoming on the way to the farmhouse seemed now to be hot and oppressive. It was hard to breathe. She loosened her collar and walked slowly back to the hotel.

In her room, she laid the package gently on the table and sat down to look at it.

Hans was married.

Hans had always been married.

The day he met her. The day he kissed her. The day he held her.

Hans wasn't torn apart by the end of the war, it was the war that took him from his family and child.

Deep inside of Marit, something seemed to vanish. Something strong and hard that she had held onto as one clutches a sword in battle, or a pillar as the ground shakes.

It wasn't broken. It wasn't lost. Something was simply gone.

And in its place was a void blacker than the darkest, starless night, emptier than the desolate barrens north of Lappland, or beyond— the ice floes where sealers fear to walk and where perhaps no man has ever been.

Marit closed her eyes.

She wanted to cry, but no tears came.

Only pain. The cold, merciless pain of a lie.

Chapter 28

Tromsø, May 1945

MARIT COULD HEAR THE SHOUTING from her room. She opened the window. The spring air rushed in, along with a thousand shouts. Horns were blowing.

"What's going on?" Lidy called from her bed across the room.

"I don't know."

"They're all shouting."

"Yes, but they don't sound upset. They sound happy."

Marit stuck her head out the window and looked down the Sjøgata. People were heading down the street towards the Storgata, towards the center of town.

"What's all the fuss?" Marit called out to a boy in the street below. She noticed suddenly that he was carrying a Norwegian flag. Not the one with the swastika. A Norwegian flag.

"It's over, ma'am! The war. It's over!"

Tomas came bursting into the room.

"The Germans have capitulated. Terboven blew himself up last night, along with several senior SS men. The last divisions are surrendering as we speak. It's all over the radio. Germany has surrendered. The German Army in Norway has been called back to their barracks under police supervision. Get dressed. Let's go downtown."

When Marit and Lidy were dressed, they found Tomas in the living room, unfurling a large Norwegian flag. Without the swastika.

"Where did this come from?" Lidy asked.

"I've been keeping it for happier days." He attached it to a long pole and held it up as best he could in the small room. "Looks pretty good."

Marit stood in the doorway, her hands resting comfortably on her belly.

"Are you alright, child?" Lidy asked.

"Of course she is! Stop being such a hen. We're all going out. You too!" Tomas called to Margret.

"Me?"

"All of us. Everyone in Tromsø will be in the street celebrating."

The sun shone brightly down, chasing away the last of cold that hid in corners or lurked behind buildings. It was spring at last, and everyone could feel it. There were thousands of people streaming slowly towards downtown. It was impossible to get to the Storgata, so they went around by the port to be able to come closer to the Lutheran church. The bells from both that church and the Catholic church had started ringing while they were still at home, and they rang continuously. They were a backdrop for the shouts and general hoopla that reigned over the town.

"Can you believe it?" someone asked.

"Can it be true?"

"Where are all the Germans?"

"They haven't gone home yet; they were here last night."

"So we're going home?" Marit said, turning to Lidy.

"Soon. Not yet, of course. There isn't much to go back to yet."

Marit's heart was torn. Leaving Tromsø meant leaving Hans for good, even though he wasn't here. Something in her made her believe he would somehow come back. If he did, and she wasn't here, he might be lost forever.

"You'll have to give us a bigger smile than that," Tomas said, taking her by the arm. "I've the prettiest woman in Tromsø on my arm, the sun is shining down, and the Germans are leaving forever. This is the best day of my life!" He grinned broadly and kissed his niece on the cheek. She forced a smile and kissed him back.

She was happy that the war was over.

Truly happy.

Inside, however, she struggled to set aside the fear inspired by the realization that a new life was beginning, a new life without Hans, in a world without any of the things she had known before.

She wondered for a moment where Bera was.

Babi, who had been so absent these many months ... Not just not with them, but somehow not there. She longed to be back in the farmhouse, to hear Babi's rhythmic *joiks* and let her mind wander to a thousand pleasant things. But Babi was not here, and the farmhouse was gone forever.

*   *   *

"You won't be going back as quickly as you thought." Tomas was putting away his rain jacket and his long rain slacks. He smelled of fish, as he often did when he came back from the boat.

"Why not?" Lidy asked.

"Even if I take you to Porsanger or Tanafjord, like we said, there's no safe road to Karasjok."

"We're big girls, Tomas," Lidy protested. "We can fend for ourselves."

"I've no doubt of that. That's not what I mean."

"What do you mean?" Marit asked as he poured himself a large glass of rum.

"The roads are mined. All of them."

"How are the police getting around then? Someone must be using them," Lidy reasoned.

"Oh yes. And they thought they were safe. I just heard today, there's been an accident in Karasjok. A big one."

"An accident?"

"A mine went off. One of the road mines the Germans left us. They're dropping supplies in to Karasjok by plane, until the river thaws enough to get people out. At least twenty dead, and quite a few wounded too."

"Well, now they'll clear the mines. Or least the river," Lidy said.

"You're a stubborn bunch, both of you. You're not listening. The roads are closed until further notice. No one is going in or out until the government decides it's safe."

"That could take months," Marit said.

"Yes. A few at least. And it's much better that way," Tomas answered. "You're better off giving birth here than in Karasjok in the snow or some dirt hut."

"I want to go back. I want my baby to be born in Karasjok."

"Talk to her, Lidy."

"I won't. She's right. Babi made it through the winter. Sami babies have been born in huts and tents for thousands of years. If Marit wants to go back, we'll go back, as soon as we can."

"Lord Almighty! What have you done to her, Marit? She'll be sleeping in the *lávvu* now, along with your reindeer herder cousins."

"Well, actually, for the first few months, she may well be," Marit smiled.

"*Lávvu* or no *lávvu*, you're both stuck with me until the summer."

Marit and Lidy sat down at the kitchen table, resigned.

"Alright," said Lidy. "But when the road opens, you'll take us to Porsangerfjord."

"You know I will, Lidy. I won't sleep until I do. I'm sure you'll see to that."

"I had a letter from Milly yesterday, Lidy."

"Are they alright?" Lidy asked Marit.

"They're fine. They're safe in Trondheim, and will get back to Tromsø as soon as they can."

"They can come with us to Porsangerfjord."

Margret quickly passed a letter to Tomas, who took it under his arm and set off for the living room.

"What's that?" Marit asked.

"Mail."

He was already halfway to the next room. Something in Margret's expression bothered Marit. It was hard to read the old woman, but there was something in the way she looked at Marit, and then would not look at Marit, that left her feeling uncomfortable.

CHAPTER 29

Karasjok, July 1945

THE BUS RIDE ACROSS THE *VIDDA* WAS UNEVENTFUL. The bus driver drove very slowly, probably still worried about the mines that were supposed to be cleared. The Germans had left behind some 60,000 mines, and the one accident had already cost twenty-two people their lives in Karasjok that spring. But the *vidda* itself was unchanged. The sun was high in the sky, and the trees had a much shorter shadow than they would later in the day. It was not the eerie *vidda* of the long summer "nights". She was happy to see that some things had not changed.

Inside of her, she could feel the excitement of her baby, kicking as they bounced along the road. He was too big to turn now, but he kicked. Or pushed rather, stretching, looking for space. Soon ready to discover the world.

A new world.

Nothing could prepare Marit for the sight of Karasjok itself. The bus stopped on the hillock that overlooked the river on the north side. It was simply where the road ended. The bridge was gone, a gnarled metal obstacle in the river that boats were certainly struggling with.

"Unbelievable," said Milly, staring in disbelief. Milly's parents were holding each other's hands tightly. Sven could hardly sit still, and kept looking out one side of the bus, then the other.

Lidy said nothing.

They stepped off the bus and took the bags from the driver, who passed them down from the roof. Milly's father collected each of them and set them in a pile by the roadside. The driver was already collecting fares from those headed back to Lakselv. The service to Finland would have to wait for the Blood Road to be cleared of mines and a new bridge to be built.

"So. Now what?" Milly asked as they stood by the roadside, staring at the desolation around them.

"We're going into the village," said Milly's mother. "There are boats to get across."

"We're going home," Lidy said simply. She picked up a large bag and began to clamber down the hillside towards the river's edge, where indeed there were a few boats tied up along the bank.

"Mrs. Enoksen!" It was Pikka, the old Sami hunter from the Tana River Valley.

"Hello, Pikka!"

"Do you need a ride home? I've finished unloading my boat. I'm going back down river in a few minutes. It's safer by river you know. The roads are full of mines."

"Thank you, Pikka. You're a godsend."

He took the bag from her, and came back up the hill to help with the rest of their meager belongings. Lidy choked back her tears thinking that this was now the extent of what they owned. They ferried Milly and her parents across the river and embraced them strongly, trying not to think of the day they had stood not far away from here setting out on the reverse journey.

The church towered over the barren fields and desolate landscape, still white, still tall. The red roof seemed redder to Marit, though.

Blood red.

"I'll come into town after we get settled at the farm," Marit told Milly, kissing her cheek.

Pikka didn't make any small talk on the river, and Lidy and Marit didn't seek to make any either. There wasn't much to be said. The houses along the river bank that had marked the miles from the village to their farm were all gone. Some had a chimney still; most were only charred piles of rubble, overgrown already by brambles and raspberry bushes. Marit marveled at how quickly nature stepped in to take its place back again.

Eventually they reached the beach. To their surprise a boat was tied up there, covered with a neat canvas.

Lidy stepped ashore first. It was their boat, undamaged, and seemingly well taken care of. Up on the hill where the farm used to be, there was smoke rising from a small fire.

"Looks like you won't be alone!" Pikka said with a broad smile that revealed a great gap between his front teeth. He put the bags onto the rocky beach and laughed as he pushed the boat into the water and scrambled back to start the motor.

Lidy and Marit stood with their bags on the riverbank, looking up at the smoke. Marit thought she could see a hut where the farm had been, dug into the hillside. The smoke came out a hole in its small roof. Outside the hut, the pens were repaired, and full of reindeer. Reindeer. In July.

"Jakob!" Lidy said suddenly.

"It has to be," Marit agreed.

Marit listened for a moment and heard barking in the distance. Star was running down the hill barking as she ran, tearing through the taller grasses towards her mistress. Marit fell to her knees and was still knocked over by the eager dog, which jumped around her barking and then buried her head in Marit's arms before turning on her back and rolling with pleasure.

Marit looked up. Over by the pens, she saw someone walking, coming to see what Star was so excited about. He stopped when he saw them and began to run down the hill.

"Andarás!"

"Marit! Lidy!"

Marit came up the hill as quickly as she could. Somewhere in the middle, they met and hugged strongly.

"You're as strong as a bear," Marit joked.

"You're as big as one!"

"Funny!"

"You're with baby?"

"You're perceptive. Where's Jakob?"

"He's in the hut. He built it for Lidy. He knew she wouldn't like the *lávvu*." They laughed.

"I don't think she prefers a hut to a *lávvu*, but we've plenty of time to build a house again. Where's Babi?"

"Hello, Andarás," Lidy said as she caught up with them.

"Hello, Lidy." Andarás' face darkened.

"You're not very happy to see me," Lidy joked.

Andarás didn't answer. He looked away from both of them. Marit could see Jakob walking down the hill towards them now. He looked older. Sadder.

"Where's Babi?" Marit asked again, a slight panic growing in her voice.

"She didn't make it, Marit. I'm sorry. We thought you'd seen it. She said she saw you."

Marit struggled to swallow. *Saw me?*

A magpie landed in the tall grasses and looked up at Marit with sharp, glassy eyes.

"She said you knew ..." Andarás had tears in his eyes too.

Jakob came forward and hugged Lidy, then Marit.

"So he told you?"

"Just now," Andarás said, wiping his eyes with his sleeve.

"She was very tired after the night of the burning. Very weak. And November was so cold. When the first snows came, very late, in December, the sleep took her. She did not wake." Jakob took Lidy's hand in both of his. "I'm sorry, Lidy. You know how much we all loved your mother. But she would want you to look to the future. Come, let me show you your new house."

Another figure appeared outside the hut, and began to walk down to them.

"Who's that?" Marit asked.

"You don't recognize him? It's Jan Erikssen. He helped us build the hut. And we let him put his horses with the reindeer. He's going to build his father's farm again."

Andarás took Marit's arm and helped her up the hill.

"I'm not an invalid, you know. Just pregnant."

"Very pregnant. I wish Babi was here."

"Me too. Me too."

The magpie fluttered behind them and flew off to find something bright and shiny.

"Hello, Jan."

"Marit. I'm really glad to see you. Are you alright?" His eyes widened as he looked more closely at her.

"It's okay. I'm pregnant. Just like your mother once was," she said, turning to Andarás.

There was a bench outside the hut made of a cut log. Marit sat down on it and caught her breath. The baby was pushing strongly against her now.

"He likes the walking," she said to Jan.

"He?"

"The baby."

"Oh. It's a boy?"

"I don't know."

"Oh."

"It's Hans' baby, Jan."

"Well, where is Hans?"

"He won't be coming back."

"I see."

Jan stood up, and then sat down again.

"I didn't know you were pregnant, Marit."

"It's okay. I didn't know you would be here."

"I've been helping Jakob and Andarás get things ready for your return. And working on my own house."

"I'm glad to see you, Jan."

"Me too."

Lidy prepared a quick lunch of dried meats with some dried fruit and berries and laid it out for the men and Marit. The bread was hard and tasted bland.

"The baker's not back, and Jakob doesn't know how to make bread," Andarás explained.

"I can teach you," Marit said smiling. "The baker taught me."

After lunch, Marit took the boat with Jan and headed upstream for the village.

"Don't you have work to do?" she asked him.

"I've been working every day for months. Even most of Sunday. I think I can take today off."

They motored along the river, passing burned farms and houses, but also a few boats. There was life coming back to the valley. At the beach in the village, a group of returnees waved to Jan from the other side.

"I think the village will need a water taxi," Jan joked. "I'll go bring them across."

"Go ahead. I want to walk around alone a bit."

Marit wandered through the wasteland that had been Karasjok. Many of the houses still had their stone or brick fireplaces, and around some of them a simple shelter had been built.

In a few places, people had started to rebuild. Besides the church, the village had another miracle: the smithy had not burned. The house it was connected to and the larger workshop were all gone, but the ancient smithy, first built when the Sami had come from Finland in 1800 to build the church, had withstood the flames. Its scorched boards, used to the fires of generations of blacksmiths, had not burned.

"Marit!"

It was Mr. Dahlstrøm. So he was back too.

"When did you get back?" he asked, coming up to her.

"I came this morning, by bus. They've opened the road again. What about you?"

"I convinced them to fly the schoolmaster in when they flew out the wounded from the mine accident back in May. I heard about the mission from a friend, and flew up from Oslo just in time to get onto the plane. You're pregnant."

"I am. I'm also glad to see you."

"Where are you staying?"

"At the farm. Andarás built a small cabin last spring. Really more of a hut. It's comfortable enough. Lidy still prefers it to the *lávvu*."

They shared a short laugh, until the sadness of the surroundings overcame them again. Marit felt her body tremble, as though ready to cry, but to her surprise, it was Mr. Dahlstrøm who shed the first tear.

"There's so much to do, Marit. There's nothing left."

"You'll rebuild the school."

"It won't be the same. They want a bigger school, on the other side of the river. They say the town burned fast because everything was so close together. Only the church was set back from the other buildings."

That isn't what saved the church, Marit wanted to shout, but her tongue stayed tightly held within her mouth.

"Don't worry, Mr. Dahlstrøm. It will be alright." She wanted to believe it would be. The desolation only emphasized her empty feeling inside.

"I found a poem that brought me solace as I walked around the village. It's a German poem."

"That's okay. I remember. Beethoven, Schiller, Goethe, all German. All nice people."

"This one is by Heinrich Heine. It's called *Herz, mein Herz, sei nicht beklommen.*"

"How does it go?"

"Let no trouble overcome you,
Heart, my heart—but bear your pain.
Spring shall come, and bring again
All that Winter's taken from you.
And how great is still your treasure!
And the world, how fair a place!
And, my heart, you may embrace
All on earth that gives you pleasure."

"It's beautiful," said Marit.

"It is."

Jan came up from the beach and joined them.

"How's your house coming, young man?"

"Very nicely. Thank you."

"Do you think we can find some flour and yeast so I can make some bread?"

Jan thought for a minute. "The butcher's got the only store in town. He can sell you pretty much anything."

"Mr. Edvardsen?"

They walked over to where the butcher's shop had been. There was a new building, set well back from the road. It was just a wooden platform with tarps covering the goods, but it was clearly a store. Harald poked his nose out from under one of the tarps.

"Marit Enoksen! And baby! Well, well, well."

Milly came round the other side of the platform. "Hi! Marit!"

Harald went over and wrapped his arm around Milly.

"Harald asked me to marry him this morning!" Milly beamed.

"You didn't waste any time."

"No. There's a lot to do. And Arnfrid's still so sick."

"Arnfrid?!"

"She's alive, Marit! She's alive. I couldn't believe it."

"You were very surprised, Milly," Harald said.

Arnfrid stepped out from behind the platform as well. Her body was very thin. Her skin seemed stuck to her bones, but she smiled and her eyes still had the beautiful blue gleam that Marit had always loved.

"Look at us," she said, holding Marit tightly. "I'm so thin and you're so fat."

She stared as Marit pulled back to wipe the tears from her eyes.

"Don't you ever disappear like that again!"

"I won't. I'm here, and I'm happy. Which is more than I can say for you."

"I'm happy."

"Eyes never lie, Marit Enoksen."

"I'm alright. It's been a long day."

"I'm sorry about Bera. And Hans."

Marit glared at Milly.

"It isn't a secret, is it?" Milly asked.

"Not anymore."

"You'll have trouble hiding it," Arnfrid laughed.

"She meant the Hans part," Milly said sheepishly.

"In Oslo and Trondheim they've been shaving the heads of women who had babies with Germans, and marching them through the streets. They spit on them," Mr. Dahlstrøm said.

"Good Lord!" shrilled Arnfrid. "Are we no better than them? Haven't we learned anything?"

"I thought things might be different here in the village, but I'm not sure. When people find out it is Hans' baby ..."

"It's alright, Marit," Harald stepped forward. "No one in Karasjok is going to despise you."

"This from the man whose own sister is still called 'whore'?" Arnfrid asked. "You can't promise her anything."

"But you helped the prisoners. You almost paid with your life ..." Marit could not believe her ears.

"Come on, Marit." Jan took Marit's arm. "We should get back to the farm. It is getting late. I have to get back to my mother too."

"We'll come visit you at Holga-njargga," Milly called out to them as they walked towards the beach. Hardly back a day, she seemed already married. Marit envied the ease with which Milly fit into the new Karasjok.

At the landing, Jan offered Marit his hand as she stepped into the boat. He pushed the craft out into the river and leaped in adroitly. His blond hair flowed a little in the wind, and to her surprise, she found him handsome, but also somehow foreign, removed from all the things she had lived these many months.

Jan steered the boat slowly through the soft current. His hurry to get back to the farm evaporated in the afternoon sun.

"Marit …"

"Jan?"

"I know it isn't going to be easy for you, with a German baby."

"He's a Sami baby, Jan."

"What I meant is …"

"I know what you meant."

"No, you don't. You're so stubborn! Will you let me finish?"

Marit gazed out over the water. Jan stopped the motor. It was hot in the boat. As the boat drifted in the current, she saw them. The water crawlers.

"I still want to marry you, Marit."

There was the net, all across the river surface, catching dreams …

"Marit?"

The ripplets covered the surface of the water. Rings linking rings to rings…

"I don't care that it isn't my baby. I don't care if he is German. I'll raise him as if he were ours."

"I won't marry you."

"Why not?"

"I can't, Jan. I still love him. I still love Hans."

"He isn't coming back, Marit."

"I know. That's why I'm so sad. I don't understand. I thought I would feel better here, but if anything it's worse."

"It'll pass, Marit."

"It won't. I know it won't. I have to go away."

Jan reached over and put his hand on Marit's cheek, but she did not move. Her gaze stayed fixed on the water's surface. Jan's hand was like ice upon her face. The boat moved into a faster part of the river, and the net formed by the water crawler ripplets loosened and disappeared.

CHAPTER 30

Karasjok, July 1945

"GET ME WATER. HOT WATER. NOW." Lidy was yelling at Andarás.

He was sweating almost as much as Marit.

Marit lay on the floor of the hut. It was the middle of the night, but the light shone brightly. July light. She was suffocating in the hot air.

Andarás raised his shoulders plaintively. "But Lidy ... There's no fire."

"Damn you, Marit, for not wanting this baby in Tromsø, in a house by the sea with a gas stove."

"Aaaaaa ... Aaaaaaa."

"Breathe in and out, child, in and out."

"The pain. It really hurts."

"I know. Take her hand, Andarás."

"I thought I was getting water?"

"Take her hand. It's almost here."

"It's easier when the reindeer mares give birth," Andarás mumbled.

Marit heard him and laughed a little, in the lull before the next contraction. She lay, legs spread, on the floor of the hut, her nightgown lifted around her hips. They had put some blankets down, and some dried grasses under them, but the floor still felt as hard as rock.

"Aaaaaa ... Aaaaaaa."

"Squeeze her hand tightly, Andarás."

"I am. She's stronger than me."

"Alright, Marit. I can see the head. How do you feel?"

"Not good ... Not good. Aaaaaaaa ... Not goooooood." Her teeth were clenched and her muscles tensed.

"Alright. Breathe in. Try to relax a little. Wait for the sharper pain. Next time you feel it get stronger, you need to push. Push hard."

"It's now ... Oh! God!"

"Push. Come on, push."

"I can't! I can't!"

"You are! Keep pushing. Alright, rest. Breathe out quickly. Short breaths."

"Aaaaaaaaaaaaaaa."

"Breathe, breathe ... Okay, now push. Push now! Hard!"

The baby came out all at once into Lidy's hands.

"It's a girl, Marit! It's a girl!"

Lidy took the string and tied off the cord in two places. Then she cut the cord with the knife, and washed the baby's belly with some cold water. The baby cried loudly.

"Here," said Lidy, caressing the baby's back. "Put her on your belly. Let her feel your heartbeat."

Andarás turned away. "I guess my job is done."

"Don't be shy, Andarás. I'm your cousin. Look at my little baby."

He stared at her tiny fingers, and the tiny toenails. "She's perfect. Just perfect." He watched her curl her little toes on Marit's belly, trying to crawl back inside to hide from the outside world.

"You have to push again, Marit. Once more. There's still something to come out."

Marit let out another yell and then leaned back on the ground. The baby was crying again.

"I think you scared her," Andarás said.

"How are the contractions, Marit?"

"Better. Much better. Fading."

Andarás stroked the little child's foot, and gazed into her half opened eyes.

"She's a little miracle, isn't she?" said Marit. "Maria. I'll call her Maria."

"Maria?" Lidy said surprised.

"Yes, Maria. Like the Virgin. Like me. Marit. Maria. It's German, mother."

She heard herself say mother and looked to see if Lidy noticed. Lidy was looking at what had come out after the baby, turning it over in her hands.

"Where did you learn all this?" Marit asked.

"Sami have been giving birth in the woods for thousands of years."

"What are you holding?" Andarás asked.

"It's called a placenta. It's what feeds the baby when it is in the belly. It's important to get it all out."

"You know this from the fox and the bear?" Marit said with some effort. "Passed down these many thousands of years?"

"No," Lidy laughed, "from Marin at the hospital, and one of her nurse friends in the maternity ward. I asked them to teach me how to do this so that you could have your baby at home in Karasjok."

"Thank you, Lidy."

CHAPTER 31

Karasjok, July 1945

THEY SAT IN THE HUT, Marit singing a *joik* to Maria, Lidy cooking over the fire. Arnfrid and Milly were rolling reindeer meat around vegetables and running long thin skewers into the rolls. Jakob and Andarás smoked a long pipe shared between them. Marit's voice floated around the hut and created an atmosphere like that of the visions. Marit could almost feel Babi back amongst them, and when she heard her own voice, it was partly Babi's voice, coming out through her.

Everyone was startled when Marit stopped. She hadn't meant to, but the face in the doorway took her breath away.

Old Man Jacobsen stood at the door of the hut.

"Come in," said Jakob. "Come in."

He stepped in and sat down next to the two men.

Jakob looked from Marit to Lidy and back to Marit.

"What's wrong, Marit? You look as though you've seen a ghost."

"Congratulations, Marit." Old Man Jacobsen held out a small packet. Marit was trembling. Jakob took the packet and set it down next to Marit.

"You're dead," said Marit.

The men in the hut laughed heartily.

"Not yet, child. I know the joke. And I *am* very old. But not dead."

"No, not the joke. The church. Hans saw you. You were burned at the church."

Old Man Jacobsen looked back at Marit. He stared expressionless for a long time and then took the pipe from Jakob. He drew in a deep breath and blew back the smoke into the room. When he blew the smoke, it formed in little shapes like houses all in flame.

"Hans *thought* he saw me, Marit. We all left the village days before. I was in the woods with the others the night of the burning. On the lake, near Gimisvarre …" He hesitated, choosing his words. "… with your grandmother," he finally added.

"I saw her," said Marit. "I was there, at the church."

"Were you? I thought you were in Tromsø, with your mother."

"I had a vision. I was Raven, flying over the *vidda*. I flew to Karasjok. I saw Babi save the church."

Old Man Jacobsen smiled.

He blew smoke out of the pipe again, but it did not take on any shape.

"You said Babi was tired after the burning," Marit turned to Andarás.

"She was," Jakob said. "They told us she was up all night praying to the *sieide* at Gimisvarre, crawling around the giant rock and walking on all fours, and chanting and singing and banging on the ground. She was in a trance for over thirty minutes. She didn't have the drum, but she banged so hard, many said they heard it. The ground shook. I wasn't there of course. We only came later. The snows came so late last year."

Old Man Jacobsen blew more smoke into the hut.

Maria cried, and Marit put the baby on her breast.

"But Donkey …" Marit said almost under her breath. Marit did not resume singing the *joik*, and the hut became very quiet.

Jakob picked the packet up from the floor and set it in Marit's hands. She unwrapped it slowly. It was a metal ring and an antler carving of a bear. They each had a deer sinew tied to them.

"For the drum," Old Man Jacobsen said. "You are our *noaide* now."

"I'm not a *noaide*. I almost killed myself flying with Raven." She set the ring and the bear down. "You can find another *noaide*."

"Relax, Marit," Lidy said, taking Maria into her arms. "You're tired. And upset."

"Yes, I'm tired. Tired of all these strange games." She was almost yelling. "Hans saw Babi, and saw you kill Donkey. Even if I was only dreaming."

Old Man Jacobsen looked down at the ground. His lips squeezed tightly together into an expression that was half smile, half frown. "Babi said you would leave."

"What?" Lidy said, alarmed. "Is it true?"

Marit picked up the ring and the little bear carving and turned them over in her fingers. It was a small ring, forged in silver. Small enough for her to wear. It had a line running in long circles all around it, like a long wave that had no beginning, and no end.

"It's true, I've been thinking of it. Ever since we came back, and I realized we were starting over again, with nothing. Alone."

"You're home now, Marit. This is home. Not Germany." Lidy looked from Marit to Jakob and Andarás. "Say something, damn it. Tell her."

Jakob and Andarás looked at each other and then back down to the ground.

"I'm not going to Germany." She stood up and took the baby back from her mother. "Maria and I are going to America."

"America? What is in America? Who do you know in America?"

"Nothing. No one. That's why I should go there. I can't stay here. I just can't."

CHAPTER 32

Traundorf, 4 July, 2013

MARIT SAT ON THE CHAIR at the window of her room, turning the letters over, not to see them more clearly, but to see them less so. Unopened letters. The envelope held three. She took each one and laid them out before her, face up to look at the postmarks. Next to the letters, she laid her grandfather's belt on the table. The silver buckle still shined after all these years.

Hans had mailed each letter to her, and each one was returned, unopened. Marit felt the pain that Hans had felt as he received the letters back again, and shut her eyes. *Why hadn't he said anything? Why had he never said* anything?

Three letters. Three tries to reach out and contact Marit. And what would he have said? She opened her eyes again. The first letter was sent on 12 May, 1945. The return postmark said Tromsø, 21 May, 1945. May 1945. The end of the war.

She grasped at something in her memory. So long ago.

My God! Margret!

She had seen the letter. That was the look on her face. And Tomas, taking it from her, keeping it from her. She had stood three feet from this letter sixty-eight years ago.

She reached for the envelope and tore at the edge.

My dear Marit,
I cannot begin to describe the desolation I felt after we parted at your uncle's house, or my despair at not being able to see you again. I wanted so

badly to tell you so many things, to make things right somehow, to set things straight. I imagined seeing you again, on the docks if you come to see me off, or even in Germany, after I came back. Your eyes would look into my soul and see that I could not leave you. Perhaps that is why God has kept us apart, kept us from telling each other what we might have otherwise said. I did not think I could leave you, but I did. I found the strength, somewhere, deep inside. It was a light. I was in the darkness.

I followed the light. I followed duty, perhaps a higher calling. Someone famous once said: "I could not love you so my dear, if I did not love honor more." It may have been noble, but in many ways my insides would have been happier to stay with you and face whatever punishment the free Norsemen could give out. I am guilty of being German, and of following my orders—and even then, not always. I do not know how to face the pain that lies before us. I wonder every day, Marit, what have we done? I did not see a way to stay, and you could not come, and I could not tell you why. Now the world has driven a wedge between us like a stake through my heart. Forgive me.

I am in a camp. It is clean and they treat us well. They are American but they are friendly. I am hopeful they will let us out soon. They have already begun sorting through those that were real Nazis and those that joined the party only because they felt there was no other choice. I like these Americans. In another life, maybe I would go away and join them. There is something to be said for fresh starts.

The bombs stopped some weeks ago, and the war is definitely over. Germany will pay dearly for her arrogance. I wish only that we not start again the same cycle that lead us to where we are now. I pray for my darling Bavaria, for her mountains and valleys, but also for her soul. We have done so many terrible things. What of the retribution Reverend Framhuis spoke so often of? And if there is no settling of accounts, how will we find our souls again? I see the village burning. I see the bodies of the men in the forests of Yugoslavia. I am haunted by what was done, but even more so by what was not done. I try to bury these ghosts, but they sleep with me, and come out in the quiet of the night.

I long in my heart to be with you. I wonder about Babi and Lidy. I cannot keep from my mind the image of Babi before the church. I know in my heart she is safe, but I still wonder. There was something in her eyes that night. She knew something, and she wanted to share it with me, but I *could not understand her message. I look for her around the camp here. Isn't that silly? It's as though her spirit is not far off.*

And Lidy. I know she did not want to go to Tromsø. I know it was hard to lose everything. She was so cold at our parting. Does she know that I love her too, with her gruff ways and dislike for all things German?

I write to you at your uncle's house, hoping you will still be in Tromsø. I know you will want to go back, to find Bera and the others. I know only too well how hard that return will be, and that it may be months before you can get back to the terrible devastation we wrought upon your world. I hope that this letter finds you first, and that you take with you the memory of my undying love, and the hope that we find each other another day, in another life, two birds in the bull rushes, or two water crawlers skipping across the surface of our dream nets.

Yours always,

Hans.

Marit folded the old paper.

It was pointless. And unavoidable.

She wanted to burn the letters. All of them. She looked at the other two. *Lies. More lies.* She picked them up and began to shred them with her shaking hands. A moment later, there were only tiny squares of old paper on the table in front of her. A pile of small paper squares. *How could he want to be with her, and yet also be with his wife and child. What of his other child, Mary?* Marit wished she had found the courage to tell him, somehow. Something in her had always held her back. More lies, or truths untold.

She was surprised by her anger. It flowed freely after all the years of sorrow. Another form of grieving. An easier form.

She looked at the pile of little paper squares and laughed out loud. Her anger vanished with the laugh, like a wave sweeping everything off the beach. The last sixty years of choices rushed past her, flashes in her mind, every one of them her own choice. And here she was, looking for something of Hans, so many years later, again her own choice. She travelled half way around the world to find her own memories and her own choices.

It was late afternoon. She stood up and took out the walking stick she had found at the little village store. It was nicely carved, with a pattern that ran all around it. It matched the little silver ring on her finger.

Outside, the birds were still flitting, but they seemed less mocking after the letter. She walked away from the church, away from the farmhouse. There was a little park up against the hill that led to the cemetery, just beneath the markers, but out of sight because of the steep cliff. There was a spring in the park, and it came out into a pool of water. The pool was paved and had a metal bar in the middle to hold and walk around. It was a *kneipp*, the girl at the hotel had explained. It was for walking in.

There was an old man walking in it now. His pants were rolled up above his knees, and he took slow steps. The water was glacial, and he seemed to be in some pain as he walked gingerly around the bar, holding it in one hand, breathing in deeply between each step.

Marit marveled at his stamina.

Why does anyone inflict this on themselves?

Even though the sun was well past the zenith, it was hot in the valley. Marit found herself breathing heavily. She looked around the park for a place to sit. Not far from the pool, there was a bench. It was in the sun, but there was a little wind.

She walked over and lay her stick against the bench. In the grass, not far off, was the blond girl from the reception. She wore one of those Bavarian dresses that reminded her so much of the Sami tunics. She held her apron out in front of her as a young man threw dandelion heads into it from a few feet away. Every time he missed, he moved a little closer. It seemed to Marit his aim was getting worse. The girl recognized her and blushed, waving a little with one hand.

There was a sparrow next to her on the bench. She sat very still, and watched him turn his little head. He seemed to smile. He had blue eyes. Marit had never seen a sparrow's eyes before. She didn't think it could be common that they were blue.

Her own eyes were heavy.

Such a long day.

She reached for her walking stick but knocked it to the ground instead.

So heavy. So tired.

She let her eyelids close and saw Hans' blue eyes inside of hers, just as she had every night for so many years. Inside, she could feel the pillar. It was back. It was her pillar, and no one else could take it away.

She heard the blond girl laugh as the young man missed again. She was home, in Karasjok, along the river at the bottom of the lower field. She smelled the fresh dandelions and alpine meadow flowers that came down to her, carried by the wind.

The afternoon sun was warm on her face, and Marit let herself drift into sleep.

ACKNOWLEDGMENTS

I MUST BEGIN BY THANKING my outstanding agent and friend, April Eberhardt, who believed from the outset in this book and in my writing, and whose support has been unwavering.

Revontuli was inspired by true stories, thus I owe a debt of gratitude to all those who opened their hearts and memories to share a piece of Norway's past. Many others helped me research this past, and I am greatly indebted to their guidance, including especially Roger Albrigsten, who translated for me during my travels to the Finnmark, including late nights reading Norwegian journals and books about the events of 1944 and translating as best he could; Leif Arneberg, an expert on maritime history and Director of the Tromsø WW II museum, who drove me to the site of the sinking of the Tirpitz and patiently answered my many questions; Anders Henriksen, who personally showed me through the private collection of the Riddo Duottar Museat (Sami Museum in Karasjok) and spent valuable time explaining Sami culture to a foreigner; Eeva-Kristiina Harlin, former Curator of the Riddo Duottar Museat and Porsanger Museum, who showed me the related collection at Skoganvarre; Tarmo Jomppanen, the Director of Siida, the National Museum of the Finnish Sami on Lake Inari, who provided information on shamanic rituals in the Sami culture and shared access to film footage of early twentieth century Sami life; Tor Reidar Boland, who on short notice came out into the cold to show me the exact location of the Serbian Camp and tell me stories of the clean-up after the war; the staff of the Municipal Library in Tromsø; the 'ghost dog' of Karasjok—you didn't make it into the book, but your spirit guided key parts of the research; and the staff of Engholm Husky Design Lodge, Sven, Christel, Kasper and Marin, for their hospitality and their stories of living amongst the Sami.

There were a few books that were of great value during the research for *Revontuli*. The book *Flukt til friheten: fra nazi-dødsleire i Norge*, written by Cveja Jovanovic, provided precious details on the Serbian Camp, and the attempted escapes during the fall of 1942. *Fragments of Lappish Mythology*, a great reference book on Sami culture, was written by Lars Levi Laestadius and is available in English edited by Juha Pentikäinen. The book provides renditions of folk tales and drawings of Sami drums. Per Hansson's *Mamma Karasjok* has excellent true stories from the war. On the unfolding of the war itself and the evacuation, besides stories from local sources, I relied on Roland Kaltenegger's German book *Krieg in der Arktis*, as well as Arvid Petterson's *Fortiet fortid (Tragedien Norge aldri forsto)* and Laila Thorsen's *Finnmark Brenner!* There are very few books or articles about the burning of the Finnmark in English, although the situation is somewhat better in Norwegian, Russian, and German.

Many thanks also to those who brought the book together: my fabulous publicist Kate Burkett, whose dedication and commitment to this project are amazing; Lorna Nakell, for her design skills on the cover and the maps; my diligent copy editor, Dawn Pearson; and the team at Booktrope Publishing for making this possible.

Thanks to my early reader's group who shared in the development of the story, especially Malcolm Johnson, Christine Gibson, Helen Sanders and Sarah Porter. Thanks also to Dad for reading the book thoroughly and offering strong support and encouragement. Elizabeth Beckett provided excellent critique on the first three chapters, and I appreciate the time and effort invested in making me a better writer. Tim Lash provided enthusiastic comment and insights on late drafts and discovered a passion of his own for the Sami thanks to *Revontuli*. Thanks to my online writer's group, Virtual Muse, who critiqued early chapters, and more especially to Steven Long, Steve Masover, and Lindy Gligorijevic, without whom the book would not read as well. Special thanks also to Stephanie Carroll, for all her platform building advice. A special thank you to my friend and proofreader Sherri Jarosiewicz, who suggested improvements, caught more typos, and provided needed encouragement.

Finally, special thanks to my wife Christiane, whose unqualified support allowed me to research and write the book, who read and cried with me, and without whom, I could not have pursued my long-held dream of becoming an author.

ABOUT THE AUTHOR

ANDREW WAS BORN IN VANCOUVER, CANADA. He grew up in Western Quebec and in the Gulf Islands, where he developed an appreciation for nature and became hooked on a rural lifestyle. He has also lived in Paris, Burgundy, Montreal, Knowlton, and Leiden. In 2010 he found a home with his family in Simiane-la-Rotonde, in the hills of Provence. Andrew is married and has five children. *Revontuli* is Andrew's first novel.

Read more about Andrew at www.andreweddyauthor.com and on his blog, Serendipity.

If you like *Revontuli*, please consider reviewing the book on amazon.com, goodreads.com, barnesandnoble.com, or the website of your choice.

A Word on Book Groups

ANDREW LOVES TO MEET READERS and is happy to visit with your book group via phone call, Skype call, or even in person when possible. Please visit www.andreweddyauthor.com for discussion questions, bonus material, and other exclusive book group resources.

MORE GREAT READS
FROM BOOKTROPE

Running in Darkness by **James Daly** (WW II Fiction) American artist Jack Martin finds himself joining a fledgling resistance group to combat Hitler and the Nazi party. But is he capable of doing what's needed? A fast-paced World War II thriller.

I Kidnap Girls: Stealing from Traffickers, Restoring their Victims by **Pamela Ravan-Pyne and Iana Matei** (Fictionalized Biography) How a phone call to one woman resulted in the rescue of over 400 victims of forced prostitution.

Sweet Song by **Terry Persun** (Historical Fiction) This tale of a mixed-race man passing as white in post-Civil-War America speaks from the heart about where we've come from and who we are.

The Summer of Long Knives by **Jim Snowden** (Historical Thriller) Kommisar Rolf Wundt must solve a brutal murder, but in Nazi Germany in the summer of 1936, justice is non-existent. Can he crack the case while protecting his wife and himself from the Gestapo's cruel corruption?

Discover more books and learn about our
new approach to publishing at **booktrope.com**.

Made in the USA
San Bernardino, CA
21 November 2013